A Red-Tailed
Hawk
Named BUCKET

A Red-Tailed
Hawk
Named

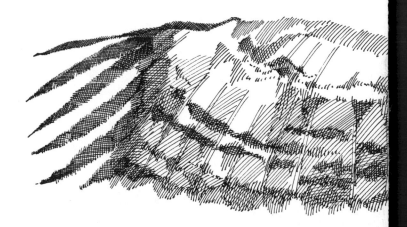

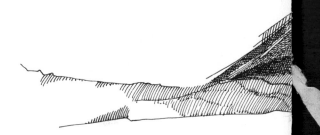

GAIRD WALLIG

Illustrations by Jennifer Dewey

BUCKET

CELESTIAL ARTS ✠ Millbrae, California

Celestial Arts
231 Adrian Road
Millbrae, California 94030

First Printing, September 1980

Cover illustration: Carlos Delgado

Made in the United States of America

Library of Congress Cataloging in Publication Data

Wallig, Gaird, 1942–
    A red-tailed hawk named Bucket.

    Half title: Bucket.
    1. Red-tailed hawk as pets.   2.   Red tailed hawk—
Legends and stories.   3.   Wallig, Gaird, 1942–
I. Title.   II. Title: Bucket.
SF473.H39W34   636.6'869   79-57546
ISBN 0-89087-276-7

1 2   3   4   5   6   7   86   85   84   83   82   81   80

To Carole Kay and her parents, Eleanor and Karl Kulikowski, and to my husband, Stephen . . . with friends like these, no creature under heaven need fear the lack of love.

1

IT WAS GETTING LATE, that Wednesday before Easter—almost time for work. Steve stretched across the drainboard in the small yellow kitchen to place his breakfast dishes in the dish water before our small Australian parrot, Ah-Soh, could land on the plate as was his habit. The gray, yellow-faced cockatiel long ago had shown his preference for people food over birdseed, but bacon and eggs over-easy did not sit well on his stomach.

The little bird was quite a character. He would make a funny series of bows with his head over any unattended plate before digging in, looking for all the world like a tiny, polite Japanese of old, hence his name.

Steve got a slice of apple—OK people food—from the refrigerator and placed it on the white counter in front of Ah-Soh; the series of bows began.

It was a beautiful morning, not the kind of day to spend at work. The sun spilled through the enormous picture windows that looked to the east beyond the flat's sun deck, and filled the wood-paneled living room, setting the walls aglow. I gave my husband a sympathetic grimace as he glanced from the clock to me, then went in to comb his hair. I got up to clear the table while Ah-Soh cavorted on top of his cage, whistling to us and to the morning in general—happy to be alive. We let the bird fly free as much as possible. Flight was his right, we felt, and we wanted him to live as natural a life as he could for a caged bird. He was a cheerful, healthy little fellow, strong of voice and wing, with a tall plume of feathers atop his head which would rise and fall as his interest in what was happening around him fluctuated.

In fact, he was such an interesting creature in his antics and bright-eyed curiosity that Steve and I had half decided to get him a companion of some sort—perhaps one of the larger cockatoos—to keep him company while we were at work and, of course, to add to our growing pleasure in his kind.

Steve came back to the kitchen, patting the last stray wisp of his dark hair into place, and gathered up his lunch and keys—all ready to leave for the discount store where he managed the camera department.

The jingling keys were the signal: Ah-Soh took off past Steve's head on the morning jaunt before cage time—all eighteen inches of white-marked wing beating up a breeze as he dipped and soared from kitchen to living room, looping through both bedrooms and around to the small pantry hall before returning again to the kitchen. Steve watched him go and as usual waited the moment it took for him to return. He stroked the gray tummy a last time, and leaned down to kiss me goodbye as the phone rang.

Ah-Soh had once been fearful of the wall telephone's loud abrupt noise—especially since we'd had to place his cage right below it—but soon after we got him we'd had a bell chime installed. Now, as its soft ring sounded, the little bird plopped himself on top of his cage to begin the ritual of feather preening while I picked up the receiver.

A young male voice answered my hello, saying, "My name is Greg Sanders. May I speak to Gaird Wallig? I got your number from Don Paquette at Oakland Pet Supply."

I thought of Don, the large, bluff, white-haired man who ran the pet shop. The week before when we had been at the shop for Ah-Soh's seed mixture, he had tried to sell us a second, bigger bird. Don had as much love for birds as we did, and he had a dozen different kinds and sizes. Unfortunately, most exotic birds were too expensive for our budget.

"This is Gaird," I said. "What can I do for you?"

"Well, Don said you might be looking for a big bird, and I have this red-tail I can't keep. I've just been accepted at a college back east so I've got to find a home for him."

2

I'd been putting Ah-Soh into his cage before he could take off again so I'd been listening with only half an ear.

"I'm sorry," (what I'd heard couldn't be right) "what kind of a bird?"

"A red-tail. It's a young red-tailed hawk. He's about four months old now, I think, and not sick or anything . . . ."

Looking at the clock, I saw I had time to talk to him—my hours at Walter Kahn's photography studio began later than Steve's—so pouring a bit more coffee into my cup I said, "I don't know about a hawk; we really hadn't considered that kind of a bird—not seriously anyway. Where did you get him? What's he like?"

"He's pretty tame," said Greg, "just like any other young bird. I was hiking a couple of months ago in the hills . . . ."

"The ones behind Oakland, here?" I asked, looking out the kitchen window at the rolling, live oak- and grass-covered coast range about five miles distant. We liked to go hiking on their slopes ourselves and had often seen hawks there.

"Yeah," he said, sounding impatient, "and I found the baby under a big old tree. Guess it must have fallen out of the nest when the parent birds went hunting for food. I'd planned to keep him, but I've got to go away to school. I only want fifty dollars for him. I know he's probably worth a lot more," he added hastily, "but Don says you're good people and I don't want to take him to a zoo or something. I could bring him to the pet shop on Friday."

I suddenly felt uncomfortable—as if I were being rushed, or being given a hard sell for goods not quite what they should be. I decided that perhaps it was just my imagination. It was reasonable that he would be anxious—going to college, probably attached to the bird and wanting him properly placed. And fifty dollars, I thought, was within our price range. But were we really in the market for a hawk?

Then I thought of the hawks I had seen in zoos: sitting like tired little brown-robed monks with their heads drawn into their necks, staring at nothing, or hanging on the side of a cage, listless, sad, looking out at the empty sky where they belonged.

If we didn't take the bird, might he too be caged forever? But we didn't know anything about keeping a hawk. Yet, neither had we known about cockatiels' needs—we had learned.

3

"Well, listen, Greg," I said, after a moment, "it sounds like a fair price, and if the bird is healthy as you say, maybe we can work something out. But first, I have to speak to my husband about it. Can I call you back tonight?"

He agreed, and gave me his phone number.

So, I had heard right: a hawk! Since our marriage four years before, Steve and I had watched every program on TV about birds of prey, raptors of any kind—both wild and captive. We found them fascinating. The last program had been about falconeers in Arabia, how they worked their birds in this sport that was possibly as old as civilized man himself. I had especially loved the birds' broad, wide span of wing that seemed to carry them so effortlessly along in the wind. Steve had marveled at their lightning quick feet, their hunting ability. He had even remarked that he would like to own a falcon for, being hunting folk ourselves, we could take a bird like that with us to the mountains during the season.

But when we had talked to Don about another bird, we had actually had one of the parrot family in mind . . . .

"It's a baby hawk?" Steve asked.

It was evening. I was preparing supper and he was sitting at the kitchen table, playing with Ah-Soh on his finger. I had told him about Greg and his young bird. As I nodded yes, Steve's eyes lit with interest.

As supper cooked we batted the idea of a hawk back and forth, pro and con; we were both rather hesitant.

How much care would a baby hawk need? It was probably old enough not to need the almost hourly feedings of a very young nestling. What about its diet? Hawks ate meat we knew, but what kind, and how much of it, did this one like?

Where would we keep it? We could possibly rent a big enough cage from Don until we could afford to buy one ourselves so we could keep the hawk safely inside during the day when we were at work. It could probably spend much of the day outdoors on the sun deck. Since it was a baby bird, maybe we could let it fly loose inside when we were home like Ah-Soh did, and it could roost on a chair back in the kitchen or in the linoleum-floored spare bedroom.

What about our landlord? How receptive would Mr. Mac, Andrew MacFarlane, be to the idea of a hawk as a house pet? He and his wife lived in an apartment below us, so we wouldn't be able to keep the bird a secret from them. Pets *were* allowed—Mac hadn't said anything about Ah-Soh. But a hawk?

How big did hawks grow? We thought of the sparrow hawks we'd seen on our hikes, and the falcons we'd seen on TV. They really didn't seem all that big—not much bigger than a cat. And a baby one would probably be Ah-Soh's size—seven or eight inches tall, if that, we thought. We had no idea.

And just how dangerous were they? Those Arabian falcons had seemed amazingly calm and manageable to us. And Greg *had* said his hawk was tame.

"What do you think, Steve," I asked. "Should we do it?"

"Well, honey, I think we can handle it," Steve said, summing up. "As it grows, maybe we can kind of grow with it. Besides, I think I'd like to try falconeering!"

Good Friday dawned drizzly, the Bay area's seasonal fog heavier and wetter than usual. As I straightened out the car in the street, starting for work, I noticed old Mrs. Greenwood sitting in her customary spot at her front window, knitting, and watching the comings and goings in the neighborhood. Plump, grandmotherly Mrs. Greenwood was not at all a busybody; she really enjoyed watching things around her and particularly liked to send her neighbors on their way with a cheerful smile and a friendly wave—"in case no one else smiles at them today" she once told me. Living alone, and being lonely I suppose, it gave her a sense of belonging. I waved first this day and was rewarded by the happy crinkling of her face, a perfect picture framed by the arch of the window above, and the pink fuschias below.

The street we lived on, Walnut Street, was mostly an area of small apartment buildings of the flat-roofed, modern sort, already aging, but gracefully. Most of the owners were attempting to maintain their investments without too great an expenditure, trying to accomplish more with love and a little effort than with money. There were flower beds, colorful and refreshing spots against the concrete and masonry. The sidewalks and driveways were swept and hosed down frequently. It was a nice place to live. Driving to work, I wondered how my friendly neighbors would react to a hawk in their midst.

Afternoon came finally. Because of a customer lingering over photographs, I was fifteen minutes late for the appointment with Greg at the pet center but still I was there before him. And glad of it: It gave me the opportunity to speak to Don about the hawk. At the library the night before, I hadn't been able to find much information about the care of red-tailed hawks but I slowly grew more confident as Don told me that he had seen the bird, and as far as he could tell, it was in good condition and as Greg described.

As we chatted in the shop's open doorway, a slim man riding a dusty motorcycle rolled into the dirt parking lot in a cloud of smoky exhaust. A large cardboard box, with a fitted top, printed with "Onions, one bushel" was strapped to the cycle's boot.

Don's face darkened as he gestured to the noisy bike and he said, "There's Greg now."

I didn't see any bird. Then it occurred to me now why Don looked so much like a displeased schoolteacher: The bird, apparently, was in the onion box—being jerked around on the rear of a rattling, popping, fume-belching motorcycle. I hoped it was a very tough bird.

When the cycle sputtered to a standstill, the rider moved off to unstrap the box's lid, and with a mad clatter of toenails and an eerie shriek onto the box's edge scrambled a disheveled creature that seemed tough enough for anything.

It was a young bird: It looked like the picture of the baby hawk I'd seen in the Audubon book at the library. Its tail was still brown, not red as a mature bird's would be, and it appeared to be beginning its first molt—white down escaping here and there from under its somewhat dull, gold-brown chest feathers. Its feathers were all messed up, and some were bent sideways—it looked as if it had had a rough ride in the onion box and had fallen over. It was petulant, angry at the world in general, and at Greg in particular. It *was* young, but in no way the little "baby" hawk—just a bit bigger than Ah-Soh—that we'd been ignorant enough to expect.

Greg lifted the bird from the box edge, thrusting a heavily

gloved hand under the bird's feet. I stared at the leather glove. It reminded me of something I hadn't given enough serious consideration to—talons. What else did I not know, I wondered. But I marveled at the bird! At the youth's first touch, the feathers on the back of the hawk's head rose into a bridling mantle. It flicked out and started to beat its gold-brushed wings at him. *The wings were at least five feet, tip to tip!*

Greg dumped the bird unceremoniously to the ground, holding on to the lead rope that was attached to the straps (jesses) bound to its ankles. It lunged, trying to get away, pounding the air with its great wings, kicking at the earth futilely with its feet for all it was worth, and shrilling its wild call again and again.

While it fought, but without saying one soothing word, Greg held the lead rope close to the ground. Obviously he was trying to show the bird who was boss. He held the rope down with one knee and put both hands on the hawk's wings, forcing them back against the brown body. He held the bird still until it just stood there—chittering in fear and frustration.

Greg lifted it to fence post beside the shop. Havoc broke loose among the finches in the screened aviary just inside the shop's door. They had heard the hawk's shrieks, of course, and had been hopping about nervously, but when Greg placed this natural enemy where it could be seen, the little birds went wild, scrambling and flying all over the place.

The hawk ignored the commotion, and flapped its wings again in exasperation at Greg. I was caught up in the turmoil and angry at Greg for frightening the birds in the shop and for his callous handling of the hawk.

But as the small birds quieted, I turned my attention back to the big bird clutching to the post. Its feet, each almost as big as my own hand, were tannish-yellow, much like Ah-Soh's, and its black claws—three forward and one back on each foot—were a good inch long! The bird must have weighed five pounds at least, but it looked thin for its size as I compared its condition to Ah-Soh's. Above the hooked, black beak, the wide-set brown eyes were furious, the irises piercing and sharp as the points of needles. The outrage in those eyes made anger again churn within me.

The bird fluttered a bit, shaking and flapping as any bird will

to straighten its feathers and wings. The movement was almost belligerent, I thought. Then it stood still. A breeze ruffled its feathers, and one rose up and separated into a tiny golden fan.

I gazed at it wonderingly. A king might have an aura created by the crown upon his head, but this bird had a majestic glow that came from within, as natural to it as were its feathers. King of a sunlit sky, I thought. King of the Winds.

"May I touch him?" I asked, watching the creature's eyes as I spoke.

"I don't care," said Greg indifferently, "but he probably won't let you. He doesn't take to strangers right away."

The big brown eyes had changed. They looked soft and gentle now, I thought. But alert, and filled with childlike curiosity too. I whistled the notes I used for Ah-Soh, and the gaze that turned to me was so much like my little parrot's that I had a sudden and odd feeling that I had known this creature for a long time. Perhaps, after all, man really *does* have a kinship with every living creature under God's heavens. I now sensed something bonding us together which, though intangible, was very real indeed—it moved across the space between us like filings within a magnet's range.

Baku, I suddenly thought. I will call you Baku, after the black African eagle with the piercing eyes I'd loved so in a book I'd once read—*The Beast Master* by Andre Norton. I spoke to him silently across that space: I don't think you'll raise even one feather against me, much less a claw . . . .

"But I'm not a stranger," I said quietly. And then, with no more thought to Greg—this person who probably stole babies like this from their nests rather than finding them, who did not feed them enough, who did not treat them with the respect due free-born creatures—I reached my hand out towards the yellow feet.

As my fingers approached, Baku arched his neck, tucked that evil-looking hook of a beak way back into the folds of feathers above his chest. This pose struck me funny—he was staring down his hook nose at me like some proper little old man might grump at an unintroduced person or perhaps at a too-boisterous child. I tickled the tops of his toes with my fingernails, talking to him with the little noises and soothing words that came so naturally when I played with Ah-Soh.

9

He seemed to accept this, so I stuck a finger and then my flattened hand under the tips of those great claws and lifted them gently up.

Unbalanced from my coaxing as I'd hoped he would be, he spread his wings slightly. And all at once he was up on my bare fingers, then he immediately sidled for the firmer perch of my wrist.

And his feet were warm. It was a pleasant shock. I'd expected them to be as cold and hard as they looked; instead they clasped my wrist like a person's soft fingers. Folding his wings then, he just sat there swaying a little in a beautiful balancing act, talons, curling but held gentlemanly away from too-vulnerable skin. I could feel the strength in those warm feet as the little muscles on the bottoms flexed to keep him upright.

And, wow, was he heavy! Maybe more than five pounds—after little Ah-Soh he felt like an elephant. He looked up at me again, those big, wild, yet incredibly innocent, eyes full of that look I'd taken for childlike curiosity. Then he quacked.

Actually quacked—I blinked, and was suddenly suspicious: The odd noise, coupled with that look, was deliberate! Maybe there was a crafty little mind at work inside that sleek head; a sly reasoning power that had summed up the peculiar scene in the parking lot, found this babbling female person to its liking, and had now decided to convince a prospective new owner that upon her arm sat not a wild and murderous-minded *hawk,* but a big, brown, baby duck.

"Quack, quack, quack," he told me earnestly, thrusting that innocent gaze to my face. He was preposterous! And then with a friendly shake of feathers that loosened more of the fluffy down, he leaned over and wiped first one side and then the other side of his beaky face on my hand, and complacently took up residence on my arm—and without a doubt, in my heart.

I paid Greg the fifty dollars.

Now how was I going to transport him? Don came to my assistance and pressured Greg to take the bird to the photographer's studio and I was grateful for that. I couldn't see myself driving three miles with the creature loose in my car—I didn't quite trust him that far yet. But I didn't want to start off on the wrong foot with the bird by forcing him to ride with me in that box.

The poor bird fought like a tiger when Greg put him back in—he hated that box. I promised him silently that it would be the last time he'd every have to ride in a box on a motorcycle; then I went to my car.

When we arrived at the studio's parking lot I asked Greg the question that had occurred again to me in the car: "What do you feed the bird? What does he like?"

Greg was untying the box. "Oh," he said, "I forgot," and he reached inside.

In an instant, Baku was out of the box and climbing up the boy's arm. Only his heavy motorcycle jacket saved Greg from a serious injury. As it was, his cheek was nicked by one of those madly scrambling claws before the youth managed to fling the bird away.

The hawk landed on his feet on the pavement a few feet away, and immediately began to fight the leash that Greg had hastily snatched up. But both boy and hawk seemed alright—I could breathe again. I looked at Greg's cut more closely; it was bleeding just a drop or two. I took a clean tissue from my purse and with a not too steady hand, I gave it to Greg. As he dabbed it at his cheek he hurried into shaky speech.

"It was my fault," he whispered, "I was careless. He didn't mean to do it—to hurt me. He just gets excited coming out of the dark into the sun. He's a good bird, not mean!" He shook his head emphatically but then he hesitantly glanced at me. I saw the indifferent young man he had been give way to an earnest boy. He sighed, "He's really not mean. But, I don't suppose you want him now . . ." Defeat was in every line of his face.

I turned to look at the bird, as he quit fighting and stood still—a small dark figure, somehow forlorn against the wide expanse of the parking lot.

"Well, Greg," I said, "I appreciate your offering me a chance to reconsider—that is very nice of you. I like to do business with people who care about others' feelings. So, I'll take your word for it that the bird isn't mean. But if he turns out to be anyway, in a week or so, you get him back and I get my money back, okay?"

Greg grinned and nodded readily—we were friends now. "Hey, that's great—you really won't be sorry; he's one of the best birds I've ever had!"

"You've had others?" I asked, beginning to feel uneasy again: Did this kid have a good little business going with wild birds?

"Only one other hawk," he answered immediately, "and it had a broken wing, somebody shot it, I guess; it was too far gone when I found it, and it died that night. That's why I was so glad to find this one, to have it live. And I'm . . . I'm sorry to have to give it up . . . ."

He looked more than sorry, sad in fact, as he stood there gazing at Baku. I realized that his apparently callous handling of the creature was due to his feelings. The turmoil inside had come out as brusqueness.

"But I've had three other smaller birds—two parakeets and a little quail," he continued, "and like I said, the hawk is the best one."

"I've never had a quail, but we did have two 'keets once upon a time. They were fun, had babies all over the place. But say," my thoughts returning to Baku, "what were you reaching for inside the box?"

"Oh, his food," Greg said, "I didn't know if you would have anything to feed him so I brought some along, just in case. It's beef," he added, reaching into the carton again and coming up with a slightly messy brown paper sack. "He gets about two ounces—that's about a small handful—of this twice a day—morning and night." He thrust the sack into my hands then turned to pick up the bird. The hawk bridled as the boy approached but stepped up readily enough unto Greg's gloved hand.

"Where do you want him?" asked Greg when we entered the office.

I looked around the small place so cluttered with fragile photographs and waved a bit helplessly. Greg pointed to a straight-backed chair near the window.

"That'll do fine," and he settled Baku on it, saying to the bird, "Now you be a good fellow; have a good life."

The bird bridled again when the boy attempted to give him a final pat goodbye and as Greg moved toward the door to leave, the fierce eyes pinned his every step.

The hackles on his neck and back, however, subsided when Greg was out of sight. He turned his huge brown eyes to the window. His neck craned, and his eyes followed first this person then that one on the street below; cars, buses, even a wailing fire engine from the nearby firehouse—nothing escaped his alert gaze. And when the noisy elevator ground into motion with its usual clanking, it was more obvious that this hawk was very unhawklike, taking everything in stride, even seeming to relish the confusion. As he sat comfortably on one foot, the other drawn up and hidden beneath his ragged breast feathers, his beak almost pressed a hole in the window glass—so eager was he not to miss a single thing going on in his new world.

After I'd watched him a few minutes (a flick of his brown tail prompted me to spread some newspaper on the floor under the chair) I began to congratulate myself on my luck. Just wait, I thought until Steve sees the bird we've got! Then the thought froze me and I winced. I had forgotten all about Steve in my involvement with the bird!

What would he say? This was not exactly the baby hawk he still expected. I stared at the sleek creature, seemingly so happy now by his window. He was so big! And I had promised to call Steve to tell him what had happened. Feeling a little guilty—and praying, that Steve would take to Baku—I reached for the phone.

I kept the information to a minimum, merely saying that our new bird, Baku, was sitting peacefully across from me, beak to window, and I described his color. Period. Better, I thought, to let Steve find out for himself when he got here. Bob Hartman, his assistant manager and a long-time friend, was to give him a lift to the studio after work and we could both bring Baku home.

While I worked and worried and waited for six o'clock to come, word of the wild bird trickled though the building, creating a parade of curious people. But despite the oohing and aahing, Baku ignored them all, eyes rapt on the ever-changing scenery outside. Customers came and went too—funny looks on their faces, they seemed to buy more than usual.

Finally, I heard a familiar step coming down the long hallway from the back stairs: Steve appeared and Bob followed him in.

I had never known what the word *thunderstruck* meant until I saw Steve's face at that moment. I tried to smile at him, but it came out crooked, and Bob started to laugh. I motioned Bob to be silent as Steve gingerly circled around the back of Baku's chair and finally came to stand beside me.

"We've been had . . . ?" he asked. There was a half-amused, half-appalled expression on his face.

I shook my head, "No, he really is only about four months old—see the brown instead of red tail?" Steve eyed it as I added, "I think we didn't stop to consider just how fast baby birds do grow. Remember the parakeets? The babies were almost as big as their parents the first time they came out of the breeding box and they were only a month old then."

He surveyed the big, sleek head, the square shoulders, and, again, the occasionally flicking dull brown tail, then he said, "You're sure it's not a baby golden eagle instead of a hawk?"

I, too, then stared at Baku. I hadn't even questioned that, but it could be, for the two species looked very much alike when young. I said, "Don claims he's a hawk, if that helps any; I *hope* he's not an eaglet—their wing span is over eight feet!" "He is a darned big thing, but he *is* beautiful."

"It *might* be an eagle," put in Bob, "he sure looks like one."

It was nice to have friends, I thought. I poked him to keep quiet. Steve was beginning to fall under the bird's spell; he didn't need to be teased just now.

The bird shook himself causing fuzz to drift from his baby down. It blew like dandelion fluff and clung to whatever it touched, especially to Steve's black pants. He bent to pick a particularly large piece off his cuff, and when he straightened up again he found himself staring right into those round eyes—Baku had withdrawn his attention from the window.

Under that fixed gaze Steve cautiously reached out his hand to the ragged breast feathers. Talking softly, he stroked the pale gold with one finger and Baku watched him carefully, eyes on his every move.

Then the bird went into his quacking act again, but this time bobbing his head up and down to punctuate, "Quack-quack-quack."

"Honey," Steve said, laughing now himself at the ridiculous sight, "it's the Easter duck . . . ."

So, Baku acquired another name—just the second of many to come—and with Steve's obvious approval his new home was assured.

Together, Steve and I managed to get our "Easter duck" into the car—Steve wadded his coat around one arm for caution's sake, and coaxed the bird onto it. By the time I got the engine started, Baku's eyes had narrowed to pinpoints again—frightened by this new roaring and vibrating "cage." He fought, flinging his wings out again and again, slapping us both with their sharp pinion feathers.

Slowly, ever so slowly, we made our way home, both of us talking softly, gently, to the terrified creature—all the while keeping his feet flat to the car's front seat between us, and easing the big wings back to his body each time so he didn't damage them in his frenzy.

Gradually, with our coaxing and soothing words, the wings strained out less and less, the big body's shivering ceased, and the huge round eyes softened into that melting, liquid brown, trusting look that was so captivating. By the time we were home our Easter duck was behaving as if he'd been born in a swaying car.

2

WHEN WE WALKED INTO the kitchen with the hawk, Ah-Soh began flapping his wings as usual and whistling his cheerful hello. Then his bright little eyes spied the bigger bird and the whistles changed to ear-splitting shrieks. He jumped to cling to the door of his cage, shaking it demandingly with the weight of his small body.

But Baku ignored the little bird, as he had ignored Don's finches, and instead looked alertly all around as I moved to turn on a lamp against the growing dark before going to calm the cockatiel. Steve, deciding the small kitchen was too restricting for the hawk, especially with Ah-Soh raising such a fuss, took a kitchen chair into the living room, and perched the big bird on its back.

Baku flapped a moment to balance himself then settled down again to continue his inspection of the premises, curious eyes minutely examining each piece of furniture in turn. Seeing that the bird was temporarily safe enough, Steve went to look for some sort of hand covering with which to handle our new friend. He returned with a stiff old leather glove that I occasionally used for gardening: It was almost too small for him but was probably the closest thing to a gauntlet we had.

He sat down beside Baku and, speaking to him, trying to make him feel at home, Steve scratched his tummy gently.

The bird arched his neck at each touch, focusing down his smooth beak at Steve's hand as he'd done at mine at the pet shop.

17

It was an even funnier movement viewed from a distance than it had been up close. Now he was a fat little man who knew *something* was going on at his feet, but who couldn't see over the arch of his pot to know *what*. We discovered much later that hawks often have trouble focusing on things close-up because their magnificent eyes are adapted to seeing details at great distances. From a height of more than a thousand feet they can see a mouse scurrying in the grass, but objects close enough to scratch on their tummies are something else again.

"I think we ought to feed him," Steve said, "do you have anything for him?"

"Oh, yes," I said, remembering Greg's thoughtfulness. Recovering the now stiff package from the car, I peeled away the wrappings, washed the meat, and cut off a slice. Steve offered it to the bird. He turned up his beak at it.

After several tries and still the same reaction, we didn't know what to do to make him eat. He did drink—accepting water from a plastic coffee cup, only after we put it up to his beak, wetting it a bit. He opened the dangerous-looking hook and dipped only the pointed lower half into the cup again and again, raising his head toward the ceiling each time to swallow. Then he shook out his feathers as if to say, "Mmmm, that was good," and wiped his beak back and forth on Steve's shoulder, using his shirt as a napkin.

The bird didn't seem to regard Steve with the hostility he'd shown toward his previous master. But about half an hour later, when Steve tried to coax him to fly, it was another matter.

Steve placed him on the wing of our upholstered green chair, then stood aside. He called to the bird, urging him to fly back to the kitchen chair, but Baku just sat and glowered. His "eyebrows," those tiny dark feathers that rimmed his eyes, knit together, just like a frowning person's brows. His mouth turned down at the pale yellow corners. He looked, in fact, just like a sulky child.

Steve returned to the green chair and sat down, talking quietly and soothingly. Baku scowled even more. Then, with a quick snap, he withdrew one strong foot from the wing and buried the four talons into the chair back, just inches from Steve's shoulder.

Steve jumped but kept his seat, clenching his fist a bit, ready to strike out in self-protection if necessary. Baku flexed his leg muscles and screamed out a challenge, head and neck feathers bristling as he glared menacingly into Steve's eyes. Then he blinked, and chirped—very like a tiny baby bird again.

He released his hold on the chair back and resettled himself comfortably on the wing, for all the world as though he had had a point to make, and once made all hostilities were over. "Let's be friends," said the big eyes, all soft again.

Steve looked at me and made a face, just as Baku decided that a shoulder was a higher perch than a mere chair wing. Up he hopped to sit beside Steve's head and begin twittering into his ear. A higher perch, we were quick to learn, was the creature's constant desire.

Feeling that we'd all had enough for one evening, I suggested to Steve that we introduce our new guest to his room. Steve nodded, and rose from the chair cautiously, Baku riding his shoulder, and slowly walked to the spare bedroom. I followed, carrying the kitchen chair that was to be his perch. I placed the chair in the center of the room, and Steve reached up with his glove to transfer the bird from his shoulder to the chair.

But Baku would have none of this being-sent-to-bed stuff. He promptly hopped up onto Steve's head to escape the insistent hand. And there he sat, quacking again, his feet firmly clutched in his new master's hair. He was really King of the Mountain now!

A smirk seemed to fill the whole of Baku's beaky face—the corners of his mouth turned up, his eyes were bright with mischief. Baku looked so satisfied and Steve so bewildered that I began to laugh. Giggling, and unthinking, I reached up to disentangle Baku from Steve's hair with my bare hand. I quickly realized it was useless; the bird had to do it himself. I placed the edge of my hand at Baku's yellow ankles, tapping them gently, and tried to coax him off Steve's head. Finally he acquiesced and climbed up onto my wrist, Steve hurriedly ducking out from under. As Steve straightened up again, Baku spread his wings and jumped from my hand to the floor. I looked at my bare wrist—I hadn't received a single scratch from those fearsome looking talons, not the slightest graze from the quickness of Baku's movements!

Baku now stalked majestically out of the spare room. Or so he would have looked if his appearance from the rear hadn't been so like that of a child with its diaper full. Back into the living room he waddled and hopped up into the green chair again and then to its wing.

Steve tossed away the uncomfortable glove—that we didn't have a predatory bird here, but a very spoiled child was apparent—and went after him. Baku played the child, obligingly climbing onto Steve's bare arm to be carried back to the spare room as before . . . but with the same result: He hopped to the floor and stalked back to the living room, with us trailing behind him.

We played this game a few more times. Each time he was quicker than either of us, hotfooting it back to the living room. Finally we gave up. Let him sit where he wants, we said to each other; he's not going to hurt anything and it's his first night here. Tomorrow is time enough for rules as to who is chief hawk in this nest. But that tomorrow never came. Baku had already claimed the position of chief.

As I washed the fish that was to be our main course for supper, I wondered why the bird hadn't touched his food. He had to be hungry by now. Greg had said the bird needed to eat twice a day because he was molting, and because his bones were still developing.

I glanced at him through the slatted room divider. He was perched on the green chair, preening his wing feathers. One by one, he drew a slender pinion through his mouth at beak tip, base to delicate end, and then he laid it smartly beside the others until each wing's feathers lay smooth and neatly shining. Steve, sitting in the chair, lightly held the lead rope that was still attached to the bird's jesses. We hadn't removed it yet because I had released Ah-Soh from his cage for his nightly exercise flight. We didn't want to take any chances even if our sweet little parrot seemed the more likely to begin any attack.

Ah-Soh darted and soared, seeming to pay no attention to the intruder. From time to time Baku would glance at the little bird as it flew by, but perhaps sensing no threat, he'd look away and go back to his preening.

The fish was half-cooked when Baku spied the TV for the first time. He gazed fixedly at the flickering screen, wriggling his head this way and that as he followed every quick movement. A commercial came on and Baku turned his head practically upside down, eyes blinking in curiosity.

An elk appeared on the screen. Instantly Baku snapped his head up and hopped off the chair. Inch by inch he crept toward the TV, keeping well to one side of the room as if to sneak up behind the elk. Suddenly he sprang at the set, claws slashing and clicking on the glass. Again and again he jumped at the bright screen, shrieking a challenge at the image of the elk.

I dashed from the kitchen, snatched up the lead rope with one hand and with the other grabbed the jesses to hold his feet to the floor. Baku screamed at me and strained toward the set. But the elk was gone, the commercial over.

"I guess he thinks the living room is his domain now," said Steve when calm prevailed once again. "He's staked out his territory and the elk was invading it."

As I reached down to pick up our now quiet and soft-eyed Easter duck, he butted my hand with his beak—didn't bite or scratch—just tapped it as if to say: "What is that you have in your hand?"

Before all the commotion I had been trimming the dry edges off the piece of meat Greg had given me, trying to make it more appealing. Now, at Baku's insistence, I opened my hand to reveal a soft and quite squishy beef scrap. In a flash Baku slurped up the messy bit, using his blunt-edged underbeak as neatly as a spoon.

"Steve," I cried, thrilled as the bird tapped my hand again, asking for more, "he's hungry! Quick, bring me some more meat from the kitchen!"

Our baby bird downed scrap after scrap, but each piece had to be dipped in hot water, to be soft and wet like the first one had been. He wouldn't accept a dry piece. After he'd eaten two small handfuls, we tried offering him the whole piece again, first dipping it in the water. But nothing doing—either he couldn't tear it up for himself yet, or he preferred to be fed like a baby, mouthful by mouthful. He would raise his big claw, under which we had placed the large hunk of meat, and let the meat fall to the floor. Then he'd gaze up at us expectantly, eyes on our hands. From then on, he dined grandly like this, with his butler and maid in attendance, until he was well over a year old.

After dinner he wiped his beak, first one side and then the other, on a towel we had the sense to provide before he tried to use the chair's slipcover, or one of our hands, as a napkin. When his face was clean, he tended to his feet, going over each claw that had touched the meat, the curved hook of his beak serving beautifully as a fingernail file. With claws spic and span, shining bright black from his ministrations, it was time again for him to watch that curious window through which he'd seen the interloper into his territory, and for Steve and me to have our own supper at last.

Baku perched peacefully on the chair wing, one foot drawn up beneath his chest, eyes on the TV. Ah-Soh cruised well away from the big bird, still seeming to ignore him. But suddenly he made a close pass, and hastily changing direction in midflight, landed in a heap right in front of the big beaky nose. The small eyes darkened with fear, and with an ear-ringing shriek, Ah-Soh took to the air again in a great flap, Baku watching with a puzzled expression.

Ah-Soh then turned buzz bomb, diving on the big bird, swooping past his head and shrilling loudly. But Baku paid little attention. After many such passes, the little parrot finally gave up and landed with all the grace he possessed right on the hawk's back!

Baku raised his big wings, stretched them out and shook Ah-Soh off, almost as if he were shaking off a gnat.

The bewildered little bird caught himself in time as he tumbled off and landed safely on the floor. Up into the air he flew again to land on Baku's broad back once more, and again Baku shook him off. Ah-Soh sat on the floor a moment longer this time, as if surprised to find himself there again, but then, bobbing his plumed head, he took off once more.

After the scene had been repeated yet a third time, Ah-Soh pecked around on the floor a bit, apparently not sure what to do next, and Baku took command of the moment; he decided to be companionable. Brown eyes still soft, he dropped to the floor beside Ah-Soh. The cockatiel took startled flight immediately.

Baku stood flat-footed, looking somewhat disappointed, as if he had wanted to play and had no one to play with, like a child whose friends had suddenly all run away.

But enough was enough—both birds could get hurt if this exercise continued. While I lifted the hawk back to the chair wing Steve caught the little bird. Ah-Soh now chose to display one of his cussed streaks. Chittering in anger, his crest laid flat against his head, he flew off Steve's finger and made straight at Baku. Before we could stop him, he bit the big hawk's toe with his sharp-edged little beak.

Steve snatched up Ah-Soh and, scolding him, returned him to his cage for the night. I soothed the enraged hawk. His toe was bleeding, but only a little, as the layer of yellow scales had deflected the worst of the attack. I talked quietly to him while he bent to run his beak over the injury, cleaning it the way a cat licks itself, before settling down again, the incident apparently forgotten.

"Well," Steve said, his eyes filled with disappointment, "so much for the idea of them being buddies."

"Maybe this was just the natural establishing of a pecking order," I said. "It could be, too, that Ah-Soh just needs time to get used to Baku. After all, he *is* the older bird, and he *was* here first. It makes sense that he would try to be dominant in any way he can."

"Hmmm," Steve said, some of the frown leaving his face, "what do you say to introducing them gradually first thing in the morning? We could put Ah-Soh's cage near the hawk's perch so that the birds could get used to one another bit by bit." Later that evening, as we turned the lights out and prepared for bed, we had no trouble carrying our sleepy new pet to the spare bedroom for the night.

The next morning dawned bright and clear. Ah-Soh in his cage was making his morning prayer music, trilling and whistling for all he was worth, and from the spare bedroom came the flap of big wings beating the air.

My first thought was that the hawk had somehow freed the lead rope we'd tied tightly to the kitchen chair that was serving as his perch. I sprang out of bed and ran to look.

But no, Baku was merely "ground testing," beating and beating his wings with feet firmly clutched in the chair's slipcover.

He quacked when he saw me and stopped his exercise with a ruffling fanfare of wing. He looked expectantly at my hands, first one then the other, and then back to my face, as if he wanted something. Breakfast! He was hungry and I'd probably slept past his feeding time.

I turned to go to the kitchen and Baku jumped off the chair to follow me, tugging and tugging at the lead rope attached to the chair, trying to drag it after him. Forlornly he gazed at the immovable chair, and with a little sigh I untied the rope, picked him up and took him, quacking with pleasure, into the kitchen.

I got out a piece of stew meat and plunked it into a bowl of hot water to warm while I put on the coffee. Baku watched my every movement with interest, but seemed to keep one eye on the slightly steaming bowl at all times. Steve wandered in, sleepily kissed me good morning, automatically went to fill Ah-Soh's seed cups, then just as automatically scratched the hawk's tummy—as if the big bird wasn't a newcomer at all but part of a familiar morning routine.

Baku seemed to feel the same way for he quacked his greeting with long-standing familiarity. Steve fed him the meat bits as I cut them and the bird took them hungrily but daintly. When he had had enough, he told us so by dropping the last bit to the floor, and wiping his beak on the towel I laid for him over the chair back.

After breakfast I filled the bucket I used to water the pots of flowers that added color to the deck before our front door. It was a scrub bucket, about a foot tall and a foot in diameter, with a metal handle. Steve carried it outside for me while I dressed for work. When I returned to the kitchen it looked to me as though Baku was yearning to go outside too, for he had hopped to the floor and was straining toward the front door, trying again to pull the chair after him. I untied him and took him with me, setting him on the deck railing, tying the end of his twelve-foot lead to it.

He quacked happily. He spread his wings to the sun; the light breeze ruffled under the gold-brushed feathers. He looked ready to take off into the crisp blue sky and soar and circle there, as he was born to do. He beat his wings slowly, rhythmically, undulating power and grace with every flexed stroke. Steve and I watched him with wonder, enthralled by the five-foot spread of his sun-gloried wings.

He was so beautiful, I could have stood there dreaming over him forever, but it was getting too late, and even though it was Saturday and the day before Easter, it was a work day for both of us. I got on with my watering, while Baku watched me as I dipped a cup into the bucket, poured water into a pot, and dipped again.

The bucket was half-empty when the hawk hopped off the porch rail and waddled towards me. The pail sat next to a camellia bush and I supposed the bush was the attraction—a natural perch for a bird born wild.

But no! In a flash of golden wings he hopped up to the edge of the pail and dove into it, head first! Before I could reach him he raised his head, looked up at me and quacked joyfully. He stood there, tail stuffed against the bucket's side and pointing upright to the sky, trying to dip first one wing and then the other into the water. He squeezed his head down, then bobbed it up again, throwing water over his back, quacking and quacking after each new bob. A bath! He was taking a bath . . . in a pail hardly big enough to hold him. Again and again he squeezed one wing at a time down into the bucket and flung it out again, water flying in all directions.

Steve came running at my call; stunned momentarily, he suddenly burst out laughing. "If that isn't the darnedest sight I've ever seen," he said when he could. "I wonder when he had a bath last? But he definitely needs a bigger tub—have we got anything?"

"How about the round pan we roast turkeys in?" I ventured. "It's big and not so deep . . . ."

"Sure, run get it; then the poor thing can have a decent bath." Steve shook his head laughing again. "A bucket—a whole bucketful of bird! Hey, that's what we should call him: Bucket!"

I put the bigger pan down beside the pail and Steve lifted Bucket out of the pail and plopped him into the roasting pan. I poured water from the pail into the pan while Bucket shook himself and squawked a second before settling into his new tub and really digging into his bathing.

Bucket finished his bath and hopped out of the pan. A more bedraggled sight I had never seen! His feathers had separated, exposing patches of surprisingly white skin. He looked half-drowned and skinny and, doglike, shook himself, drops of water flying everywhere.

I lifted him back to the railing and tried to dry him off with a towel, blotting gently. He was agreeable, but I wasn't too successfull, so I draped the towel around his shoulders. He stared over his beak at it and just as I was expecting him to shake it off he raised one big foot and clutched the ends of towel together in front of his chest. Then he scrunched down under the towel, the picture of a hunched over little old man. Steve and I were delighted by this very expressive, unhawklike creature who seemed to be taking to civilization better than we could have dreamed possible.

I would have liked to allow Bucket the freedom of the porch and sunlight all day, but I had to go to work. So, shining claws curled gently around my wrist, gleaming feathers soft and fragrant with the clean odor of outdoors, I carried Bucket into the spare room where he would spend the day while we were at work.

He glanced wistfully back at the porch as I carried him away, and in the spare room I pulled back the curtains and dragged his chair close to the window so he could look out, at least, to the street below. Bright-eyed, he settled down, seemingly content.

As I left for work, I looked up from my car to see him gazing down at me curiously, a solitary brown figure etched against the dark room behind him.

My boss, Walter Kahn, made one of his rare visits to the office that day. I was bubbling over with the glory of our new "child," and I chattered away about Bucket while he tried to work.

After a while, he looked up at me over his thick-rimmed glasses, pulled thoughtfully at the tip of his goatee, rubbed his ear, and said in a slight accent: "Geerd, I'm going to make you a present of the rest of the day. Go home to your hawk and have a happy Easter."

Touched, I jumped up to hug him, then, quickly gathering up my purse and coat I left the office and started for home. On the way I thought about a holding cage for Bucket, and so headed for Don's pet shop.

Don led me to his small, dim, crowded storeroom and pointed out two beat-up old parrot cages.

"I need space in here," he said, "so if you want to clean these up for me, you can borrow them until you get your own." He extricated them from the confusion of seed bags, smaller cages, other odds and ends and said, "They'll fit together, bottom to bottom, if you remove the trays and make a larger cage. Just wire them together and you'll have a holding cage big enough so the hawk can even stretch out his wings in it. And here . . . " he added, dragging out a two-foot tall wheeled cage stand, "set the cage on this—it will keep it off the floor and make cleaning the cage easier."

Once home, I had a hard time getting the cages out of the car, but finally I hauled them to the house near the stairs. Washing off the top layer of dust and at last getting a good look at them, I had to wonder if I'd been too hasty in accepting them; they were in worse condition than I'd thought—bent bars, no perches, no holes for water cups, patches of rusty welded-on screening, and just plain filthy from previous tenants. The hose was having no effect.

Finally I left them there for Steve to look at, knowing that no one in their right mind would steal them, and went upstairs.

As I walked in Ah-Soh called out his usual greeting of happy whistles, and Bucket had hopped down off his chair and was now peering around the doorjamb. He quacked as I came over to him, just like he was really glad to see me. I knelt down beside him and offered my hand. He stepped up readily and as I rose he bounced up to my shoulder and began a cheerful cackling in my ear.

I scratched his tummy a moment. And then, untying his lead, I walked slowly toward the front door and out on the deck. I was careful not to unbalance him for fear the huge claws might reach for a tighter hold. But I need not have worried—never did he once latch on to my arm, my shoulder, my head. If he lost his balance he would simply jump to the floor then wait patiently to be picked up again.

I tied his lead rope to the railing directly across from the apartment door. From this point he could perch on any of the three rails. Talking to him, though saying nothing at all as one does with a pet—"silly bird, such a pretty thing, what a beak face you are, a big-footed, feathered kid, all nose and eyes"—I saw for the first time that his jaws worked similarly to a human's. They not only moved his beak, they enabled him to appear smiling, sad, angry, innocent, and, at times, surprised. His posture and balance, and of course those eyes and eyebrows, were also indicators of his emotions at any given moment. Just then everything told me that he was happy to be out in the fresh air again.

I walked over to the flower pots near the front rail to pull a few weeds and pick off the dead blooms. Right behind I heard the patter of little feet—Bucket. Up onto the nearest rail he jumped and began quacking in a somewhat strident tone as if to say, "Why did you walk away and leave me?" I tickled his tummy reassuringly and when I bent over the flower pots again he jumped onto my back. He shook out his wings and sat there contentedly, his warm little toes spanning my waist. Short of knocking him off, there wasn't much I could do, I decided, so I tended the pots while Bucket basked on my back.

Suddenly, Bucket let out a wild shriek and sprang from my back to the porch rail; he had gone into full mantle—the feathers stuck out straight from his body—and he looked twice his size. I stepped beside him quickly and firmly grasped his leg jesses. George Haskins, our downstairs neighbor, had seen Bucket and was excitedly rushing up the steps. Seeing I had control of the bird, George stopped on the stair landing just below, his boney face suffused with red, and his bushy hair going in all directions. And even from where I stood, I could smell the odor of liquor on him.

"What in hell is *that?*" he roared, swaying a little and blinking his eyes in what I thought was a bleary attempt to see Bucket better.

I introduced him to the bird.

"What do you want him *for?*" he bellowed then, trying to make a joke of the words with a sticky grin.

Ruth, George's wife, came outside to see what the fuss was all about, calling up, "What's going on up there, George?" Ruth was a saucy old girl, who had a way of speaking that was at once soft-toned but authoritative.

"They've got a big ugly bird up here," he yelled down to her, leaning way over the rail to look at her as he spoke. "Hold on a sec," he added, "I'll show you."

Excitedly he lurched forward, reaching for Bucket.

But Bucket was having none of this grabbing stuff and before I could react, he sprang to my shoulder. He dropped his big wings around me like a cape lifting and drawing back one of his feet—like a man ready to throw a punch—the sickle-shaped talons spread wide. And he screamed a warning so that even George, drunk as he was, should have been able to understand. But George, apparently thinking the bird was attacking me, came rushing closer.

Scared for the man, I shouted, "No, George, stay back! He thinks *you're* trying to harm *me!* Go back downstairs before he jumps at you! It's really alright—really! He's only defending me . . . I think."

George's face had turned pale, and obviously he was in a quandary as to whether or not he should heed me. At last on another call from Ruth he retreated downstairs.

My knees were shaking hard as I shushed Bucket, trying to calm him—I was almost deaf from his screeching so close to my ear. I was more than a bit sick: Our funny new pet had suddenly turned into a real threat to a human being's safety. He may have been protecting me, but if George had come any closer . . . well, those claws had meant business, and they were capable of inflicting grave injury. And while I had seen him use them before, climbing up Greg's arm, and clutching at the upholstered chair back, the reality of the danger they represented hit me now for the first time. How could we keep him?

I talked soothingly to the creature on my shoulder, gently stroking the foot I could reach, and coaxed him to fold his big wings back to his sides. After a few minutes Bucket relaxed; I could feel the tension leave the warm feet on my shoulder. He shook out his feathers and began to softly chirr-up into my ear, almost as though he was reassuring me that I would always be safe with him.

George and Ruth were both on a lower landing now, and staring up at us, eyes big and round with wonder. "It's mothering you, Gaird," Ruth said, in a tone of disbelief, "if I hadn't seen it with my own eyes . . . . "

Bucket had been in the family less than twenty-four hours but he had treated me like I was his "chick": defending me, talking to me as if I was one of his own kind, and now giving me "hawk kisses" on my check with soft touches of that cool, black hook of a beak.

We went inside, and while Bucket watched from his perch on the chair, I began my Saturday housecleaning and worried. There was so much we had to learn about this bird! Would we really be able to keep him? I thought of all the people who came and went in our house. How safe would they be? What if they tried to hug me? What would Bucket do? Was there *any* way I could find out more about these red-tailed hawks?

I thought of Park Ranger Covel at the bird sanctuary near Lake Merritt in downtown Oakland. He was an expert on raptors I remembered, and the cages he maintained at the sanctuary for sick or injured birds had often held birds of prey: eagles, owls, buzzards, and even hawks. I'll call him right now, I said to myself, maybe he'll be able to answer our questions—perhaps he'll even answer questions we didn't know enough to ask!

"He'll be back in about two weeks," said the young ranger who answered the phone, "can I help you with anything?"

I hesitated but then decided that one ranger might be just as good as another, so I told him about the new addition to the family, then asked my questions, beginning with what should we really be feeding Bucket.

"Here at the sanctuary we feed our hawks white mice;" he said, "they don't have to be live mice—the birds accept dead ones just as readily. Hawks are lazy, you know, and that makes them almost as good scavengers as buzzards."

"Won't butcher shop meat do?" I asked, "our bird has lived on beef for several months now. . . ."

"Oh, no, hawks need the whole of a kill—the bones, the intestines, the fur or feathers—because of the mineral and roughage content. Your bird is already probably sick and weak from the lack of these things in his diet."

I looked at Bucket. He was now gazing interestedly out the front window at the neighborhood. And I thought of the uproar he had just caused. Our bird hardly seemed sick and weak.

The man continued: "They take what they need from all that stuff, you understand, and regurgitate the rest. All raptors are the same—and without the whole kill the birds deteriorate in temperament and physique very rapidly."

Boy, just what I needed, I thought: a bird upchucking slightly used mice all over the place. Stomach rebelling, I hastily changed the subject.

"Can you tell me anything about how to actually raise our bird? Anything we should watch out for? And how are these big birds around strange people—can they eventually get used to just anyone they might see from time to time?"

"Well," he answered, "first, how are you keeping him? A lot depends on what kind of facilities you have."

"Facilities?" I wondered aloud, "Well, we just got a holding cage for him but mostly he's been here in the apartment with us or on the sun porch. Nights he sleeps perched on a chair in the spare bedroom."

"Lady, do you mean to tell me that you're keeping that bird like a dog or cat?"

"Well, yes, I suppose so," I said, hesitantly, "though I hadn't exactly thought of it that way. Why?"

"It's a hawk, that's why! You can't keep it in an apartment. It's a wild bird: They're too restless, too unpredictable, too fierce!

Man's civilized world moves too fast for a hawk's nervous system; they can't handle it—they go crazy. With any abrupt noise they're liable to lash out and hurt anything within reach or even themselves. No, it's no place, no way, to keep a hawk. You'd better bring it down here; we'll put it in with our other red-tails.'' Then casually he added, ''By the way, where do you live?''

''In Oakland . . . '' I began, then remembered that hawks were federally protected birds—if someone in authority thought a captive hawk was being ill-treated, the bird could be immediately confiscated. I shuddered at the thought of a confiscated and permanently caged Bucket. The ranger's casual question now seemed ominous. Hurriedly I brought the phone conversation to an end: ''Thanks so much for your time, and the offer of a home for our bird. And I'll think over everything you've said.'' And with that I hung up before he could say another word.

For a moment I stood in the kitchen and contemplated Bucket as the sunlight from the window turned his feathers to rusty gold. Were we really doing this bird a disservice by keeping him in our apartment? Our ''facilities'' were nonexistent, true, but Bucket seemed perfectly happy as a ''house bird.'' I *still* had my questions, as well as a couple of new fears.

I made myself a cup of coffee, took it into the living room and sat down beside Bucket.

''What should we do, bird face?'' I asked as I stroked him.

But he was more interested in what I had in my cup than in deep questions. He dipped his beak into the hot coffee, then quickly jerked away as the steam assailed his nostrils. He quacked plaintively, unquestionably telling me that he did not approve of the ''funny water.'' I chuckled in spite of everything, and went to get him some proper refreshment. He was so funny, so quick to learn. Even after such a short acquaintance, I knew I would feel horrible indeed if we were forced to give him up.

3

W HEN STEVE ARRIVED HOME from work, Ah-Soh whistled out
his greeting from his perch on the room divider as Bucket
from his kitchen chair and I at the sink smiled ours. I knew without a doubt now that the hawk recognized Steve as he had me earlier that day, and was happy to see him. As I went to give Steve a
big hug, Bucket went into his quacking, head-bobbing routine and
then jumped off his chair toward us, trying to get into the act. Ah-
Soh took flight and landed on Steve's shoulder.

"You guys have a good day?" Steve asked us all as he bent to
pick up the big bird at his feet.

Bucket hopped up onto Steve's hand and then tried to climb up
to his shoulder but was forestalled by a sudden, furious shriek
from the cockatiel. The big bird eyed the small one for a moment,
and decided to stay where he was. Shaking his feathers and drawing one foot up under his chest feathers, he acted as if he'd in-
tended to perch on Steve's wrist all along.

"I see Ah-Soh's got things under control," Steve said, petting
the little bird then the larger before transferring Bucket to his chair
perch and Ah-Soh to his cage top.

"I got off early today and everything was fine when I got
home. But we had a few problems after that . . . . " I told him
what had happened on the porch with George, and about the

phone call to the ranger, then recalled one more worry, "And there is also Mr. Mac."

"Whuups, forgot about him," he said, "but we can settle that soon enough!" He picked up the phone. The doorbell rang in a few minutes and Steve answered it while I stood next to Bucket. We'd put Ah-Soh in his cage; the little bird had a habit of taking advantage of distractions so we didn't want to take any chances that he might make the situation worse.

Steve led our landlord into the kitchen. He was dressed as usual in workingman's khakis, complete with hat which he politely took off when he saw me.

"Mac," Steve said, pointing to the creature beside me, "I'd like to introduce you to the newest addition to the Wallig household: Bucket. Bird, meet Mr. Mac."

Steve was so graceful, so sincere in his mannerly exhibition, that Mac reacted the same way, with a sniff.

"Well, well," he said, "so it's a chicken hawk. Haven't seen one of those since I left the farm in Kansas. What are you going to do with him—eat him?" He jokingly growled the last, leaning close to Bucket who had been sitting peacefully on his chair, gazing at the stranger.

Bucket drew his head into his neck seeming to wince, almost as if he understood exactly what Mac had said. Mac's bushy gray eyebrows waggled in mock emphasis at the bird's reaction.

"See," he said, "the critter knows what we farmers do with pests like chicken hawks."

"Then you won't mind if we keep him?" I blurted, unable to wait a minute longer to know.

"Can't imagine what you want him for," Mac grunted, "but any bird that can scare George half-sober has my vote." He took another look at Bucket and shook his head before he turned to go. *Bucket could stay!*

"At least Mac likes our 'Easter duck'—one problem off our minds," Steve grinned. "Now for the next . . . that guy at the sanctuary. Did he seem to know what he was talking about?"

"He sounded very sure about what he said," I sighed, "but he wasn't Mr. Covel, and maybe not an expert either." Perhaps one ranger *wasn't* as good as another in this case.

"But he *did* say the same things the library books did about a hawk's inability to cope with a human kind of life, didn't he?" Steve looked pensive.

"Yes, but honey, our hawk seems to do just fine wherever he finds himself," I said, "at the pet shop, at the office, and now here. Even when George started all that commotion on the porch, Bucket withstood it really well."

"I know," said Steve with a sigh, "but what if the bird *had* jumped at George?"

"Maybe we could put a gate on the landing, a sign and a bell for people to ring. Then we could make sure the hawk was in a safe place before anyone came up on the porch or into the house."

"We could do that," Steve said, "but we'd still be liable, as far the law is concerned, if Bucket did anything to someone who climbed over the gate and came in unannounced." As a reserve deputy with the sheriff's department, Steve was all too aware of the consequences that could befall an irresponsible pet owner.

"But you know," Steve said as he turned to gaze at Bucket, who was delicately preening those long feathers at the ends of his wings, "I don't think Bucket likes George, I don't think he trusts him. That man isn't a person animals trust. You know how he teases that poor little kitten of Ruth's and gets all scratched and bitten." It was true; George always had scratches on his arms.

"I don't think Bucket would behave that way with anyone else. Maybe we're creating a tempest in a teapot where there is only a slight breeze!"

"Oh, Steve," I cried, "I hope you're right."

"I think I'll have a talk with George tomorrow, and explain to him that he isn't to come on the porch when the bird is out. That should solve *that* problem; any others?"

"Well, what about those mice?" I asked. "Do you think we really have to feed Bucket whole, dead mice?" The idea still repelled me. "He's never had them before, why should he need them now?"

"Bucket's still very young," said Steve, "maybe he's still living off the vitamins and minerals in the kills his mother fed him when he was a baby. I would guess he *will* need them again. But perhaps we could get around those mice and feed him that tonic we used to give the parakeets. It's pure vitamins and minerals."

He opened a cupboard and after a bit of searching brought out the old bottle of Avitron. "It says here it's for all birds, from canaries to parrots, and for dogs and cats too. What will it hurt to try it?"

And so all our pressing problems were more or less solved. At least for now. Even the cage, which had seemed such a disaster when I left it at the bottom of the stairs . . . After an hour's work, Steve had it clean and shining, and assembled in the corner of the deck closest to the living room window. The bird would be protected from the sun by the roof's overhang, and because the cage was tall, he would be able to watch the street and backyard as well as look into the apartment. The cage also had a strong latch; Bucket could sit inside in comfort with only his jesses on; there would be no need for the lead rope, too.

As soon as Steve had finished setting up the cage, what did the bird do but take possession of it, hopping up to its top and then, with those big feet firmly clutching the narrow bars, beating his wings, screaming again and again.

"Looks like he's trying to fly away with it," Steve laughed, and he put up his hand to stroke the clutching toes.

But Bucket wasn't going to have anybody's hand near his new possession. He nonchalantly lifted one big foot, beating his wings all the time, and wrapped his toes around Steve's wrist before he could pull away. The bird held on, and Steve, even though Bucket's hold was just firm, not painful, didn't care to have his hand held, so he tugged while Bucket resisted by leaning the opposite way. Then Bucket started to cackle—a high pitched peep, a kind of squeaky laugh.

"Gaird," said Steve with his eyes full of frustration mixed with laughter, "talk to him—he won't let go."

Saying things like, "Come on, goofy goose, turn Papa loose—there's a good bird—let go—sure, sure, Papa doesn't want your old cage—there now, there, let go." I tapped smartly on the yellow-scaled leg. Finally Bucket was tired of the game himself and let go. Then he went into his quacking act, bobbing his head at Steve as if to say, "No hard feelings, OK?"

I went about getting the rest of our own dinner ready as Bucket's warmed. We had planned a ham for Easter Sunday, so we would have chicken tonight. I had finished washing the big pieces and was starting on the giblets when Bucket hopped to the sink's drainboard beside me.

"Well, what do you want, goofy?" I asked him, surprised.

He quacked, and his big eyes rested on the chicken gizzard I held. Gizzards were my particular favorite, but I reached for a knife to cut off a small taste for the bird. He gobbled it up, and then seemed hardly able to wait for another. I was glad that he didn't try to snatch it from me, but waited patiently, although eagerly. I cut him off another piece and then tried to give him his own dinner of warm beef.

Nothing doing! Bucket wanted the rest of the gizzards.

Steve, who had been watching the entire episode chuckled, saying, "Afraid you're going to have to fight him from now on for your share. Remember Mac called him a chicken hawk."

"Chicken hawk, nothing," I said, starting to laugh at the greedy eyes that watched my hands, . . . "*pig* . . . that's what!"

Easter Sunday dawned soft and clear, with that special freshness in the air that is so typical of the Bay area in spring. I was up before Steve and Bucket awaited me as he had the previous day—the sound of his big wings beating the air filled my first waking moments.

After church we had breakfast—Bucket had the last of the chicken gizzards from the night before—and little Ah-Soh had his morning flight before Steve put him back in his cage. It would be a warm day; Steve went to open the front door. Bucket hopped off the back of his chair and tried to follow him. I untied the lead rope from the chair leg, half wondering why we kept him on the leash because he hadn't flown since we'd had him.

"You want to go outside, bird?" Steve asked.

Bucket raised his wings and began to quack, nodding his head as if begging. Steve picked him up and opened the screen door. Out of Steve's arms hopped the bird and, striding out onto the porch like he owned the world, he headed straight for his bucket.

I brought out the big roasting pan again, as Steve pulled the hawk, quacking mournfully, out of the bucket. Steve decided that our bird might like a nice warm bath so filled the pan with tepid water, thinking it would be perfect. Bucket took one look and turned his back on the waiting bath. Clearly he was very annoyed.

"What the heck is the matter with him?" Steve asked, scratching his head. "He was so hot to bathe, and now he acts like we've done something wrong."

"Maybe he doesn't like warm water," I suggested. "Yesterday's water was cold. And in the wild, a bird wouldn't have a warm bath. Water this temperature would probably be stale and unclean."

We dumped out the warm and refilled the pan with cold.

Sure enough, with a little new water splashed on his toes, Bucket's eyes went big and happy, and he bounced into his bathtub. He wallowed joyfully in the pan, dipping first one wing and then the other into the icy water, splashing it over his back and tail. And when he hopped out finally, again he accepted the kitchen towel placed over his shoulders.

A little later that morning—Bucket sun-dried and preening his feathers—Steve discovered another characteristic that made the hawk different from Ah-Soh.

"Watch his eyes a minute," he said. "When he nuzzles into his feathers, do you see what I see?"

"Why, he's got two sets of eyelids!" I stared in surprise. The outer set was covered with tiny white feathers and moved to cover the big eyes from the bottom up. The other set was underneath and moved sideways, from the inner "corner" of his eye to the outer. This set was a milky-white membrane and seemed opaque; it looked almost as if Bucket had suddenly developed cataracts.

Bucket glanced at me, his eye covered by this odd lid. Though I couldn't see through it, it was obvious that he could.

"He probably used that inner lid as a wind screen when he flies," Steve said after a moment, "like a natural pair of goggles."

This double eyelid is, in fact, nature's protection from dust and wind for the swiftest of all flyers, the raptor, and particularly useful in high-velocity dives for scampering prey. Without the flight lid the birds could be blinded by their own speed.

But Bucket now was using the flight lid to protect his eyes from his own feathers as he buried his beak deep into his wing in his preening ritual.

"Happy Easter," Ruth called up to us with a grin, one hand shading her eyes from bright sun. "You folks still have that pretty bird?" She waved something in her hand, "I bought this a few days ago for my little cat, but she doesn't like it, scared of it, I guess. Would your bird care to have a toy to play with?"

A hawk playing with a toy? I didn't know about that, but then I didn't know hawks used towels either. "How nice of you," I said as Steve went down for it. It was a long-tailed mouse of squishy pink rubber that squeaked when squeezed. Steve put it on top of the cage beside Bucket.

First Bucket eyed it, beak turned up suspiciously. Steve wriggled it and pinched it, making it squeak.

The bird took a hasty step backward at the noise, then lowered his head, peering hard at the pink "enemy." And then, in a sudden flash, his big claws snatched up the mouse, and he began to jump up and down on it: squash, squeak, squash went the toy. Bucket tossed it into the air and caught it, jumped up and down again, and then danced around on the top of the cage, wings aflap, tossing and clutching at the toy, doing his best to "kill" this mouse that wouldn't be killed. He looked up quizzically at us, almost as if asking us what to do with this thing that wouldn't submit; then with a final shake he tossed the mouse aside and regarded it disdainfully.

"Bucket doesn't like his new toy . . . ?" Steve asked the bird teasingly. "Awww, poor bird. Can I have it then? Pretty little mousie . . . " Steve made as if to remove the toy from the cage.

Bucket snatched up the mouse again, turned his back on Steve, and spreading wings and tail wide, looked mischievously over his shoulder at his master.

"You gimme that mouse," commanded Steve, reaching first one way then the other around the flared feathers.

Bucket twitched his feathers, ducked his head, and peered up at Steve. Steve yanked gently on the tail. Bucket pivoted, and, facing Steve, but hunkering his shoulders in an effort to hide the mouse in his tummy feathers, he screamed out his own mock challenge.

"Awwk, yourself," said Steve, laughing. He grabbed the toy mouse's tail. Bucket tugged, and Steve tugged back. Then Steve let go to try another tack. Poor Bucket! Off balance, he fell in a heap on the porch deck. Both Steve and I jumped up to see if the bird was hurt. But Bucket took this as part of the game and leaped up to go racing around the deck, lippety-hop, mouse in claw. Soon he came crow-hopping back to us and sprang back to the top of the cage to begin the baiting game all over again, offering us the toy and snatching it back, hoping to entice one of us back into the battle.

"So this is a dangerous raptor!" said Steve puffing a bit after succumbing to Bucket's challenge and giving him chase. "I had no idea hawks could be so much fun."

It was obvious that Steve liked the game as well as the bird did, and also neither of them wanted to lose the competition. After a few more rounds, he rolled up a penny-saver newspaper that had been lying on the stair landing. He held it behind his back and approached the bird. He waited for Bucket to offer him the mouse again, and when he did, Steve swung at it with a quick sweep of the paper.

But it was not quite quick enough. Bucket caught the paper, yanked it out of Steve's hand, and screamed in triumph. Then the victorious bird bent his beak to his new prize and began shredding it. No beagle could have done as thorough a job.

Pieces scattered and blew all over the place, and I hurried to gather them up, trying to catch them in midair. Bucket paused in his attention to the paper and eyed me with marked satisfaction when I glanced away from my futile snatching at the flying scraps. His head bobbed up and down and he smirked, actually smirked, the corners of his mouth seeming to turn up in glee. Then he tore busily into the remains of the roll.

"Enough of this," I said at last to my howling husband. "*You* lost the game—*you* clean it up."

"Hey, you bought him some more toys," Steve said as I put the sack of groceries on the counter. He took the hard rubber ball and the rubber spool with the jingle bell inside out to the cage.

"He distrusts them just like he did the mouse at first," he said when I returned to the porch after putting away the gizzards I'd bought for Bucket's dinner.

"But look what happens when I do this. . . ." He whipped up the hand mirror he had held hidden at his side. He clicked the glass to Bucket's beak and then drew it slowly away.

42

Bucket bridled, his eyes fierce, and screamed in full challenge as he snatched up the spool, ball, and his pink rubber mouse. He spread his glorious wings out fully, displaying their white and brown underfeathers.

"Why he looks just like the top of a totem pole," I exclaimed. His talons clutched hard at his possessions and with his wicked beak he tried to rake the new "enemy" in the little mirror.

"Keep him that way," said Steve, handing me the mirror, "I'll be right back."

I hid the mirror again, and Bucket looked all around suspiciously: *"Where did that enemy bird go?"* Steve returned with a camera and focused, but the bird, seeing his reflection again, this time in the camera lens, turned on it. Neck feathers bristling, he dropped his head to his chest, and darted a big foot out to the camera, claws wrapping around it.

"Hold the mirror up to him, honey," asked Steve. "Let's see if he'll do the totem pole bit again."

And Bucket did. He danced around in great style, wings outstretched, the sun picking out the gold glints just above the dark-banded flight feathers.

"Hello," sang out Bob Hartman as he, his wife, Cathy, and daughter, Kimberly, gained the top landing of the stairs. "We're on our way out to dinner but I thought I'd bring Kimmy to see your Easter duck."

Bucket had put his drawn up foot down as the group mounted the steps and now screamed a warning as they came up on the porch. I hurried to him, half afraid he would repeat the behavior he had exhibited towards George the previous day. But he didn't—he wasn't even interested in moving from his cage top—he just shrieked piercingly a couple more times as if it was something he thought he should do, then proceeded to watch the visitors curiously.

Bob's pretty wife, Cathy, looked a bit pale when she saw Bucket, but Kimmy's round, blue eyes were huge with interest.

"Can I play with him, Mommy, can I. . . ?" she begged, tugging at her mother's crisp linen shift.

"I don't think Uncle Steve would like . . ." Cathy began nervously, but Steve interrupted gently.

"It wouldn't hurt to introduce them, Cathy," he said, "I'm sure it's alright. Don't worry, Bob and I will watch her."

Cathy relaxed somewhat and Bob, giving a nonchalant shrug, strolled up to the cage.

"What are you doing, funny face?" he asked the bird with a grin, putting his hand out to touch the big feet.

Bucket must have thought he was being asked to step up, for up he stepped to Bob's wrist and sat down complacently. Bob pursed his lips a bit and looked from the bird to me. I smiled encouragingly.

"Heavy little thing, isn't he?" he said, managing a smile of his own.

"*Little!*" Cathy sniffed, backing toward the apartment door. "Well, if Steve says it's okay, it is," she said to Kimmy. "But be careful! Mommy will watch you through the window."

Steve held Bucket's lead and I went inside to keep our nervous guest company. Through the window Cathy and I watched Steve relieve Bob of Bucket so Bob could pick up his daughter. Kimmy was near to bursting with anticipation and the moment she was high enough, her little hand darted out to the hawk.

Bucket blinked at the quick movement, and his head flinched back. Steve stroked him reassuringly and Bob held Kimmy's wrist. When nothing else upsetting happened, Bucket allowed the little girl to touch his soft tummy. She giggled with delight when one of the downy baby feathers stuck to her moist little hand as she drew it away.

Clutching her prize in one hand she reached out to pet him again with the other. But Bucket seemed to have had enough of this small person, whose voice grew more excited by the minute. He stared down his beak as her hand came close, and then snapped out one big foot to enclose her tiny wrist in a no-nonsense grip.

I headed for the door; Cathy froze where she stood.

Steve and Bob started with the movement, but then quickly realized the hawk's intent. "He's not hurting her, Cathy, just holding her hand," said Bob.

And so he was. The sharp talons were carefully held away, and all that touched the vulnerable little wrist were warm, yellow toes.

After only a second or two, Bucket obligingly drew his foot away and shook out his feathers, releasing more of the filmy down. It drifted to the porch deck, and the child wriggled in her father's arms, asking to be put down so she could catch the feathers to keep for herself.

Steve put Bucket back on top of his cage, and Bob moved to take Kim's hand and bring her inside.

"No," the little girl tugged her hand away, "I want to play with the bird some more. He likes me; he gave me his feathers. Maybe he'll give me some more!"

"Kimmy," I said, "Look at Bucket's eyes; see how they're all scrunched up in the dark part? That means he doesn't want to play anymore." The little girl considered the idea and peered closely at the nervous bird. "And you know," I added, "it's hot out here on the porch. I bet Bucket would like a drink of water. Would you help me fill his water cup? And then maybe you would like a cold drink yourself."

Kimmy nodded. "Can I give him the water?" she asked as we went inside.

I hastily shook my head. "No, honey, but you can watch Uncle Steve give it to him, through the window, see . . ." I pointed to the cage plainly visible through the sheer curtains.

Steve gave Bucket the cup of water, but it turned out he didn't really want it. He hooked the edge of the cup with his beak and dumped most of the water out. Steve left the cup on top of the cage, and Bucket, now with an audience and a prop, once more turned into the silly self we were getting accustomed to. He took hold of the cup with a foot and walked with it all around the cage top, head pulled into his neck, wings held close to his body, and the foot with the cup stretched out. He hopped to the edge of the cage top and dropped the cup over the side. Watching it fall, he went into his quacking act. Kimmy squealed with delight.

"He wants someone to pick it up," Kimmy cried, "I'll do it!"

"No, Kimmy," Steve ran to the door and caught her before she could reach the porch.

Steve played this new game of Bucket's several times, picking up the cup and giving it back to the bird only to have him jump around—clink, hop, clink, hop—with it and drop it again. Kimmy clapped with glee.

Cathy turned to me. "You guys ought to have kids," she said. "You'd make terrific parents, you're so patient."

"We'd like to," I said, feeling a bit sad all of a sudden. "But nothing ever happens."

The little family left and in the late afternoon we sat down to our Easter dinner. During dessert, a luscious strawberry torte, the phone rang.

Steve and I exchanged looks. Both of us had half expected it and we both knew who it was. With a sigh, Steve got up to answer it.

Sure enough. A holiday—some men had called in sick—and the Alameda County Sheriff's Department was calling on its reserves. Steve hurried into the bedroom to change into his uniform and I began to clear the table.

Little Ah-Soh spread his wings and fluttered from his perch on the curtain rod, landing on the plate I was carrying. He eyed the leftover gravy and bits of ham greedily, but I handed him off to his cage top and offered him a slice of boiled carrot instead.

Steve came out of the bedroom and laid his dark blue cap on the seat of the green chair. He then went to put on his service belt in front of the big mirror on the living room wall. As Steve turned his back, Bucket jumped down from his perch on the chair's wing and clutched his big foot around the shiny brim of the expensive hat. Steve dropped the heavy belt, and giving a yell dashed for the cap.

Bucket took one look at Steve, shifted his talons for a better grip on his prize and sprang with it back to the chair wing, defending what he claimed as his own just as he had done earlier with the pink rubber mouse.

Steve tried in earnest to retrieve his hat before the big claws or the sharp beak ripped it but after a few minutes I saw that he needed help. I came over and tried to distract Bucket. Finally, taking the bull by the horns—or in this case, the bird by the legs—I was able to lift Bucket up and nudge his claws open. Steve quickly reclaimed his hat.

Needless to say, Bucket was more than a bit put out by the defeat. I sat him down on the chair seat and, shaking his feathers into a fan of indignation, he screamed and screamed his protests.

"Poor Bucket," said Steve soothingly, the picture of fatherly support now that his cap was safe, "poor bird . . . but you've got to learn what is a toy and what isn't." Steve offered him the toy mouse and Bucket, snatching it from his hand, seemed to forget his anger. He went into his playful routine, begging Steve to try to take the mouse back. Steve played for a minute or two before picking up his belt and precious hat and leaving, reluctantly, for work.

Meanwhile, back in the kitchen, little brother Ah-Soh found in the confusion an opportunity not to be missed. He stood knee deep in the unattended bowl of gravy, greedily slurping away. Half in anger, half in fear that he'd be ill, I caught him up and scolding him, grabbed a paper towel to sop up the mess.

It was still warm in the apartment after the heat of the day, so under the tap went the hapless little bird, squawking and struggling. Attracted by Ah-Soh's racket, Bucket abruptly appeared beside me, quacking and nodding, big eyes taking in the whole scene.

Finally I managed to rinse most of the greasy mess off Ah-Soh but when I reached for a towel to dry him, the little bird slipped like quicksilver out of my grasp and landed on the drainboard right beside the hawk. He then flew at the big bird with a vengeance, taking his revenge out on the closest thing. Bucket jumped to the floor while I quickly threw the towel over Ah-Soh. Sensing yet another new game, the big bird hopped back up to the counter and flashed a foot out toward the towel. I reacted instinctively. I threw out my arm, sweeping Bucket off the counter. I grabbed the little bird and thrust him into his cage.

Bucket hopped back to the counter and reached out his beak and banged it against the bars of Ah-Soh's cage. The little bird was furious anew. He shrilled at the top of his voice and tried to bite Bucket, sticking his sharp little beak out through the bars as far as he could. Bucket grabbed a bar with a foot and shook the cage, as Ah-Soh ducked away.

"No, silly, I know he deserves it for attacking you that way, but you are too big to start a fight with him." I tapped on his outstretched toes. He looked up at me, eyes going from my finger to my face then back again. Finally he released his hold on the cage and allowed me to coax him back up onto my hand.

It was 11 P.M. and bedtime. I got up from the green chair and lifted Bucket from its wing to carry him to his night perch in the spare room. We passed in front of the TV when suddenly he screamed and bounced off my hand to land on top of the set. Craning his neck upward, he tried to peer into the mirror that hung on the wall above the console. He had caught a glimpse of something, that "enemy bird" of the hand mirror, and wanted a closer look. But from this position he couldn't see a thing, so I lifted him up to face the mirror.

He leaped at it, talons flashing and clicking, and fell back on the TV. He renewed his attack again and again, slashing out at this other hawk invading his territory. I was fascinated as he furiously attacked the bird in the mirror, this creature who was fighting him back, bloodlessly with duplicate, though reverse, strikes. By and by, after many leaps at the enemy, Bucket must have decided he'd scared the other off and he fell back to the TV shaking the fighting stance out of his feathers.

I talked to him softly for a moment then picked him up again to carry him to his room, being careful this time that he didn't see himself in the mirror.

With Bucket settled, and Ah-Soh asleep also, I settled myself down to wait Steve's return. I must have fallen asleep in the chair for when I awoke Steve was incredulously examining the bird prints on the looking glass.

And from that day on, looking at that mirror became a matter of peering under, over, around, or through our Easter duck's toeprints. He took to the battle at every opportunity; he would eventually even fly at it, taking on the enemy from the air as is natural for hawks. But flight, that happy Easter night, was still a long way off.

4

BUCKET QUICKLY BECAME ACCUSTOMED to the holding cage into which we placed him each morning. He would flutter his wings, as if trying the cage on for size, and then would wipe his face on the smooth two-by-two piece of wood we had fashioned into a perch for him. We'd draped an old beach towel over the sunny side of the cage top. It seemed to be working well and each night when we returned home, we found the bird calm and comfortable.

One Saturday when I arrived home, a different scene awaited me. As I reached the deck, it was obvious that Bucket was nervous, very nervous. He jumped at the least abrupt movement, and when I let him out of his cage he sprang to its top, to the deck, and then to the porch rail. There he stood and screamed his eerie cry at the street below and the neighborhood.

When Steve got home an hour later, the bird was still on the rail but calmer, almost his old funny self. But he was, for some unapparant reason, still keeping one eye on the street, and he didn't seem to want to go far from the front rail.

There was no sign that anyone had been on the porch while we were gone, nothing was missing, the door hadn't been tampered with . . . . nothing had changed except Bucket.

From below, in the parking strip, came the sound of Mr. Mac pounding on his old gray truck. He'd been repairing it, exchanging motors and transmission, for the past few weeks, working on it every chance he got.

"Think I'll go down and ask Mac how the truck is coming . . ." Steve said, "maybe someone *was* up here, maybe he saw something." When he came back a few minutes later, Steve shook his head, "Mac's been out there almost all day. He didn't see anything but George wandering in and out of his own place."

The weeks went by with no repetition of the bird's nervousness. But then, one Saturday, again I came home to find his eyes narrowed down, his wings jumping, as if he would take off and fly at every slight noise.

By this time both Steve and I were sure that no unusual noise, such as Mac's constant hammering on the truck or even the test-roaring of the new engine, was responsible for Bucket's uneasiness. The bird would have been in the same condition every night when we returned home, if such was the case, for Mac was always home, day and night, and had been doing the same things for a month.

The Sunday morning after the second incident, while we sat at breakfast, Steve suddenly looked up and stared hard at Bucket, who sat as usual on his green chair. "Honey," he said, "do you think that maybe Bucket needs to go out and stretch his wings a bit? Could the fact that we've never flown him be causing these weird fits of his. He's a bird, for all his unbirdlike ways. . . ."

Of course! Bucket had never been given a chance to do what comes so naturally to hawks. I had never seen him use his wings for anything but the marvelous "ground testing" he did each dawn and often during the day. He did use them to aid him in his hops to this or that perch, but he'd never actually flown. We had almost forgotten that a bird needs to fly, and now we felt a little guilty.

"I think we should take him out immediately," I replied. "Poor bird . . . all that glorious wing power and nowhere here to use it. No wonder he has fits . . . he probably sees a seagull or something flying over, and is dying to join it up there."

But where could we let such a big bird fly freely and safely? Where could we attach an extra-long lead rope to something until we trained him to return on call?

Steve had been boning up on falconry during the past weeks

and thought he could train Bucket to respond to a special whistle. If the lead rope was reeled in just after he made the sound, perhaps the bird would soon get the idea to return to the arm at the call.

We rejected the street below us as too busy, the parking lot across the street as too small for the hundred feet of tether Steve planned to use, and the hills behind our place as full of brush. Steve picked the field behind the airport as the ideal spot for training and for flight.

Bucket took to the car like it belonged to him. He'd watched Steve come and go in it for many days, of course, and when the bird saw Steve carry a kitchen chair down to the car, Bucket was ready and waiting to go too. He climbed up on Steve's hand almost before it was offered, one eye still on the chair in the car's back seat.

We took the chair with us to provide the hawk with something he would immediately connect with us and our care of him—a link to the place and to the people from whom he got his food, should the line break and the bird get loose. We hoped that if he *did* get free he would sooner or later remember the chicken gizzards he so loved and return to a familiar place—the perch where he sat on when he got them.

During the ten-minute ride to the field, Bucket for a while sat on the front seat as he had that first day, but then, whether he was nervous or because of his natural nosiness, he suddenly hopped up to perch beween us on the back of the seat.

Concerned that his big, sharp claws would damage the upholstery, I tried to get him back on the seat, to again sit on the protective blanket I'd brought along for the purpose.

But nothing doing . . . the assertive bird claimed the high perch, and then totally ignored my tugs on the line as his eyes watched every car, every bus, every person we passed. And when a man out walking his big dog passed us, while we stopped at a traffic light, Bucket raised his voice to demand what right they had to cross in front of us. The poor dog jumped nearly out of his skin, the man stopped dead in his tracks to stare.

Steve and I, as if by common and silent consent, looked back at the gentleman with a "Hello-and-we-don't-know-how-to-shut-him-up smile" along with a "Sorry" shrug. The fellow smiled back and seemed about to drag the dog over to our open car window for a closer look, but the light changed, the car behind us began to honk, and we drove on.

Pulling away, we noticed the cars on either side of us were keeping pace with our careful slow speed. We didn't want to travel too fast for fear it might upset Bucket and make him jump around. We needn't have worried, however, for Bucket, rode a car as he might a tree limb, never so much as once losing his dignity or his footing.

Everyone was looking at us, and of course at Bucket. I felt my face going red with embarrassment, Steve ducked his chin into his neck. It was like being at a circus when the clown suddenly sits in your lap.

And clown we had with us for sure. Bucket stared back and then went into his quacking act. First he'd nod to one window, then to the other, and then he shook out his feathers as if to say, "See what a pretty fellow I am." And then the silly creature sidled along his perch going from one window to the other, as if to give everyone a better look, nodding and quacking all the while.

In a few minutes we were at the deserted field. I climbed out, taking the lay of the land. Despite the field's closeness to the airport, all around us was the silence of wild places. Small birds twittered and flitted from bush to bush. Somewhere a pheasant warbled to his mate. And jackrabbits, long of ear and soft gray, hopped about in the tall grass already turning the yellow-gold of summer. We walked up the dusty, dirt road, and then turned into the first flat meadow. The rabbits seemed totally fearless. They sat and watched as we settled down to train Bucket.

When the hundred feet of 60 lb. test line was firmly attached to Bucket's jesses, Steve took him up on his arm. After talking to him, moving his arm up and down to make a breeze under Bucket's wings, Steve held the bird still for a moment. Then with a mighty thrust, Steve launched our "falcon" into the air. Up and out into the blue sky went Bucket . . . only to crash, in a heap, not five feet from where we stood.

Well, maybe he wasn't ready, we told each other, picking him up, maybe he didn't understand that he was being allowed to fly, being "launched" to soar and glide high above his earth-bound friends.

Bucket chirped, shook out his feathers, and then laid his beaky nose on Steve's chest.

We walked back to stand beside the chair and try again. Once more, the bird was catapulted into the air. He spread his huge wings . . . but to little avail. He landed on his beak-nose in the dusty grass, and then stood up shaking his head with a great sneeze.

We tried it a couple more times, before admitting failure. The bird couldn't fly! It wasn't that he was being ornery, he just couldn't get into the air. It was obvious from the way he tried to use his wings—just fluttered them—that he didn't know how. Feeling very sad and perplexed, we gathered him up and the chair and went back home.

Steve set Bucket on the porch rail and stood gazing at him. With a lithe and sinewy movement his thigh muscles beneath the pale and amber feathers flexed, long and strong; he stretched the leg, and curled the talons—glinting black and sharp in the sunlight—into a fist.

"Useless," Steve said to him, "five-foot spread of wing, feet capable of catching and killing anything that can't eat him first, and the bird can't fly. Poor bird . . ." Bucket was now quacking and doing his dance again. It was more than Steve could take; he grabbed the bobbing beak and wiggled it gently, "Look at me," he said, "this is how it goes. . . " And with that Steve spread out his arms and flapped like a bird.

"Like this, dummy, like this!" he said, again and again.

And to give a devil his due, Bucket did watch. And then he obligingly spread his "arms" and flapped, the perfect picture of a baby imitating his parent.

I noticed then what his feet were doing while he flapped. When, Ah-Soh, a small bird, exercises his wings, his feet remained very firmly clutched around whatever perch he was on, so as not to take off by accident. But Bucket's big feet were relaxed, toes flat on the porch rail. His wings had no lifting power at all; the balls of his feet barely moved off the rail for all his flapping. Maybe his shoulders weren't strong enough, not developed enough, to allow him to fly. I pointed it out to Steve.

After a moment he mused, "He's not even six months old yet.

Didn't you tell me some book said that these birds stay with their parents for two years?"

I nodded, "And they have to be taught to fly—it doesn't just come naturally."

Steve gazed at me a long moment. "Okay . . ." he flatly said, "then that's what we're gonna do. Equipped like his real mama and papa we're not, but we're gonna teach him to fly!" And he reached for the red and orange throw rug we kept beside the door to wipe feet on.

"Toro! Hey, toro," he said, and jiggled the slightly dusty thing right in front of Bucket's beak, tweaking the bird like a bullfighter would a bull. I stepped back, out of the way . . . quickly. For Bucket took one look and leaped into this new game, a big foot flashed out and snagged away the prize.

Steve grabbed, he retrieved an end, and the tug of war began. Back and forth pulled man and bird, Bucket digging in his toes, wings flapping like oars in a rowboat, hunkering down his neck, grabbing at my poor rug with his beak, even, to get more of it in his possession. Finally, Bucket managed to get close enough with his beak and claws to force Steve to let go of the last piece that he held. And with a scream of triumph, the bird plopped himself atop the wadded-up rug, beating his golden wings in a victory salute. Steve sat on the deck and laughed.

"This is going to teach him to fly, huh?" I asked, laughing at the satisfied looking bird.

"I figure that if his muscles are still too weak, he needs all the exercise he can get. Playing tug of war is hard work. The more we can get him to use those wings of his, like he did just now to pull the rug away from me, the stronger his back, chest, and shoulder muscles will get. At least that's what I think."

It seemed logical. "In the nest," I said, thinking aloud, "a young hawk would have been fighting for his share of food, each baby trying to drag whatever he could closer to himself to get more to eat."

"Sure," Steve agreed, "and I think if we see that Bucket is stimulated as much as he would be in the wild, well, I'd say one day he'll be strong enough to fly from my arm."

The next morning I called the Oakland sanctuary first thing, with fingers crossed that I'd get the expert this time. He was there. After he listened to me about Bucket, adding a word or two at intervals, Ranger Covel sighed.

"Mrs. Wallig," he said, "I'm sorry to have to say this, but nobody but its mother teaches a hawk to fly. A captive bird either knows how already or never learns. That's one reason the law forbids taking baby hawks from the nest until, at the earliest, late September. By then the birds are more or less able to survive on their own, having had the benefits of the mother's teaching all that time."

"Well, couldn't we try to duplicate that teaching somehow?" I asked.

"I don't know of any way you could," he answered. "Besides, in captivity the bones, and the chest, neck, and back muscles of a young bird don't develop properly. The bird needs the months and months of the squabbling and training it gets in the nest, as well as the example set by its parents."

Then he added, "I'm just afraid you got your bird too young. And I'm afraid he'll never be any good for falconry, even to the limited extent that a male red-tail ever is. He'll probably never even be able to care for himself in any way, he'll get loose, get his jesses caught in a tree and be helpless. For his own good, I suggest you bring him down here, before he escapes only to starve to death, unable to catch his own food."

"Don't worry," I assured him, "Bucket's not going to get loose, we'll see to that. And even if he did, all we'd have to do is walk over and pick him up. But," I added, since despite my depression over his words I was also curious, "what did you mean when you said something about male red-tails and falconry . . .?

"Males are independent," he said, "feisty roosters who don't usually form the attachments to a master that are so necessary for a bird to be a good falcon. Females are better, and generally even in the wilds they're better hunters. Male red-tails are very lazy; they'd much rather be fed then hunt for themselves or a master."

"Yeah," I said, "I can see that; this one won't even tear up his own food, likes it warmed, then cut into bite-sized pieces."

"Oh, you shouldn't let him get away with that," Covel said immediately, "hawks need to tear up their food by themselves or the hook on their beaks grows so long that they literally become cripples and die because they are unable even to open their mouths."

I realized Bucket's hook *had* grown more than a little since we got him.

"Otherwise, it sounds to me like he's doing fine. You might add some bonemeal to his rations, that would help him. And you might even wind a few strips of old toweling around that perch in his cage so he can tear it up and eat it—to replace the crop-cleaning feathers and bones he isn't getting from that butcher meat he's eating. Make sure the cloth is clean, of course. . . ."

"I'm afraid Ranger Covel thinks Bucket will never fly," I told Steve that evening and watched the disappointment seep across his face as I explained about the mother bird's teachings. "He also confirmed that even if Bucket already knew how to fly he wouldn't be good as a trained falcon because he is a male."

Contemplating the peaceful bird who sat, one foot drawn up, beside his toys, watching the world around him, Steve's face became unreadable.

"He is a good pet, anyway," I ventured, "we can just enjoy him as he is . . ." I mentioned then that Mr. Covel had said we needed to obtain a "hawking" permit, to make our keeping of Bucket legal. "He was specific on that; we're supposed to write for a federal application then return it along with the $15 fee—so they can keep track of how many of the protected hawks are in captivity."

I made a mental note to do it myself because I could tell Steve's thoughts were elsewhere. His eyes had turned again to Bucket and lingered on his gold-brushed wings.

"It's just not right that he can't do what he was born to do." he said abruptly. "He's a bird. He belongs in the sky. And no matter what anyone says, I'm going to do my damnedest to make up for what he hasn't had, to see to it that he has his chance! And you know what? I feel that we should think about what he really is—a wild, free-born creature. Is it right of us to keep him? Is it right that he spend the rest of his life as just a pet for us?"

56

I knew very well what Steve meant, all too well the feeling of wrongly imprisoning a wild animal, but it was as if a cold, great hand had closed roughly around my middle, leaving me breathless with sense of loss and sorrow.

"We should think about setting him free one day. Just imagine it: to look up into the sky one day and see a hawk circling and soaring; and to know that maybe we had a hand in making that happen, that we helped to add such a beautiful creature to the world instead of subtracting one from it. It would be the right thing to do . . . to give Bucket back his birthright. . . ."

I agreed, but I couldn't, even though we'd had Bucket only a short time, face the thought of not ever again being able to touch him, never to feel his weight land on my back as I leaned over a pot of flowers, never to have him sit on my shoulder again or touch his beak to my hair or cheek or neck in a hawk kiss, never to feel his soft feathers under my hand or my cheek, never to have him chirp his hellos at me as I came home, never to have him eat from my fingers, never to have him to love again. I was being selfish I knew—but I just couldn't help it.

I gazed at Bucket silently. A light breeze had come up. As usual the bird had spread his wings to it, waving them gently up and down, waggling the long dark feathers at their tips like fingers which might touch the face of the warm south wind. And the corners of his mouth turned up as if the gentle draft beneath his wings was a pleasant feeling.

He was a wild thing. Every inch of feather and bone cried it, and the oddly inward-turning look of the soft, brown eyes whispered to me, told me he might be wheeling in a dream of flight, even though he had no idea how to spring himself with his strong legs from the earth. And he wasn't mine; he belonged only to himself; every bit of the independent personality in him proclaimed this, loud and clear. But he would let us touch him and love him, because he was growing more each day to love us, because he trusted us. And then a different sense of what that trust meant suddenly curled around my feelings—along with a wistfulness that would never leave me.

"All right," I said, all at once determined to shake away my growing depression. "Okay! He's a wild thing being forced to spend his days with people and not be free, but there's so much he doesn't know about being a hawk, that I don't see much hope of accomplishing the goal. But let's see if we can't at least give him a fighting chance. . . ."

Bucket was definitely a household pet, but he grew stronger all the time. A few months passed, and Bucket decided he'd had enough of sleeping on the chair in his bedroom. One evening after we'd put him to bed, we heard the big feet go plop on the floor, followed by a patter, patter. And then came the sound of flap-flap, thump, flap-flap, thump.

After this had gone on for a few minutes I become curious. The bird had often left his perch before settling down for the night to hop up to the window and gaze for a while at the quiet street. But this noise was different. Whatever he was aiming at with his leaps was higher than a window sill.

I crawled out of bed and went to look.

The street lights outside illuminated the room enough to see, but my eyes couldn't find Bucket. At last I looked into the dark corner behind the half-open door and there he was. He chirped as I spied him, and then he raised his pointed face to the ceiling. I snapped on the light, trying to determine what he was looking at, and with that his big wings again beat two quick strokes and he sprang up at the face of the door. But, thump, he landed again.

On the next attempt he managed to hook the door top with his beak, but quickly lost his precarious grip, and the swept-out wings played parachute to let him down easily.

"He wants to sleep up there," Steve, beside me now, said, "It might do him good to use his wings that way to get down from high places . . . Look, he's trying to use them now to get up there. . . . " And he was. It was the first evidence we'd had that Bucket *did* instinctively know he had to use his wings if he wanted to go up. And it was obvious his wings *were* getting stronger, that his chest, neck, and back muscles *were* responding to the continuous games we played with him, for the wings had helped him gain a few inches up the door.

Bucket gazed at me from the floor and then eyed the door top longingly. I pressed my cheek against one soft wing as a sign of praise and approval, then hoisted him up to his objective. He shook his wings happily, stretched out one leg after the other, tucked his foot up and then closed his eyes.

The next evening, I was a bit late in getting back from work. Steve had arrived before me, but he was not home, I saw, as I pulled up at the curb.

Across the street in the gravel parking lot behind a sporting goods store stood Steve, two of our kitchen chairs, and Bucket. The bird was perched on the back of the chair with his eyes on his adoptive parent. Steve was flapping his arms, calling to his child, and patting his glove-covered wrist. Encouraged by the scene of last night he had obviously decided to waste no time starting Bucket's flight training. Half the neighborhod seemed to be watching them.

I got out of the car and strolled over to the lot, waving hello to the enthralled neighbors who lined the balconies of all the buildings within sight. Even little Mrs. Greenwood had come away from her knitting to watch. She was standing at the corner of the lot and I stopped to speak to her.

"Dear child," she said, taking my arm in apparent delight at seeing me, "I have witnessed many strange sights from my window, but never one like this. I just had to come out. And your husband is so dear and polite. He said your Bucket wouldn't mind if I watched. But what is the matter with him, if you don't mind my asking? Why won't he go to your husband?"

Just as I was about to explain to her that the bird couldn't fly, the elderly woman said, "Oh, look! Now he's behaving. . . . "

Bucket, who had been cheerfully waving his wings in imitation of Steve's frenzied movements, had hopped down from his perch on the chair and was obligingly walking over to him.

"There's a good bird . . . to come when I call," Steve said, "But, dummy . . . that's not how it goes! You gotta fly, wings are for flying . . ." He ran his hand down one of Bucket's wings, lifting it out and away from his golden body, and then moved it in a flying way. "Come on," he cajoled, "let's try it again." He put Bucket back on the chair. Then he returned to the other chair and whistled, patting the chair back encouragingly. Both man and bird seemed oblivious to the audience; not once did either of them so much as glance up to see who was watching.

Again Bucket spread his wings. And again he closed them before hopping down to trudge over and jump up onto the chair by Steve. This went on for some time. Finally, Steve picked up the bird for the last time, and raised his head to discover all his neighbors, who began to show their appreciation of the show by applauding.

Steve's face turned pink, but he grinned when he saw me. He tried to appear casual as he walked over with Bucket on his arm, but I could see that he felt like dashing for the house.

"Bucket was kind of nervous when I came home," he explained. "You know, that same old scared mood where he'd jump if I even moved my hand too fast; so I thought I'd try to give him something else to think about."

The bird's odd fits were rare but they hadn't changed too much in the past months. And we were no closer to the solution of the mystery than to its cause.

From Steve's arm Bucket was serenely gazing around the neighborhood, taking in all the cars and people who were now returning to their homes.

"What would make such a pretty bird nervous? The lucky bird has even his little friend to visit him, so he shouldn't be nervous," Mrs. Greenwood cooed, still standing beside me gazing at Bucket curiously.

"Little friend?" I asked her what she meant.

"Why, your neighbor downstairs brings his little kitty up to play with your Bucket. He did today," she said. "They have a wonderful time. Bucket jumps up and down in his cage. At first I was worried about it, that they might hurt each other, you know. But your neighbor told me that he always holds on to the kitty so she wouldn't get too close. So it was all right, I thought . . . Isn't it all right . . .?' she asked, a little apprehensively.

"Sure, Mrs. Greenwood," Steve murmured, handing Bucket to me as he gently took her arm. "Everything's all right. And we really appreciate your concern for Bucket. With a good neighbor like you watching out for him, we won't be so nervous about leaving him alone in the daytime."

He began to walk her home while I tagged behind. "One thing, though, Steve said as we walked, "Bucket needs to be quiet when the sun is on the porch. He shouldn't have too much excitement or he might get too warm and then maybe get sick. I'll mention this to George, but if you would continue to keep an eye on our place, in case anyone else decides Bucket needs company, I'd really be grateful."

"Oh, certainly I will," she said at once, "and I'll come right out and chase them away too! We can't have Bucket sick. You leave it to me."

"Oh, no, please," Steve said hastily. "I wouldn't hear of your running over to our place, disturbing yourself. Tell you what . . . why don't I give you Gaird's phone number at work, and our landlord's number. Then if you see anything, you can call either him or us?"

And with this, we acquired what we came to call our "guardian angel," because that's what the sweet little lady turned out to be, averting possible catastrophe a number of times.

With Bucket once again secure to the porch rail, and the two kitchen chairs back in the house, Steve and I sat down on the deck chairs and pondered the problem of the meddlesome George.

"I'd like to go down and bust him in the mouth!" Steve said tightly. "Damn fool! That's what he is! What does he think we have the gate for? What if someone had gotten hurt?"

"We don't know anything . . ." I pointed out, trying to keep calm. "Maybe the bird likes the cat. It's only a kitten, after all. . . ."

"We *do* know that he doesn't like George," Steve said, as the first flash of fury was ebbing. He took off his glasses and rubbed his face dispiritedly with both hands.

"Hey, Steve, Gaird . . ." Speaking of the devil, we heard George's door close downstairs and then his foot hit the bottom step.

"Man, how I'd like to teach him some manners!" Steve muttered, and then putting his glasses back on, he said, "Well, we have *got* to get across to him that no matter what he does with his own animal, he has no right to tease ours."

Bucket shrieked for all he was worth. He bounced from cage top to deck to front rail—like a coiled spring gone amok—wings, head, back and neck more swollen than I'd ever seen before. I raced to grab his lead and jesses. George came onto the porch, finding nothing unusual in Bucket's behavior I supposed, glancing indifferently at me as I fought to hold on to Bucket's lead as the bird screeched and threatened like he'd actually gone crazy. In exasperation I yelled at George to go back to the landing until I could get the bird into his cage.

Steve walked over to George and waved him downstairs in no uncertain terms. After a few minutes of coaxing, and the enemy out of sight, I was able to persuade Bucket to step up on my hand. Once the cage door was latched, I draped the beach towel over the cage to cut off his view hoping to calm him.

"It's all right now, George!" I called as I walked over to stand beside Steve, half expecting to have to put another towel over him too.

"Boy, he's fierce!" George, gaining the porch again, grinned. "Our kitty and I have been playing 'get-the-cat' with him every once in a while, and he raises such cain it tickles me. Have you seen what he does when you poke a stick at him through the cage?"

A sick chill enveloped me—the man didn't consider it wrong to torment or tease a caged creature. Talk could prove useless.

"And you think that's fun?" Steve cut in, too quietly.

"Oh, sure," George said. "It's good for him, too. Gives him a good workout."

I put a warning hand on my husband's arm and said, "Well, George . . . I kind of think we'd rather you didn't give him any more workouts. One reason is that Steve might want to make Bucket into a falcon, and in order to do so, he, and only he, must work with him. It's the way a hawk is, George," I continued, hoping he'd understand and not get so angry that perhaps he'd sneak up one day and do something worse. "They only serve one master, see. And if you keep on playing with him like that, he might even grow confused and then not recognize *anyone* as master. It might even make him useless as a pet: He might turn mean and try to attack everyone who comes near him. Then we'd have to have him destroyed because even a zoo doesn't want a mean animal. Will you help us out? Will you leave him entirely alone from now on?"

"Well, I didn't mean any harm," said George. His voice was blustery, but also edged with a bewildered defensiveness that made him seem very like a little kid who was becoming aware he'd done wrong.

Steve patted my hand resting on his arm, tried now himself to ease the situation. "No, we know you didn't," he said in the mild tones I'd heard him use in his role as policeman, "not many people know much about hawks. Tell you what," he clapped George on the shoulder, "now that you know, and live so close, how about you keeping an eye on Bucket while we're at work on Saturdays? You wouldn't have to do anything, of course, but if you did hear anyone walking around up here when we're not home, maybe you could run them off or something. . . ."

I held my breath. Would George think we were patronizing him? Then I began to wonder why he'd come up right now. So I casually asked if there was any special reason for this visit, seeing as how he didn't come up to visit very often.

He slapped his hand to his forehead and exclaimed, "Wow! I'm gonna get killed! Ruth sent me up to borrow an onion for her chili and told me to come right back. You don't have . . . ?"

"Sure, I've got an onion," I laughed at his expression and went to get it.

He took it from me with hasty thanks and then made a beeline for the stairs, saying, "And don't worry, Ruthie and I will keep an eye out for Bucket. See you later."

Several weeks passed without incident. Steve worked Bucket every night after work in the parking lot. It got to be so common a sight that the neighbors stopped watching. And all Bucket did was the same old thing: hopping off the chair and walking over to Steve. At least we could congratulate ourselves on one accomplishment: The hawk had learned to respond on call. A single old-fashioned "wolf whistle", preceeded by a high-low note to attract his attention, would bring Bucket waddling over. This very unhawklike hawk didn't limit his responding to Steve alone. I, too, could whistle in the same way and onto my shoulder he would spring. So much for what experts said about a falcon's loyalties, at least where this particular bird was concerned.

Talking about it later, Steve worried that the bird might respond to just anyone who whistled to him so he asked Mr. Mac to try to call Bucket. But at Mac's whistle, the silly bird stared at the man, then drew his beak into his chest, as if to say, "Humph, who do you think you are?" And turning his back, drew up his foot,

definitely not interested. Mac sniffed in droll rejection at his re-
sponse and returned to his truck.

Steve and I were rather pleased. At least Bucket wouldn't inad-
vertently leap onto some unsuspecting wolf-whistling person's
shoulder. And we were sure now that he couldn't be lured away by
anyone intent on "hawk-napping."

Bucket spent many of his days fighting with the throw rugs— he'd
taken to jumping on them. He'd wad one up into a pile, pounce on
it, claws snapping and flashing, spring away from the enemy, return to shake it, and jump up and down on it, beating at it with his
big wings. When he'd enough of the battle, he'd plop himself
squarely on the enemy and scream in triumph—big, mean, hawk-
faced hunter.

Soon Bucket discovered that Mr. Mac's black and white cat
was a much more interesting opponent. The cat had long known
we had a bird, in the house, Ah-Soh. The little parrot liked to
warm himself in the morning sun and would perch on the table

lamp beside the window. Cat had found that if she came and sat outside the same window, she could *almost* have a bird in her clutches. She would stand on her hind legs and, with paws stretched against the glass right next to the little bird, she would rub her head against the window, lap her tongue on it (and then make the most disappointed face), and hope that the bird just might, just *might* find a way to get outside.

Ah-Soh seemed to think her silliness great fun. He would rap his sharp little beak on the glass every time she seemed about to lose interest and turn away. And he'd obligingly flap his wings at her when she drew her claws excitedly across the glass, and then he would begin bowing to her. This drove the poor cat almost crazy and she would fling herself, thump, at the window again and again.

The hawk had watched these morning charades for quite some time. Bucket had never done more than watch Ah-Soh tease the cat, however, until one early August morning when the poor puss, apparently baited beyond endurance, abruptly flung herself from the offending cockatiel's window and unthinkingly sprang atop the cage to which Bucket was tethered.

I saw it happen and started to run outside, to grab one or the other of them, I didn't know just which. But then I saw that each animal was as puzzled as the other by this confrontation. Cat looked at bird, eyes going round as saucers; bird stared at cat, just as surprised. Then bird screamed at cat: "Hey, you, get off *my* cage!" And cat didn't wait to be told twice. She scuttled for dear life, off the cage, across the porch, and lickety-split, down the stairs, with the very curious hawk in pursuit. Bucket stopped at the porch rail, though his 100-foot line allowed him much more room, and then followed with his eyes the cat streak away, stretching straight out from the rail toward the street in his desire to see where she was going so fast.

Later, I was relaxing with a book in the green chair beside the window when I suddenly realized that Bucket, who had been peacefully roosting on his cage top, had come alert. Every line of his feathered self seemed pointed toward something beyond the top landing of the stairs. I leaned to look.

And there, inching along on her white belly, was the cat. Having recovered her courage and having finally figured out that she was a cat and Bucket a bird, she was stalking her prey in the most businesslike manner. Black and white fur blending with the shadows between the flower pots and the apartment's stucco wall, she put one foot at a time before her. Her eyes never leaving the juicy prize atop the cage. When she had made it to the front door, where her cover vanished, she froze. And then making herself as small as possible, she darted to the shade of the pot nearest Bucket's cage.

All the while she was sneaking her way towards him, Bucket just calmly watched her. I wasn't the least bit afraid for him—he was equipped to handle a cat—but I was a bit worried for her safety. Bucket, by then, had demonstrated many times with little Ah-Soh that he would live and let live as long as no one picked on him. But if this sneaking cat did mean him harm, he was sure going to teach her what a hawk was all about.

The cat hovered, scrunched down, by the side of the flower pot, her black and pink nose pointing and sniffing toward her objective. And then, either realizing what the cat was about to do, or deciding to have a little fun, the bird stepped off the cage to drop right in front of the questing nose. As if that surprise wasn't enough, he thrust his hooked beak to the quivering nose and then he let out a quack.

The startled puss leaped straight up and, with a single movement, swiveled in midair to land on the other side of the flower pot. Then she scooted for the safety of the stairs and the street.

For Bucket it was "chase the cat" time. With mighty hops with his strong legs, he raced her down the stairway, the cat taking two stairs at a time, the bird leaping along above her on the hand rail. They both made the concrete together, and the cat, recoiling abruptly as she landed only to find the bird suddenly again beak-to-nose with her, leaped backward right into a small rose bush, and from there to the fence that led into the backyard and the safety of the apple tree. Poor cat, of course, had no way to know that she was safe from this particular bird once in the tree. She scurried out to a tiny limb that overhung Mr. Mac's open screen-less bedroom window. From there she dangled until she managed to get a foot on the window casing. Zip, into the house she went.

Bucket's eyes were wide when I bent to pick him up, and he

had the strangest look on his face, almost as if he couldn't believe that anything could be as peculiar as his departed friend.

This incident was the first of many such encounters: Every time the cat would find the courage to attempt a "hunt," and the bird was free enough to give chase, the two of them would play their game.

Steve and I were both at work when the game changed a bit. It might have been, in fact, the end of the cat's career, but for our "guardian angel."

I had left in a rush that morning, after having played with Bucket a little too long. Discovering I was almost late for work, I'd hastily put him into his cage, forgetting to check that the door was truly closed. It had a tricky double catch, one notch of which only held the cage door closed; the second notch really latched it.

Steve got a call at work. "Could you possibly come home—right now!?" Mr. Mac asked, "We have a small problem here. Your bird is chasing my cat. . . ."

Steve ran for his car. He found Mr. Mac's face pressed against the window overlooking the side yard, straining to see around the corner of the building.

In a moment it became quite clear what the trouble was. Cat had, in our absence, decided to try to regain her reputation as mighty huntress and had apparently started the game up. The un-tethered Bucket had pushed open the cage door, and was now loose. No lead rope to stop him short at the fence under the apple tree! And this time, Cat had missed her footing on her "home base" window sill.

Here Bucket came—leap, hop, run, leap—in hot pursuit of the racing cat. Around and around the building they want, Bucket us-ing his strengthening wings to aid his pumping legs.

"How long have they been at this?" Steve asked Mr. Mac, per-plexed and solemn, but trying hard not to laugh.

It was a comical sight, cat streaking for all she was worth, hawk with his beak almost touching the end of her tail, and both of them totally enrapt in the chase. Dumb cat never thought to leap into any of the several trees she passed, and the hawk never thought to leap onto the cat, which he could have easily done; just round and round they raced.

As they raced by, Mac answered, "Oh, about fifteen minutes that I know of. Mrs. Greenwood, across the street, called me wanting to know if I had seen how cute they were."

The two came around the corner again, and suddenly the cat stopped. The bird also applied the brakes and stopped behind her. He held out his wings, letting the cooling breeze flow through them. Steve started towards them. No sooner had he made two strides then the cat jumped up and raced away with Bucket again pursuing her.

Steve looked questioningly at Mac, who said, "Yeah, that's what they've been doing. They run like blazes, then stop to rest, then get up and run again." He shook his head as Steve snorted with laughter. Mac then added, "I couldn't get close enough to even touch my cat, much less the bird. They veer away when I try."

Steve thought over the situation, then said to Mac, "Why don't you open your front door. I'll stand by the corner of the house, and when they next come around I'll jump out in front of Bucket to stop him while you call in your cat."

The sound of toenails on concrete was soon heard again. Around the corner came the cat. As she passed Steve stepped out and quick as a flash scooped Bucket into his arms. The big wings struggled. Steve got one hand around a leg, then the other, and it was all over. He held the flapping bird up to his face and yelled, "Quit, already."

Bucket took a good look at who held him and with a final flap he closed his wings. Steve had just settled him on his arm, when the cat came running around the corner again. Mac hadn't been successful.

Steve and Mr. Mac watched her race around the building a couple more times. Mac shrugged his shoulders; what could he do? The cat was crazy. Mac laughed out loud but then he stepped outside in front of the cat and caught the silly beast as she careened into him. She collapsed in his arms, no fight left. Mac told us later that it took her two full days to recover from her ordeal, and even then she didn't want to go outside.

But Bucket seemed to suffer little if any ill effects, though his heart was pounding heavily under his feathers when Steve recovered him, and the bird's beak gaped open, revealing his pointed tongue, panting like a dog.

Toward the end of August I was not feeling well and blamed it on the uncomfortably hot summer. And everyone and everything around me, including the birds, irritated me, expecially since Ah-Soh had lately taken to picking on Bucket more than usual. In his morning flights the little bird would "dive-bomb" the bigger one, smacking Bucket on the top of his head with a wing or a foot, or sometimes even a beak if he felt daring. I have seen wild birds doing the same to cats camouflaged in the tall grass. They dive-bombed the cat, closer and closer, more and more daringly, and then suddenly a clawed paw would go up—end of divebomber. But Bucket never raised a claw.

Evenings, little brother would flit back and forth from living room to kitchen, upsetting Bucket's water bowl by landing on it with a determined bounce or two. And Ah-Soh would then, if his efforts had been successful, land on the divider and shriek in his shrillest whistle, almost as if he was a laughing gleefully at his mischief. Even perched atop the open living room door poor Bucket could have no peace, because the little bird would tease him and try to coax the hawk into reaching too far out to snatch at him. Off balance, the big bird would have to jump down to the floor forced to be low man instead of King of the Mountain. Bucket would then shriek and shriek his eerie cry until someone came to pick him up and hoist him back up to the door top.

Thinking back, I realized it must have been the noise the two of them made with their bickering that upset my nerves most. A two-bedroom apartment, containing a loud-voiced parrot competing with a screaming hawk is not the most restful place.

I even took to picking on Steve when he arrived home a few minutes late from work, or when his games with Bucket seemed a bit rowdier than usual.

And Bucket, of course, caught an extra share of scolding for not accepting Ah-Soh's teasing, and the scolding seemed to incite the big bird to attempt to settle the score even more.

One of these occasions proved too much. It was after work, a drizzly evening. I had a headache, and needed some aspirin. I left

Bucket loose in the house, but had shut Ah-Soh in his cage. Both birds would be safe, I was sure. Bucket had tried, more than once, to get at the little cockatiel in the cage, but the bars were very closely placed and he'd had no luck. Besides, he hadn't liked being scolded for shaking the cage around. So I walked to the drugstore for a bottle of aspirin, feeling certain the two of them would be all right, and brooding on my miserable day at work—an expected shipment of pictures hadn't arrived, and all day people had been calling, upset at not getting deliveries as promised. My stomach was churning from so many apologies, and my head ached. To come home and find an empty aspirin bottle did not help me toward a better mood.

With the aspirin in hand I came home again. No sooner had I reached the top step than I heard the cockatiel squealing in his most distressed voice, and I heard a thump-thump.

Quickly unlocking the door, I was horrified to see that Bucket, one big claw firmly clutching the bars, had dragged Ah-Soh's cage to the doorway of the spare room. It was lying on its side, caught against the doorjamb. The little bird inside the cage was terrified, as Bucket, who had seen me change paper many times, now decided that if I could pull open a cage bottom surely he could do the same, the better to extract the little pest and chastise him. Bucket was so involved with what he was doing that he hadn't noticed me yet. I picked up a newspaper from the coffee table, rolled it up and furiously descended upon the big bird, smacking the floor before him.

He at last retreated to a corner of his bedroom, me chasing him, smacking at his tail as he ran around and around the room trying to escape the raining blows. I threw down the paper, raced over to Ah-Soh's cage, snatched him out, and then stomped back to thrust him into the big bird's face. Bucket cringed.

"You see him?' I shouted at Bucket. "This is my bird—mine! Don't you ever in your life try to eat him again, or I'll pull every feather out of your rotten hide and have you for dinner myself! You got that!'' Then I thrust my poor little, very mussed-up cockatiel back into his cage.

Bucket looked away from me and stared into the corner, inspecting it centimeter by centimeter, for all the world like a kid who's in disgrace, and knows exactly why, but hopes if he doesn't call any more attention to himself, the grownups will pretty soon forget. My ill temper evaporated. I rubbed my still aching head and went to kneel beside the big bird. He dared a glance at me and then chirped inquisitively as I stroked his soft tummy.

"It is all right now, Bucket," I said to him. "Mama's sorry to be so cross with you; but you just can't eat little Ah-Soh . . ." I picked him up, his big toes curling softly around my wrist. "Come on now, you come sit with Papa, and I'll go take my aspirin."

Steve had by this time arrived home, picked up Ah-Soh's cage and placed it back into its niche. The little bird was none the worse for wear and was busily preening when I reached into the cage to pet him. He kind of eyed me with one eye as if he thought I might snatch him up again but when I didn't his little world seemed to be all right again and he nodded his head to me, begging as usual.

I still didn't feel well, and nothing seemed right as it always had been. I went to Steve and cuddled up, hugging him, feeling sad, and suddenly worried that I might be sicker than could be accounted for by hot and muggy days.

The next morning at Steve's insistence, I called the doctor. "You better come in," said the desk nurse. "How about two o'clock?"

Steve came home that evening to find me sitting in Bucket's green chair, with Bucket right beside me on the wing and little Ah-Soh flying happily around the house.

"Nice to see all three of you pals again," he said, smiling as he noticed that the small bird's swings through the living room were giving the large bird a wide berth. I gazed almost unseeing at Ah-Soh and nodded absently. Steve came over to me, and put his hand under my chin.

"What did the doctor say, honey?" he asked me quietly.

I looked at him, noting the scared calm on his face. He was trying so hard to be ready for what he clearly expected to be bad news. I grinned, almost evilly.

"Oh, nothing much," I told him, suddenly bursting with excitement. "I'm just quite, quite pregnant!" His eyes went a bit glazed.

"Oh, yes!" he said, and then he grabbed up the beak-faced bird and babbled, "A baby . . . a baby . . . after five years, Bucket, we're going to have a baby!"

Attracted by all the noise, Ah-Soh landed on my shoulder to watch the sight.

"One's quite as crazy as the other, you know," I said to the little bird. "Look at them: We're going to have a baby, he crows to the hawk . . . not to the mother, you understand but to the bird."

"Well, why not?" Steve suddenly stood beside me, Bucket still on his arm. "After all, it's all his fault. . . . Adopt and you're sure to find one of your own on the way!" He waggled his eyebrows at me, and I could almost swear Bucket did the same.

5

THE BABY MEANT that certain changes would have to take place. Babies were welcome as far as Mr. Mac was concerned. But, we only had two bedrooms. We needed three bedrooms if Bucket was to continue to have one of his own. We began to consider the idea of moving.

One day I was folding towels in the small pantry room that served also as linen closet and connected the bedroom to the bath and kitchen. Bucket, as usual when I was home, sat on the nearest door top, watching my activities with interest.

Lately he had taken to trying to help me with every chore around the house. He would help me sweep, sitting spraddle-legged atop the broom's bristles at the handle base, adding his weight to the broom's efficiency. He would help make the bed, tugging at the corners of the sheets with one big foot at one end while I tugged at the other, his wings spread wide and rowing to help him in his struggles. And he would help me iron Steve's shirts, planting himself atop the ironing board and then trying to grab the iron's handle when I set it down. Looking up at him as I folded, I decided he would soon be helping me next with the linens—who know exactly how. But his eyes never left my hands. He seemed perfectly content sitting on one of the double doors of the linen closet.

I stopped what I was doing and gazed around the small room. The only piece of furniture it held was a chest of drawers. Most of the wall space was doorways. The floor was linoleum—no problem for easy cleaning. Why couldn't this do for Bucket's bedroom?

When Steve came home I told him about it. "Perfect," he said after a careful examination. "I think it'll be great. And so now we don't have to move!" That was a decided relief.

"Shall we inititate the change right away?" I asked, "So maybe he won't think he's been ousted by our new arrival . . . ?"

This was a growing worry of mine. How would Bucket react to a new baby in the house? Would he accept it as one more family member, or become jealous and try to harm the baby?

All kinds of old wives' tales had been descending on us as friends and relatives heard about the impending event: "The hawk will scratch out the baby's eyes;" "hawks eat babies;" "the baby will get sick from having a nasty, dirty, wild bird in the house;" "hawks carry off babies, then drop them and kill them."

I didn't believe any of them, of course. I couldn't see Bucket, funny little Bucket, ever harming an infant. And Bucket wasn't a dirty bird; even his stool wasn't harmful, for unlike some birds, most raptors' feces are sterile. No bacteria live in it. Bucket had no "bird" diseases either. He had never even been sick. And he never had lice or mites, because we constantly inspected him for these and had yet to find one. And, of course, Bucket wouldn't carry off the baby. He couldn't. Hawks can't even lift a thing as big as themselves. Yet such tales, once told, tend to stick in a person's mind and they had left me with a somewhat apprehensive feeling.

Bucket took to the little room just as if it had been his all along. We did have one small problem though, with his staying in the only room that gave access to the bathroom; the occasional overnight visitors we had, making their way through the darkened house and into the bathroom past a flutter of disturbed wings and two big eyes peering down at them, found the experience rather unsettling, though Bucket did no more than chirp inquisitively.

As we prepared for our baby, Bucket got into the act, of course. He took to building a nest, a most peculiar nest. It was a rainy day and I'd kept Bucket in the house. It was near Christmas and I had gift wrapping spread out on the coffee table.

Bits and scraps from my cutting littered the floor. I was afraid he might decide that gift wrap was as good as newspaper to play with. He had also littered the floor with his paper tearing that day, but he walked over to the rose bucket—a wooden bucket on a three-legged stand in which I kept an arrangement of artificial roses—and stood there a minute as if he were Socrates listening to some inner voice. Then he hopped up onto its edge. His beak bent to one of the red roses. Plucking it out of its clay base, he hopped to the floor and pattered over to the kitchen table. Up he sprang, deposited the rose, and then went back to pluck another. One by one, all two dozen roses were carried to the kitchen. He had made a huge circle, more or less, with the flowers atop the table, covering all but the corners of it.

He had gone back into the living room as I went to the kitchen, and now he came back with a fork in his mouth, the fork from the lunch I had just finished in the living room. He carefully laid it atop the rose circle and went back to get my knife. When the spoon, too, was added to his artwork, he moved over to the nook where I kept my mop and broom.

First he tugged on a strand from the dust mop. When he couldn't tear it off, he turned to the broom, managing to snap off a couple of straws. These he also added to his "nest," along with more silverware from the sink which I hadn't yet washed from breakfast. When he had also gathered up some of the tearings from his last bout with the newspaper and tucked them into the nest's center, he then tucked himself into it, happily fluffing up his wings and chest.

Shaking my head I decided to let him be. He could play house if he wanted to, as long as he wanted to. I settled down to finish my wrapping. About an hour later, I got up to bring my lunch dishes into the kitchen and what did I see but my broom on the kitchen floor, with only half its bristles left attached. The rest were spread all over the floor and all over the table-top nest. With bird, of course, plopped in the midst, looking ever so pleased with himself.

I couldn't even scold him. I just swept up the mess on the floor with what was left of the broom and put the sweepings into a box. Sure enough, those big eyes had watched. Within five minutes he was carrying the rest of the bristles to his nest, bit by bit. And as the day wore on, he decided he would need the rest of the broom, too. When I caught him at it, I quickly shooed him away lest there by yet another mess for me to clean up.

He turned his back on me, went into a half mantle and looked over his shoulder as if plotting revenge. He seemed at that moment a mischievous child, determined to have his own way, and just waiting for me to turn my back.

I grabbed a handful of tail and gently tugged. Then it was open warfare. He jerked his precious tail out of my loose hold and ran at me as if he would attack me, but instead of pouncing on my bedroom slippers as I expected him to do, he abruptly put on the brakes and went sliding on the waxed floor right past me, to pounce on his primary objective, the broom. He spread out his wings, fanned out his tail over the poor broom, just as he did when his pink rubber mouse was threatened.

Finally, after many minutes of coaxing, I got him to let go of the broom, and I went over to the box to break up the rest of the straw into it—at least there wouldn't be such a mess.

When Steve came home that night, Bucket was still sitting in his nest; Steve circled it curiously. After a moment he patted Bucket on the head, saying, "A nice nest, so nice . . . all birds are entitled to nests." Then to me he added, "But in the kitchen? With the silverware?"

We left his nest for that evening, but the next morning I recovered my silverware. Bucket decided, however, that meant I was helping him build his nest. He began to bring me all kinds of odds and ends: thread from the spools on my sewing machine, bits of yarn, little strips of cloth deftly torn from bed sheets and curtains and such, and, naturally, those nice green leaves, twigs, and blossoms from houseplants and porch, just perfect for nest building. One by one, anything green and growing was reduced for the nest.

New Year's Day came crisp but clear, with a breeze that tended to strengthen occasionally into strong but short-lived gusts. We let Bucket outside for his bath, the first he'd had in several days because of the weather, and Steve had spent the morning on the porch, too, sanding a crib for our new baby.

Bucket looked on, helping where he thought he could, wadding up any laid-down sandpaper (so it wouldn't blow away, of course), carrying back to the kitchen any rags, dropping them into the dishwater as he often saw me do; making sure any tools such as screwdrivers and pliers didn't get lost by carrying them in and tucking them secretly into his nest; and there was an occasional beer can Steve would set down on the porch rail—Bucket would push it over the side to keep *his* porch nice and neat.

By about two in the afternoon, Steve had had all the "help" he could take. He turned to the bird. "How about it, pest," he asked, "are you ready for your flying lessons?" Ready or not, Steve hauled the two kitchen chairs downstairs and over to the parking lot.

Bucket still seemed to like the "calling game". At every whistle he would chirp, hop down to the gravel obligingly, and waddle over to his master. His wings had by this time grown strong enough to enable him to make the door-top perches he preferred. So Steve, after all the flightless months, still had hopes of convincing the bird he could learn to fly. But Bucket seemed to think he should forever walk.

77

Watching the bird beat his wings, imitating Steve's flapping, I noticed Bucket was doing something new: The big gold-brushed, forward "elbows" were bending at the joint as he flapped. It was almost a swimming motion, like someone doing a butterfly stroke. But then I saw that the big feet were still flat to the chair back, not even the claws were curled in as they were when Bucket took his early morning exercises.

Holding my hair out of my eyes as a particularly strong gust of wind hit us, I glanced to see if the bird and chair had weathered the blast, only to find Bucket rising up into the air! The gust had caught under the outstretched wings. I stood frozen with disbelief, as, airborne at last, off went Bucket.

He squealed. He called. He screamed to us to get him down, his big eyes round with fright. Higher and higher the gust took him, and I knew in a moment he was too dumb to close his spread wings. He'd always used them open to get down from high places, parachute style; how could he know he had to close them this time?

I looked toward Steve, expecting to see him rolling in the lead, but he had been left in shock as the bird rose and he abruptly swore as he scrambled for the line in the dust stirred up from the gravel. And then he was running and jumping for the line as it dangled in front of us.

"The lead!" He yelled, "I dropped it—help me!"

But it was too late. The end of the line had passed me and had risen beyond our reach. Bucket cried and cried for rescue. The wind was carrying him away, toward the distant hills. Steve gave chase, with me right behind him. Past the side of our building we went, across the backyard, over the three-foot fence, right through the neighbor's rosebushes—craning our necks to keep the wind-blown bird in sight. Once beyond the neighbor's house, we crossed the next street, ran down it past a few houses to plunge into another yard and out onto the next street. Suddenly, we could see that Bucket was coming down. As we broke through one more hedge, he disappeared from view behind a house. We made a bee-line for the bird's probable landing spot, dashing past the house's owners busy with yard work. Steve reached what we thought was the last fence—a five-foot tall span of redwood slats—and came to a halt. I rushed up, puffing for breath, to see what had stopped him. On the other side of the fence, a very startled Doberman stood beside a bright red doghouse. She wasn't at all welcoming the mass of scrambling feathers trying to gain footing on the tin roof of the doghouse, nor did she appreciate the warnings to stay away, screeched in answer to her barked demands.

The dog lunged toward the bird. Teeth snapped. Talons flashed in return, and the dog yelped. A pinion feather from one jerked-back wing came away in the dog's teeth. She jumped back and paused to lick a few drops of blood from her black nose, then resumed her violent barking, while Bucket screamed and screamed, making feinting charges along the roof toward the dog.

After what seemed hours, the shade of the windowed back door was lifted and a middle-aged, heavyset man peered out. His sleepy looking face quickly became as startled as the dog's. He jerked the door open and called his pet into the house. With the dog out of sight, Bucket quieted down. Steve climbed over the fence to retrieve the bird, as I explained to the man what had happened. Steve gathered up the lead line, then offered Bucket his arm. Still very upset, the bird was more than happy to climb onto the familiar perch and from there he sprang to Steve's shoulder, twittering his ear, one eye on the door behind which the dog had vanished. Steve handed Bucket to me and climbed back over the fence.

So Bucket's first flight ended. In fact, the accidental takeoff and ensuing flight had filled us with great expectations now. What had once seemed fraught with frustration now seemed a near possibility.

Bucket's training was intensified. Every evening the chairs went to and from the parking lot. Whether Bucket didn't relate spread, wind-catching wings to flight, or he was now frightened of the sky, he couldn't seem to get off the ground again. We tried, we coaxed, we flung him into the air from our arms, only to have him land immediately and then sit happily in the gravel, waiting to be picked up again to play this new game. He loved it. But, for us, frustration returned.

One day several weeks later Steve had to work late, and Bucket had to forego that day's flight training. When Steve didn't arrive home at the usual hour, Bucket remained on the front rail. For the last few months, he had sat there each evening about homecoming time, peering down the block to the corner, waiting for the car's red nose to turn into our street. By this time, too, all the neighborhood cars and people were familiar to the bird. He recognized each and would chirp and cackle at his friends in greeting. But most emphatically he greeted Steve, flapping his wings, anxiously calling while Steve parked the car.

No car came that evening. Bucket's eyes searched and searched every movement at the end of the street, and he would often turn his head to look inquisitively at me in the living room.

As dark approached, Bucket didn't even seem interested in his supper. He remained at his perch, and seemed to be growing nervous, more nervous by the minute. He began to shift uneasily from one foot to the other; his wings began to flick out at intervals and more than once he screamed at strange cars passing. Then all of a sudden he let out a trememdous shriek; those huge wings flexed and began to beat. I jumped to see what had caused the change, and there was the familiar red car at last coming down the street.

As it turned into the driveway, Bucket's wings spread their widest; he flapped twice, his feet left the rail with a mighty thrust, and down off the porch he soared to land perfectly on the window of the car door as Steve was opening it.

It had been a deliberate act, not a jump and a parachuting to get down from a doortop. The two flaps he had taken had propelled him over the outer handrail of the top landing and given him momentum to glide to his objective.

Steve, needless to say, was startled to step out and find himself nose to nose with his feathered friend. He quickly glanced up to where I stood on the landing by the rail, nearly jumping up and down with delight.

"He flew," I shouted, "all by himself!"

That evening, as was soon evident, something had clicked in Bucket's mind. He now seemed to know that his most natural and expeditious way of travel was by wing, not foot. He began to fly at every opportunity.

The trouble was that he couldn't always seem to coordinate those huge wings properly. Most often he made them go like a seesaw, instead of working them up and down together. In the apartment, where his operating space was greatly restricted, particularly going through doorways, the problem was at its worst. His body would cant sideways, one wing dropped while the other raised high, then halfway through the opening he could change the position of his wings, jerking his tail in the opposite direction; left wing up, right down, right up, left down, and fanned tail wagging as he went.

It was quite comical to watch, but such a peculiar means of flight was very hard on Bucket. After each flight—no more than ten-foot jaunts—he would need to sit and rest, beak open, tongue hanging out, and breathing very hard.

We worried about it, wondering if his heart could continue to stand such a strain, but gradually this odd method of propulsion made his chest, back, and neck muscles very strong; we could feel the rounding bulges grow very firm under his feathers.

And now the ground testing of early mornings, during which he used his wings correctly, changed to where the kitchen chair on which he sat would be lifted slightly in time to his beating wings, causing it to bump up and down on the floor. Afraid he'd waken the neighbors, one of us would sit on the chair until he was finished with his exercises.

It was quite an experience to sit that close to five feet of powerfully undulating wings. The wind from them was surprisingly strong, and his warm scent filled my nostrils. So much movement so close to my eyes and ears was a bit frightening, probably a bit dangerous, and more than just a little enthralling. I would fancy owning such wings, spreading them to the sky if I wished—free.

As I sat on his exercise chair one day, I began thinking about the bird's scent—he smelled like . . . it was a warm, sweet, sun-filled odor, but I just couldn't place it. Steve came up with the answer: Watermelon. Bucket's clean, soft feathers had much the same scent as the aroma from a ripe watermelon when first sliced open.

Bob Hartman had stopped by to pick up Steve for work and was having a quick cup of coffee with us. Bucket, still busy exercising, didn't pay any attention.

"Yep, smells exactly like that," Bob said, "makes me hungry . . .'' And with that he raised his voice and said teasingly to Bucket, "and what fine, fat drumsticks he has, too!"

Bucket abruptly stopped his flapping, turned his head toward Bob, and stared hard up at the man who now pretended to drool above him. The bird lowered his head and the feathers on his neck expanded as if he was ready to do battle to defend his "drumsticks." Bob and Bucket were actually pretty good friends in the wary sort of way that Bucket gave his friendship to anyone other than Steve and me.

"Oh ho," Bob continued as Bucket half-screamed. "He wants to fight, does he? Well, maybe I don't want to today. Maybe I'll just eat the pink mouse here instead." And with that Bob stepped over and scooped up the toy out of Bucket's table-top nest. The fight was on.

Bucket leaped into full if peculiar flight and launched himself at Bob, who dashed into the living room.

Clumsy as Bucket yet was in flight, he didn't quite catch his prey, but landed instead on the green chair's wing, gulping air as fast as he could. Bob came back and waggled the mouse under his beak. Bucket flung out a foot, big claws snatching to recapture his possession, but he missed. Bob retreated again as the bird caught his breath and flashed into the air, wings seesawing.

After this pattern was repeated one more time, Steve decided Bucket needed some help. Bucket sat with his wings outspread to cool them, while Steve knelt beside him. He put his hands to the bird's wing tips.

"You gotta flap right if you're gonna win," and he made Bucket's wings move up and down in the proper flight pattern. Up and down, up and down. When the bird didn't do it on his own accord, tried in fact to snatch his wings away, Steve then made the wings move in the seesaw pattern just twice, saying "No!" each time in a very loud voice. And then grasping the wings closer to the shoulders, he moved them again in the proper way, telling Bucket, "Good bird . . . do it like this, up and down." Finally, after a few more half-hearted attempts to fight off the hands on his wings, the hawk seemed to get the idea at last. Quick as a wink, Steve put his hand under the big feet, trying to get the bird airborne while his wings were working properly. Bucket stopped flapping immediately.

I had a notion. I motioned quickly to Bob. "Tease Bucket with the mouse," I whispered, and took the bird on my wrist. Holding his jesses down tight to my arm so he couldn't snatch at the mouse, I told Steve to work his wings. As they moved rhythmically up and down, I moved my arm up and down too, hoping to stir up a natural reflex that would make Bucket move his wings properly by himself. Bob thrust the mouse again, then yanked it back.

It worked. All of a sudden the wing-tip feathers were jerked out of Steve's hands and the huge golden wings were beating. I let go the jesses, and then on the next upward stroke drew my hand quickly from under his feet.

He started to drop like a stone, but then the wings bent in a flight flex, drawing back, out, and down, again. Two strokes carried the big bird across the entire twelve-foot width of the living room, to come to rest on a chair. He lit, squawked once, turned back to face the room and was again airborne—headed directly at Bob—using his wings as if he'd been born flying.

Bob pitched the pink mouse onto the couch and dropped flat to the floor, just in time. The great wings swept over him, and Bucket pounced on his toy with gleeful satisfaction.

A problem solved—Bucket could now fly properly. The following weeks were to find him giving up walking entirely. He flew from chair to chair, from his door-top perch to his kitchen chair. He still flew through doorways, but now he soared, sideways, the tips of his wings clearing lintel and sill with very little clearance. And he discovered that his wings would take him from the porch rail to the roof of our building . . . from which vantage point he could see forever.

6

FLYING, THOUGH TRULY A TRIUMPH for a house-kept bird like Bucket, also posed problems. We continued to keep him jessed and on a long lead for safety's sake. But even double-jessed, he more than once jumped farther than his lead allowed, ending with a small crash and loss of dignity. So we decided to jess only one leg, and to change the jess from one leg to the other at regular intervals. He seemed to like the extra freedom, learning to break falls by putting out the unjessed leg and to cope with the imbalance caused by the lead tugging at only one leg instead of two.

One evening, several weeks later, Bucket's puckish temperament was manifested with a vengeance. I had his dinner ready and started for the porch. I glanced at the cage and there he was, oddly mantled over something. Thinking that he had probably picked up another of the endless throwaway papers, I hurried toward him before he made another mess to clean up. He glanced over his shoulder, then jumped away from me to the porch rail, and then his rapidly strengthening wings carried him quickly to the roof. But the glimpse told me he didn't hold paper in his sharp black claws, but something tan-colored.

"Bird, what have you got?" I demanded, apprehensive about his newly acquired habit of picking up almost anything, from litter on the street to the rags Mr. Mac left on his truck fender and laundry Ruth hung on the clothesline—people had this odd habit of getting annoyed when we returned their possessions with strange new holes in them here and there.

From behind me came a thin voice: "He's got my hat."

I glanced around and there, below me, was an elderly gentleman whom we often saw taking an evening walk past our house. Only the top of his head and his eyes were visible above the porch floor. Behind him stood Jim Ellis, who had owned and run the sporting goods store across the street for years.

"Your hawk swooped down off the roof," Jim said, "and swiped this man's cap, then flew away with it."

"Never saw him coming," the old man chimed in, and to my relief he seemed more amused than anything else, "just saw my hat sailing away. Uh . . . can you get it back for me, lady?"

I couldn't believe it; Bucket had stolen a hat right off a man's head. The man had to repeat his request before I turned to gaze up at Bucket. He had his back to us, and all I could see was a red tail fully spread out and the arch of a back that indicated he was busy at something he had between his feet. I knew he was trying to tear up the hat. I called for him to come down, but the only thing that came down was a feather from one of his molting wings.

Just then, Steve's car turned into the driveway and Bucket hippety-hopped across the roof to the edge, then spread his wings and glided down to the street, cap clutched firmly in one big claw. He landed on the opening door as usual. Stepping out of the car, Steve immediately saw the tan hat and started to reach for it, but Bucket bounced around and turned tail to Steve, too.

I came down from the porch and told Steve what the bird had done. His face flushed; "Bird, give me the hat!"

Bucket spread his wings still more, hiding his new possession. Steve reached for the nylon tether, and running his hands up it to the jess, he held the bird's foot still while I, ducking under the protesting wings and grabbing the free leg, managed to remove the hat from his grasp.

When the bird was securely back on the porch, installed in his cage, we apologized to the man for any fright Bucket may have caused him and for the damage to the hat—a hole or two in the crown and the once crisp brim rather crumpled. In the cage Bucket quacked mournfully, bewailing his loss. We offered to replace the hat, but the old man graciously refused our offer, saying he wouldn't trade the experience for anything. He hurried home, to tell his adventure to his family during supper.

"He's going to be the talk of the dinner table," Jim Ellis chuckled after the man had left. Then he sobered a bit; "But you folks had better shorten that hawk's leash, if you understand my meaning." We understood. Steve tended to the tether, leaving Bucket enough line to reach the roof, but not enough to go beyond the top landing of the stairs.

That evening as we sat reading the newspaper, I discovered the next crisis. Jim had mentioned an ad he had placed in order to sell a large collection of camping gear. As I glanced through the list of equipment, an adjoining news item caught my attention. The words "exotic animals" and "to be banned from the city of Oakland" fairly leapt off the page. The story said that the city council of Oakland would hold their regular monthly meeting the following Tuesday. The ordinance banning exotic pets—from squirrels, snakes, exotic birds to elephants—would be up before the council for a vote. We could lose Bucket!

Steve shook his head, "No, it won't ever pass; too many kids have pet mice, snakes, spiders; too many people keep parrots and birds like that. It'll never pass. Forget it."

But I couldn't forget it. And I began to worry about what would happen if no one showed up at the council meeting to protest; it could pass just because no one opposed it! On the day of the meeting, I felt I had to attend.

There were already about twenty people in the council room and more coming in. The members of the council were busy with another issue for which there seemed to be only a few interested spectators. I sat down near a group of people who seemed to be together. After a few minutes one of the women glanced up, smiled, and came to sit in the empty chair next to me. "You're here for the exotics question?" When I nodded she handed me a sheaf of stapled papers. "This is a copy of the ordinance and the schedule of meetings. We don't expect to get the bill defeated in only one session, so . . ." she hesitated then, and regarded me a bit suspiciously. "You are *against* banning exotics from Oakland, I take it. You *are* sitting on the 'con' side of the audience."

"Oh, yes, absolutely! We have this hawk, you see. . ." I

paused, wondering if she could tolerate the idea of someone keeping a hawk as a pet.

"*Great!* An owner!" She beamed. "Maybe later we could talk and I could tell you about our club, Exotics Unlimited. I'm Shirley Nelson, the club's president. We've come from as far away as Novato to fight this bill. We all love animals, you see, and if this bill becomes law, Oakland will be just one more place where people like us will be banned." She laughed abruptly, and added, "Well, forbidden to pursue their lives as they wish, anyway."

With a good deal of emotion in her voice, she went on. "Oakland would be one more place where no exotic creature is welcome, and people who do have them will be forced to give them up, or move. And if the law goes through, it will be one more step against the preservation of wildlife. Some people have animals that are basically healthy but unable in some way to survive in the wild. Zoos don't want them, so they'd just be destroyed. That the animals are really OK, and able to reproduce to perpetuate their species, makes no difference; they'll just be killed."

She sat back then, as the committee chairman, a sandy-haired, middle-aged man with glasses, had stepped to the dais and announced the exotic pets ordinance. He glanced at a sheet of paper in his hand, then asked if the first speaker registered on the agenda, Miss Shirley Nelson, would please take the floor. Shirley moved to the podium and introduced herself.

She spoke for about five minutes on the right of people to keep whatever kind of pet they wanted, as long as the animal was well cared for and didn't infringe on others' rights. Then, surprisingly, she suggested that some sort of bill governing the keeping of exotics was actually needed. Such a law, she added, should be strictly enforced. That way, no one could keep any potentially dangerous creature unless they could prove that the animal was adequately and safely caged, or keep a naturally very noisy animal that could disturb neighbors if not housed in soundproof quarters.

The next speaker, Mavis Denchot, was an older woman, plump and neat in appearance with carefully groomed black hair. She wore a lavender business suit and placed a tote bag full of flyers beside the podium with a deliberate motion. Then she launched into a half-hour tirade on the tragedy of unaltered dogs and cats.

"I run a shelter for homeless animals," she began. "Every day I see the victims of senseless breeding, poor little things, thrown out to fend for themselves. . ." and she went on to tell how they starved to death or were cruelly exterminated in the "death chambers" of the SPCA. She went on and on.

"That is all very interesting, Madam," the chairman said in a kindly tone, "but as time is growing short, could you please make your point in relation to the current bill?"

"Well, certainly," she beamed sweetly at him and then continued as if she had not heard him.

"Madam. . ." said the chairman again. "are you for or against the banning of exotic animals from Oakland?"

"Oh, I'm for banning, of course," she said, nodding vigorously. "This city shouldn't spend money to police a very small bunch of people to make sure they don't let their wild animals hurt people. What this city needs to do is crack down on the number of unspayed, un-neutered dogs and cats on its streets!" She continued as she had previously, speaking so fast that the chairman had difficulty saying another word.

"Mavis *always* does that," Shirley explained, after the chairman had finally managed to close the meeting and postpone the decision to the next month's meeting. "She's a professional lobbyist, and goes to any meeting on any animal bill, anywhere in the state. She knows just how to disrupt any proceeding so that nobody else gets a chance to speak. Ordinary citizens don't have the time to waste, nor can they afford to come back again and again while she holds the floor, so she usually gets the bills she's interested in passed or defeated. And it all revolves around her hopes of getting money for that pet project of hers, that home she runs."

Shirley was distressed but not defeated. "Listen, have you ever thought of joining a club like ours where you can meet others who have the same interest in exotics? We really need to band together now!"

"I didn't even know such clubs existed," I said.

She nodded, "Most people don't. Come to our meeting next Sunday. Give me your name and address and I'll send you an invitation."

Sunday was beautiful, perfect for a drive forty miles southwest of Oakland to Cupertino, where the exotics club meeting was to be held. I went alone, as Steve had to work. Bucket had been invited, too, but I decided this time I would leave him home.

The redwood ranch-style house was in a quiet neighborhood. A small, tree-lined creek ran by it, and the lot was surrounded by a tall cyclone fence. There were numerous cars parked in the gravel driveway. Walking up the path, I saw another "parking place." It was a pine tree, and at its base was a spotted cat, a *big* spotted cat, snoozing peacefully in the sparse grass. Later I learned this was Caesar, a cheetah, who belonged to a club member.

The door of the house was ajar, so I knocked and went in. The house was crammed with people, animals, and food. Shirley handed me a cup of fruit punch, and I wandered about meeting both people and their pets. A diapered monkey sitting on a man's lap chittered at me. Samson, a cougar, lived with a couple and their twelve children (he played and even slept with the kids.) There were two shy, gentle foxes, Sweetheart (gray) and Red (red) belonging to a man very much like his pets in temperament.

Shirley had brought a raccoon named Wild Child, who promptly went after the goldfish in the backyard duck pond. There was Pele, another cougar, named for the fire goddess of Hawaii's volcano; an African spotted leopard, Schezada, who loved her owners so much that she would purr like a common house cat, a purr that made nearby windows quiver.

There were ocelots, bobcats, small jungle cats, opossums, wolves, more monkeys, and a puma named Junior with a motor-balance problem that kept him lurching instead of moving with the grace of his species. They all got along together beautifully. It was a unique and wonderful experience. I made the decision for us and joined the club. At future meetings, Bucket fit in perfectly, adding his magic to the already special magic that surrounds people who love all animals enough to spend the time, money, and love necessary to bridge the gap between civilized man and the wild.

The following Tuesday found me again at the Oakland city council meeting, convinced more than ever that the proposed ordinance was unfair.

"Since we are running a little late," the chairman said as he opened the meeting, "we ask that the speakers on this issue limit their comments to five minutes." Then he called the first name on the list.

A neatly dressed young man stepped up, obviously ill at ease. He said he had a tame wolf. It didn't bother anyone. He loved it, and he couldn't understand why anyone would want to discriminate against his pet when so many of the dogs in his area caused far more trouble. He abided by the law, while most of the dogs didn't even have licenses; his wolf was under Department of Fish and Game regulations and was always kept behind a high cyclone fence in his backyard, while many of the dogs ran loose.

The next speaker was an elderly lady, with shopping bag and cane. She was afraid of "horrible wild animals." What if one got loose and attacked a child? There should be a law against keeping them, and when her friend, Mrs. Denchot, had asked her to come and tell her feelings to all the lovely people at this meeting, she had been happy to do so. There were already so many poor cats and dogs who needed good homes because nobody had "fixed" their mothers or fathers. Why couldn't those people who now had wild animals just get rid of them and give a home to some of these poor cats and dogs? Beaming at her friend, Mrs. Denchot, she then hobbled back to her seat.

My name was called next. I could only say what I felt: "I don't think the ordinance is fair. We have a wild bird, a red-tailed hawk, that we have raised from a baby. He's a lovely creature. Everyone in our neighborhood enjoys watching him, too.

"None of them would appreciate it or understand if the law is passed and Bucket has to be sent away. He's a pet, with the outward appearance and idiosyncrasies of a wild animal, perhaps, but he chirps to those he knows and lets them watch him up close, and hold him, and touch the soft feathers that few people ever even see. My husband and I have had dogs and cats in the past, we have a domestic bird, a cockatiel, now, but as to the previous speaker's suggestion, we greatly prefer to keep the 'wild' bird we've raised from a baby. I would feel guilty, totally crushed, in fact, to suddenly have to abandon him to a zoo, when practically all his life he's known the close companionship of my husband and me in our home. He could die for lack of the personal care and love he's used to . . . making one less beautiful, wild creature in the world. I think this ordinance is very unfair."

Two more people spoke, each expressing their opinion against the bill, and there seemed to be no one else to speak for the other side when once again Mavis Denchot took the floor.

I heard Shirley Nelson, sitting in front of me, groan, and several others around us made hissing comments. I thought that surely the woman would not go on and on as she had the last time—the chairman, had, after all, limited the speakers' time to five minutes. Five minutes passed, then ten. She didn't even look at the members of the council, but continued on about the spaying of cats and dogs.

When the chairman managed to interject a mild remonstrance that she be brief, she told him very sweetly that she was almost finished, and she went on. An older man in the front of the room abruptly stood up. His hair was thin, as was his face, but both were quite red, and bespoke a temper. His finger jerked in a staccato beat pointing at her, and he said loudly, "Lady you *are* now finished! You did this last week, and again you are doing nothing more than wasting our time here! I'm a busy man! I can't keep coming here for nothing! You should now give someone else a chance to speak! Have the kindness, please, to go and sit down!"

All eyes were on the two. If someone had spoken to me in public like that, I couldn't have said another word, but she gave him a cold stare as if to say, "What a rude person you are," and began to speak again.

The man made sputtering noises, then took one furious step closer to the dais and shouted, "I don't give a damn if cats and dogs overrun the world and sleep in *your* bed"—she'd just made a plea for homes and warm beds for them—"Now, you will sit down, right now, or if these good people here won't throw you out of this room, I will!" and he took a determined step in her direction.

The chairman hastily pushed back his chair, stood up, and waved a nervous hand at the irate gentleman.

"Calm yourself, sir," he said with a hopeful but weak smile; then he turned to Mrs. Denchot. "Thank you, madam," he told her, "I think you should please return to your seat now."

"But I haven't finished. . ." she began.

The angry man stamped his foot and took another stride toward her. Mrs. Denchot gave up.

"Oh, all right," she snapped, "but I have never in my life been subjected to such. . ." and her voice went on and on as she gathered up her things and huffily walked down the center aisle and out the door.

A few more people spoke for five minutes or less on various sides of the bill, and then the chairman returned to the dais. He said apologetically that there would be no vote this day, but that it would be taken first thing the following week, when the council had had a chance to review the statements and give consideration to the ordinance away from the heated discussion.

Unfortunately, when the next Tuesday morning arrived, I awoke with a cold. All day I lay in bed and worried. I'd kept Bucket in the house where I could keep an eye on him, and he seemed to know that something wasn't quite right in his little world. He sat for a while on the living room's streetside window sill, then came swooping into the bedroom to land beside me, and chirped and cackled as if to encourage me to get up and play with him. When I wouldn't, he walked all over the bedclothes, his big claws wadding them up, and gazed at me as if to ask what was wrong. He had seen me sick in bed a few times, but when I refused to play he had returned to staring out the windows, or snuggling into his nest, or harassing the throw rugs and his toys. Today he just kept coming back in to see me, and once the covers were disarranged to his satisfaction, he'd perch on the end of the bed, draw up one foot beneath his chest feathers, and keep me company.

Shirley had promised to call me after the council meeting, but five o'clock came, when the meeting generally ended, then six o'clock, and the phone didn't ring.

Steve came home from work and came in to sit beside me.

"Maybe the vote was delayed again, and. . ."

"Or maybe we lost," I answered miserably. "And because I'm sick she doesn't want to tell me."

Steve patted my hand, then turned to pet Bucket, who had come flying in. "I won't believe that we lost, until I hear it for sure," he said grimly. "Poor old hawk . . . he can't, just can't survive on his own yet. . ." The doorbell rang.

There was Shirley, grinning so broadly that she didn't have to say a word.

"I've invited myself over for a victory drink," she laughed. "I wanted to tell you the good news in person: The bill was defeated by a good majority, then amended into a 'nuisance' ordinance; *all* animals are now safe in Oakland as long as they don't bother the neighbors."

Bucket swooped from the bed to the living room. And to our surprise, since he didn't know her, landed gently on the wing of the chair where Shirley had seated herself. She glanced up at him, saying, "Well, hello, bird." He eyed her, quacked a few companionable notes, and then before we could stop him, he leaned over and with his beak snatched the black silk scarf she wore casually tossed over her shoulder.

Airborne, he went from the living room into the spare bedroom, into our bedroom, and into the kitchen, then around again to land neatly in his nest with the scarf clutched firmly in the foot now securely under him. When we caught up to him, he ducked his head and mantled, with that look in his eye that said, "I have a new treasure; wanna fight for it?"

Shirley was not at all upset at the loss of her scarf. She was chuckling, obviously understanding what the bird was up to, for she curled her lips into a mock scold and shook her finger at him, "That's mine, bird," she told him. "I came all the way from Marin County to save you from extinction, and you treat me this way?"

Steve tugged on the outspread tail, trying to distract him, while I tried to get him to stand up, but nothing short of destroying his nest would get him out of it.

As the black beak dipped down to begin to shred the new "bedding," Steve raced across the living room and snatched up the evening paper. He rolled it and thrust it under Bucket's head as he looked to see what we were about. Bounce, up out of the nest he came, one big foot lunging at the furled edge of the paper. Steve tossed it into the middle of the living room floor, with Bucket in hot pursuit. I quickly retrieved Shirley's now-forgotten scarf. With the bird happily tearing up his newspaper, the scarf no worse for wear, Steve poured the victory drinks.

For the next few months, life settled into a calm routine. I made baby clothes, while Steve put the finishing touches to the baby's room, and Bucket helped both of us whenever he saw an opportunity, tidying the house by neatly tucking any stray fabric scraps, and sometimes even the new baby clothes themselves, into his nest.

Standing on the shower curtain rod as either of us bathed, he would cackle inquisitively as if wondering why we were standing in the "rain." He even helped me cook each evening, landing in the middle of the stove top, lifting one foot and then the other to keep them from the warm metal above the pilot light, until I shooed him away and put on the pots for dinner. In fact, everything I did found him right beside me, almost as if he caught the excitement in the air, and wanted to be a part of it.

I was cooking dinner one night, after a day of scrubbing the kitchen following a messy session of canning strawberry jam, when I bent down and could not straighten up again for some moments. I had started labor, and soon we were on our way to the hospital, Bucket watching us drive away from his perch by the front window.

We named the baby Edward Stephen after his father and grandfather. He was a beautiful boy, chubby and strong, with a shock of hair much the same color as a bright copper penny.

While I lazed around in the hospital for three days, waiting to go home, Steve was left to cope with our other two "sons"—with flight time; clean-up, which is not inconsiderable when dealing with a bird as big as Bucket or even one of Ah-Soh's size; bathing and feeding; to say nothing of playtime. When Steve came to visit us each night, the first thing past his lips was some variation of, "Wow, we miss you!" And he said it seemed that Bucket spent most of the time he was cooped up in the house sitting at the front window, peering in the direction I had left that night. Ah-Soh was more subdued, probably because he spent so much more time in his cage. But Bucket was off his feed: by the second evening I was gone, he was only eating one and a half chicken gizzards, down from the four or five he generally ate morning and night. By then the three days passed, and Steve came to bring me and our new little son home.

During the short drive home that beautiful morning, I was bubbling over. Life seemed so good. Unlike in the hospital, my baby was all mine to watch over now. My husband had missed me, and my birds were waiting; even my house was neat and clean, so I would have nothing to do but tend the baby, be with Steve, and play with the birds.

As we turned into the driveway, I thought Steve grimaced a bit, as if there was something wrong and he didn't want to tell me. I looked up and there sat Bucket by the front window. Nothing seemed wrong. His beak was pressed to the glass, his mouth was open, screaming in welcome. His eyes were big and excited; he'd been watching for me. Even in the car I could hear him calling and calling.

Steve carried the baby up so I would be free to greet the bird. I had no more than stepped in the door when Bucket with a mighty spring, leaped onto my shoulder, cried into my ear, nuzzled my neck and hair gently with his beak. I tickled his toes, his tummy, scratched the back of the neck he bowed for my attention. The sweet, watermelon odor was all around me, and he pressed his beak against my cheek, telling me in no uncertain terms that he had missed me. Steve came back, having settled little Eddie in his bassinet, and Bucket abruptly spread his big wings around my shoulders—in his defense stance—and decidedly warned Steve away from me!

"He's blaming me for your absence?" Steve laughed, "What an ingrate!"

Steve stretched out his arms and flapped them as if to fly, and Bucket's eyes blinked, and then turned to the soft look I loved so. He put down the threatening talon, leaned forward and chirped.

Being off work the last few months, I'd been taking the bird down to the field behind the airport during the day, sparing Steve the usual twilight-time flight exercises. The daylight excursions had been satisfactory, but Bucket much preferred his jaunt with Steve, as hawks in the wild generally hunt at dawn and dusk. The bird had become fairly good at flight, and he was improving with each week that passed. He loved it. He would spread those gold-brushed wings, catching the wind, and he would climb ladders in the air only he could see, spiraling up and up until he would glide in lazy circles on the thermals that blew over the field. And when the return whistle was given, he would press his wings tight to his

body, wingtips pointing towards the heavens, shoulders low, beak pointing to earth again. Down and down he would plummet, eyelid "goggles" protecting the vision, until he was just twenty feet from the ground. Then the red-brown tail would fan out wide against the wind, the wings would lift to form parachutes, the long legs would extend beneath him and stretch forward, the great talons spreading—front toes up, heel claw straight back—and he'd land on the proferred arm or shoulder with all the grace of his wild nature, not one claw touching skin. Balanced grandly, he would then chirp and shake out his feathers, waiting to be launched again.

But for three days now no one had had time to take him to the field. "Perhaps he's missed his flying lessons more than I thought," said Steve. "that bird has been acting crazier than ever lately. He even dragged your plant off the kitchen window sill this morning just before I left to pick you up. He tried to put it, pot and all, into his nest." He was laughing, but suddenly he stopped, and turned guilty looking.

"Uh, oh," I knew then what Steve had been holding back from me. My nice clean kitchen!

The flower pot, too heavy for the bird to carry far, was in small pieces in the sink, and potting soil was all over the place, from sill to counter to floor, covered with bird footprints.

"For Pete's sake, get the broom," I said, then hesitated, "or don't we currently have one. . . .? I glanced at the nest, and then into the corner where the broom was kept. Sure enough, the bird had been busy at that too—bits and pieces of straw were spread all around, only half a broom left.

"He didn't hurt the plant, he only carried it around a little while, and I got it away from him before he ate it," Steve said uncertainly, watching me from the broom corner.

"He doesn't eat them, Steve," I said, and started to laugh.

Bucket hopped down from my shoulder and, with a happy look on his face, was now busily pacing back and forth, gathering up the straw and depositing it in his nest, leaving neat if dusty toeprints in his wake. His world was right again.

I assured Steve that the plant would be just fine—tough stuff, that grape ivy—and plunked it into a pot of water for later care, then turned to prepare for the first baby feeding at home.

The baby awakened a few minutes after I was ready for him, but as I went through the living room to get him, I paused a second and wondered how Bucket would react to this new, noisy little stranger in my arms, being fussed over? All the old wives' tales flashed through my mind.

Steve came up behind me, and he also gazed at Bucket now sitting quietly on a green chair wing, preening his chest feathers, the hooked beak buried itself in the soft white beneath the upper gold and drew each small feather out just like a comb might separate a single hair from its mates.

When Steve had short-tied Bucket to a chair, I brought out the infant. Little Eddie's eyes were closed, but Bucket's big brown ones were wide open. He watched me carry the small bundle to the couch, watched the child held close to nurse, chirped inquisitively as I laid him over my shoulder to burp, and when I finally sat just gazing at my new little boy, Bucket seemed suddenly unable to contain his curiosity. Down from the chair wing he hopped to the seat cushion for a closer look. When he went to jump to the chair's other arm, the short-tied line kept him from it, one leg out away from his body. Steve went over and gently urged him back to the chair's wing, then sat down beside him, talking softly all the while, explaining that I was holding his new "brother" and that it was nothing to fret about. They would be friends.

Bucket peered and peered and the baby slept. Finally Steve looked at me and said, "Do you think it would hurt to give him a closer look?"

My first instinct was to say no, but looking at the inquisitive bird's stance—it was calm—and the big soft eyes in the head that screwed itself upside down for a better look, it occurred to me that perhaps now was the most opportune time to introduce the two . . . before Bucket could decide that the baby was, in truth, an interloper whose presence in the house meant that a bird wouldn't be treated as he had been. Bucket was all eyes as Steve brought him close to the couch.

"It's a baby," I told him softly, "see, a tiny little fellow, small fingers, small toes. . ." I showed him. "You musn't hurt him. He's mine, remember." I reached up to stroke the golden chest, the darker feathers under the beak. I went on like this for a minute or two, and whether it was the sound of my voice, my praise, my warning of just who owned this new thing in my lap, or from curiosity satisfied, the big hawk shook out his wings, gave a chirp, a nod, and then lost interest in the baby. He craned his head to the top of the open front door, indicating to Steve that was now the desired perch.

"I think it's going to work," Steve said tentatively.

News of the new baby had reached our immediate neighbors even before we had time to tell them. The MacFarlanes phoned with their congratulations; George Haskins came up to meet the new arrival the afternoon of the next day.

George was by this time as good a friend as we could wish. He was always looking out for our interests, but Bucket still hadn't forgiven him for the kitty incidents. The bird would scream and scream in hatred every time he saw the man, though George seemed to accept it as just the way the creature was.

I was sitting on the couch, relaxing after feeding little Eddie when I heard the bell ring loudly at the porch door and George calling to me. I got up and went to catch Bucket, loose on the porch, and to hold him until George got inside. Once he was out of sight Bucket settled down, flying up to the roof as if giving no more thought to the visitor.

George and I talked while he admired the baby who was sound asleep in the bassinet I'd brought into the living room. When he had finished his pleasant reminiscing about his own children's babyhood, he started to leave. Moving to check the baby, I told him to invite Ruth to come up when she arrived home. When I turned around again, he had his hand on the screen's latch and was starting to open it.

"Wait, George," I yelled, "let me first catch Bucket!"

"Oh, never mind him," he replied airily, with a negligent wave of his hand, "he knows me, he won't bother *me*."

George stepped through the door to the flash of wings and a shrieking scream of hatred and triumph. Bucket had seized the chance to get back at his teaser. George glanced up to see Bucket swooping down from the roof, talons outstretched. The claws met the bare skin at George's temple and clenched.

The victim roared, ducked and slapped the hawk away with a mighty stroke. Then he collapsed on the deck, his eyes closed. My thoughts froze on the word *dead*.

The bird landed six feet away and instantly turned to attack again, rushing at the fallen man on foot. George's eyes popped open and he scrambled up to grab Bucket's lead line.

Cussing vehemently, he pulled the line taut with a snap of his wrist. He swung the bird by the leg in circles in the air, and then tried to dash him to the porch with all his strength.

Numb with the horror of the bird's attack, George's fall, and now his retaliation, it was a while before I could move and catch the line away from George.

"Enough, George!" I gasped at him. But when he tried to push me aside in his blind fury to get at the bird, my own anger rose. "Stop it, George! You're at fault as much as he is! You should've let me catch him, you know that! He's just a bird, George. And don't you discipline him, I'll do it; you're too angry!"

But he didn't even hear me, bellowing obscenities as he was. Finally, I got a hold on Bucket and thrust him unceremoniously into his cage. George quieted down and stood panting for breath. I went over to him to see how badly he was hurt.

He was bent over holding the side of his head, moaning. I persuaded him to let me have a look. Bucket had put three gashes about a half-inch apart on the man's temple and one lower down by his ear. Fortunately, the bird hadn't done as much damage as I had feared; no blood was gushing as if an artery had been punctured. I tried to soothe George, telling him that the injuries were not serious after all and looked like they would heal without even a scar. But George was still angry and in shock, and not to be soothed.

"I'm going to sue you!" he said, wrenching away from me. "That ugly bird is a menace to society! I'll kill him next chance I get! Claw me will he! You'll hear from my lawyer by tomorrow! And you'll have to pay my doctor bill, too!"

I stood staring after the furious man for a long moment, my emotions pulling me this way and that. Should I go after him and try to calm him? Should I call a lawyer myself right now? Should I call Don Paquette or Shirley Nelson to try to find a new home for Bucket right away before George rounded up an animal control officer to come take the bird away? Maybe I should do that, if George really meant what he said about killing Bucket!

Sick at heart and stomach, and weak anyway from the recent

birth of Eddie, I had to sit down before I could do anything more.

About an hour later, I felt well enough to call Steve and tell him what had happened. "Well, honey, since the animal control man hasn't shown up yet, perhaps he won't come at all," Steve said, reassuringly. "Could be that it was just an idle threat, said in the heat of anger. Let's just let things alone until I get home. I'll talk to George then." Relieved, I let it stand at that.

Luck and love, it seemed, were on Bucket's side during this awful time. George, it turned out, had gone downstairs and poured himself a drink or two to ease his nerves. By the time Ruth got home, George was feeling no pain at all and was happily babbling about the various ways of stewing foul. He had not called his lawyer, or the pound, and he hadn't gone to a doctor. Ruth called me and got the whole story, and then convinced her husband that he owed me an apology. She was truly a loving and remarkable woman.

When George called the next day, sober and more than contrite, he delivered his apology in a voice so shamed I wanted to hug him to tell him it was all right. He wasn't an evil man, just a human being who had been given a shock and who had become very angry, understandably so. But his anger had been excessive, and it was fortunate that no real harm had come of it.

"George," I said, when he finally finished explaining how he'd never meant to upset a new little mother, "everyone here is just fine this morning. And just so you know that your apology is one of the biggest-hearted gestures I can think of, if we ever have another child, we'll name it after you!"

"Uh!" He grunted, "Poor kid, don't stick him with that."

"Yep," I said, warming to the idea as my father's name was also George, "that's what his name will be. Or how about it for the middle name?"

George started to chuckle. "Or what about Georgine if it's a girl?"

The world was suddenly a good place to live. And Bucket was safe ever after from any carelessness from George: the man was scrupulously cautious from then on.

I had been home several days and was beginning to feel like myself again when friends started coming by to see our new baby. The first visitors were my younger sister, Diana, and her husband, Bob Jones. They brought their little girl, Lisa, who was just ten months old herself.

Diana waved, coming up the steps, and then paused, laughing, as Lisa, in her arms, seemed determined to undo her mother's up-swept blond hair. Diana handed Lisa to Bob, and then hurried up the stairs to hug me. Bob rubbed Lisa's head in a caress and then directed her attention to Bucket. The bird sat on his cage, shriek-ing his hellos, while Steve held on to the jess. The child gazed at the bird, the bird at the child. One screamed, the other cried and tried to wriggle closer to her father.

"Bucket, shame," Steve scolded him, "not to scare Lisa."

Bucket looked at him as though to say, "What did *I* do?" Then he went into his quacking act, head bobbing, wings dipping, and he was suddenly a duck. Even Lisa laughed.

They stayed to supper, and in the excitement of showing off the new baby we missed Bucket's regular feeding time. But Bucket hadn't forgotten. When I glanced out the window, he was pacing back and forth on the top of his cage, eyes fixed on the house. I pointed him out to Steve, who laughed and waved to him. Bucket stopped pacing and cackled.

"He's hungry," Steve said, "and being very polite about it. Is his dinner ready?"

"Oops, not yet," and I hurried into the kitchen to get his meat out of the refrigerator. I returned to the living room to chat while the meat warmed up in a dish of water. I got involved in the con-versation and again forgot all about Bucket. This time Bucket in-terspersed his pacing with loud clicks of his beak on the window. He became pretty insistent before we noticed him. Both Steve and I jumped up at the same time. "I'll get it!" "No, I'll do it!"

But by that time little Eddie woke up and Lisa, who had been put down for a nap, woke too. In the confusion of both babies cry-ing, poor Bucket was forgotten once again.

As I sat in the kitchen feeding Eddie, I heard the screen door rattle. I called to Steve to shut the door so the babies wouldn't take a chill, and then saw that Bucket was charging at the screen door, bouncing off it and kicking at the metal frame with his feet. He was *very* determined to have his supper now, and was running out of patience. He gave a mighty leap, flapped those huge wings of his, and with both sets of sharp black talons attached himself to the screen. He beat his wings and rattled the door violently with every magnificent, powerful stroke.

Steve opened the door cautiously and caught Bucket's line, offering the bird his wrist. Bucket screamed, but then unhooked first one claw, then the next from the wire mesh, and grandly took his place on the wrist. He glanced from one of us to the other with a woebegone look that plainly said, "Well, it's about time!" Diana and I cleared the kitchen of babies. It was Bucket's turn at last.

We quickly learned that with or without a new baby in the house, Bucket was not going to allow us to forget about him. He was determined to have his own way and developed any number of tricks to recapture our attention the moment it strayed. This new determination of his was, ironically, the beginning of his growing independence—independence he would one day need.

7

IN JULY I RETURNED TO WORK, and since the office was quiet most of the time, Walter was kind enough to let me bring Eddie with me. It worked out fine, as far as the studio was concerned, but Bucket didn't much like spending his days in his cage again. More often than not he'd fight going into the cage, and then refuse to look at me, sulking, when I left. I didn't blame him. I wouldn't have liked it either.

At first, when I came home from work, Bucket would call to me even before I reached the stairs, happy bird that he usually was. But one day in late August this changed. I came home, lugging Eddie and some groceries, and heard no "hurry up and let me out" call. Instead I was greeted by an irate scream and a hawk obviously in a very bad temper. I stood before his cage and talked to him, and gradually he recognized me; his hackles smoothed out, but his eyes were still angry.

After I'd taken the baby and groceries into the house, I came back to let Bucket out. When I reached inside the cage to attach his lead line, he almost looked as though he would strike me. Then I saw the trouble. The top of one of the yellow feet and the foreleg had been cut, ugly gashes half an inch long. I could see nothing in the cage that might have caused them. Cooing to him, and gently petting his chest, I examined the injuries. Though the cuts didn't appear to be deep, they were probably painful, for he wouldn't let me touch the leg. The wounds looked clean, as if he'd licked them well, but I thought some antiseptic wouldn't hurt.

Eddie was sleeping peacefully in his room, so I brought Bucket into the house to treat his foot. He still didn't like me touching it, but with much soothing and petting I was able to apply ointment and wind a piece of gauze around it so he couldn't lick off the medication. Then he stood wth his hurt foot drawn up to his chest and just gazed at me unhappily, his feathers all fluffed out as if he were cold.

I had been sitting next to him and soothing him for about half an hour when I heard footsteps on the stairs. Bucket screamed and flew to the front window, eyes narrowed to pinpoints. I petted him, trying to quiet him. It was our neighbor from across the street, Mrs. Greenwood, who had come over to chat many times before. He had always tolerated her, so I couldn't understand why he was upset now.

"My dear," she said, "I haven't come over just to chat today, but to speak to you about your pretty bird." Her plump face was red from her exertion climbing the stairs, and her eyes were flashing indignantly. "Bucket didn't just hurt himself," she said with a snap. "A group of young men were standing on your stairs throwing rocks at him. I've seen them before, throwing rocks, but the bird was out of his cage then, and able to get out of harm's way, or catch the rocks with his feet. I never dreamed the boys were actually trying to hurt him, but I saw today that they were. I ran out and told them that wasn't nice, and they should go away. When they wouldn't, I said I'd call the police if they didn't leave immediately!" Then her face flushed even more, as she said primly, "They were very rude and nasty young men, but they did finally leave when I went back in my house and picked up the phone!" It was obvious to me that she had been through an ordeal and she nodded gratefully when I offered her a cup of tea. I returned Bucket to his cage, and Mrs. Greenwood followed me into the kitchen and sank down in a chair. As I made the tea she gazed in awe at the untidy mess on the table. Her eyes took in the many "treasures" in Bucket's nest.

"Is this his bed?" she asked after a minute.

I shook my head and explained the nest, handing her one of the molted feathers. It was a golden chest feather, about an inch long, the end of it fuzzy with down.

As she felt the soft, white fluff, she smiled. "It's so beautiful," she said, her voice little more than a whisper. "We lived in the country when I was a girl, and my mother kept geese, but none of their feathers were even half as soft as this one. Why did he discard it?"

I smiled and said, "He changes his dirty or damaged feathers twice a year. See how raggedy the edges of that one are?" I pointed out the tiny breaks in the feather's individual barbs that comprised the solid banks on either side of the quill. "When his preening has worn out the feather's usefulness, nature takes over and grows him a new one to replace it. He's just now going into his winter molt, even though it's only August; he'll be at this stage about a month. His winter coat will have heavier down on the feathers than is on the feather you hold." Mrs. Greenwood was fascinated, and by the time Steve arrived and escorted her home she was relaxed and calm.

However, when Steve returned he was not. His face was dark and furious.

"How can we cope with that kind of thing—kids throwing rocks at Bucket when we're not home!" he exploded. He pointed a finger at me, "Do you really *have* to go on working? We could get by if you didn't and wouldn't it really be best all around if you and Eddie stayed home?"

"I'll call Walter right now and quit," I said. It was either that or keep Bucket tied up in the house all day, or worse, give him up before he got badly hurt or even killed. So I quit.

It was probably fortunate that the boys did not reappear immediately, for in the meantime we saw a problem developing, one that was never to be solved, no matter how we tried. Bucket began to repel *all* visitors to the porch. Whether it was from a natural maturing process that increased his territorial instincts or was a direct result of the rock-throwing incident, Bucket turned fierce and possessive when anyone dared climb our stairs.

The next visitor—before we were aware of the change in Bucket—was Cliff Jones, my sister's father-in-law. He was a short and robust-looking gentleman whose round, rosy cheeks and nose bespoke his jolly temperament. He was the kind of person it was easy to love, and both Steve and I did. But Bucket didn't love anyone but us anymore.

Cliff arrived at our house late one morning to drop off a favorite old footstool I had promised to recover for him. My non-working days were long, and I'd taken up upholstery as a hobby and to earn some money now and then.

Bucket screamed a welcome as usual, but I didn't know his scream that day wasn't hospitable.

Cliff brought the footstool into the living room where we talked for a while before he got ready to leave. As he moved through the door, Bucket took flight from his cage, swung up and out around the screen door, and braked in, red tail fanned wide, with both sets of talons stretched out as though to land on Cliff.

Cliff yelled, "Hey!" and ducked but nevertheless the big bird skidded on closed claws across the man's bald head.

Startled, I swatted at Bucket, sweeping him off Cliff in an instant. I really wasn't sure what Bucket's intention had been, but as he was now in half-mantle I was afraid he had deliberately attacked Cliff as he had George.

I rushed after the bird, stepped on the lead line, and snatched Bucket up by his legs. I shook him slightly and scolded him and then quickly put him into his cage. The whole scene had taken no more than thirty seconds, but it left me feeling limp. I returned to Cliff. There was a one-inch cut on the bare pink head, and not much blood, I noted with relief. I wondered what to say; an apology seemed inadequate.

"Jeez," he said finally. "What an experience! I must look like a tree to him. What a way to be friendly—scared the heck out of me! Does he always try to land on people's heads?"

"He does sometimes land on our heads, but you're the first person other than ourselves. And I'm really sorry about it, Cliff. It's just an awful thing. . . ."

I got him a wet towel, and taking it he gently patted my hand. "Now, never mind," he said and dabbed the towel across the wound, "it's all over. He didn't mean to hurt me. This old head of mine has no hair on it, so he skidded. No harm done."

That night Steve and I decided we'd better catch Bucket whenever anyone wanted to come on the porch, just in case, and hold on to him when the visitors left. That became the procedure. With the sign on the outer porch rail, the gate at the first landing, and the very loud hand bell attached to the gate, for a while we had no problems.

One morning, Bob Hartman came over for coffee before work, as he did so often. We'd kept Bucket in the house because of the cold, drizzling weather.

While Bucket was inside, he behaved like his old self. From his door-top perch he greeted Bob, then flew down, obviously wanting to play. He offered his pink mouse, then his rubber spool with the jingle bell in it, and his ball. Steve and I gave little thought since Bucket had always minded his manners—and his claws— perfectly while playing. Bob had been playing with him only a few minutes when Bucket's temper changed.

They were playing "tug-on-the-bird's-tail," where Bob took hold of the handy tail feathers before Bucket could catch the darting wrist with his foot. Whoever won would let go and the play would begin again. Bucket always seemed to enjoy it very much.

We were all laughing and urging Bucket not to let Bob catch him when Steve abruptly lowered his coffee cup and started to say, "Watch it . . ." But before the words were out, Bucket—eyes narrow and hackles up—had flashed his talons; a claw caught on Bob's wedding ring and the bird reacted to the sudden dilemma by trying to slash at it with his other foot.

Steve thrust his cup between the striking foot and Bob's hand and deflected the sharp talons. As the hot coffee spilled, Bob managed to twist his hand enough to free the claw from the ring.

Steve started to apologize, but Bob waved him to silence. "It wasn't his fault," said Bob, gently stroking the bird. Bucket's eyes were still narrow but he let his old friend pet him; then, with a surprising mood change, the big eyes went soft, he shook out his feathers, and he chirped, almost as if to say he was sorry and was glad to be friends again. But obviously something was transpiring within our pet. And sadly, for whatever reason, that was the last time Bob would ever play with Bucket. The bird was willing, but the man was not.

By this time Bucket was two years old and Steve had begun the hunt training, letting him fly free at least every two days so his wings would maintain their full strength, and so he would have the healthful exercise that his body required.

Steve and I had grown very attached to the sometimes ornery but generally sweet-natured creature. I didn't want to think about not having him around, but even I had to admit that he seemed ready to begin this last phase with us.

On the days I accompanied them to the airport's back field, I would watch Bucket's huge wings carry him into the air where he could now stay for as long a time as any of his wild brothers. Around and around they would all soar in lazy, broad circles against the blue sky, spiraling up and down as the thermal winds strengthened and waned in turn. The other hawks didn't seem to mind Bucket, or perhaps they did mind but hesitated to drive off a newcomer so much bigger than they were. They soared and spiraled as if he belonged there.

When Steve first got the idea of hunt training, we were able to do little research, for we kept running across the line, "The red-tail hawk is not among the best birds for serious falconeers."

Well, we told each other, Bucket did have the same kind of "sail" (his wings were square-tipped) as the goshawk, which made him a short-winged variety versus the peregrine's "long-winged" (pointy at the tips) classification. This meant that luck had been with us during Bucket's original flight training since short-winged birds were always launched into flight from an arm instead of hunting while already aloft when prey was flushed, as were the peregrines. Bucket had also already been *weathered,* in his case adjusted to open country in the company of man; therefore all he still needed was the *manning* (the term for the preliminary hunt-flight training), and he didn't really need that because as a well-tamed bird taught to fly by adoptive parents, he already knew he was to come out of the sky when we called.

What he *did* need to learn was the actual mechanics of hunting prey for man, and for himself eventually.

Falconeers train their birds to attack by use of a lure, a heart-shaped leather bag on a swiveling line to which is attached rabbit fur or a set of pigeon wings, depending on what prey the bird is being trained to hunt. The lure is swung around and around the falconeer's head during training, with the hawk coaxed to chase and "kill" it.

Since we were very hopeful of the capabilities of our large redtail, and we had read that some big hawks could bring down pheasants, we decided to start Bucket right out after this bird so plentiful in our area. Steve fashioned a lure out of an old rag and some pheasant feathers from my best hat. He tied some of Bucket's extra nylon lead line around it. When the creation was ready, Steve introducted Bucket to it.

The hawk was sitting atop the front door that evening, with one foot drawn up beneath his chest feathers. Steve walked casually past the perch, dragging behind him the "pheasant." The odd-looking pile of white cloth and russet feathers bounced along and flipped every time a quill touched the rug.

Bucket, of course, spotted it immediately. His wide eyes examined it with interest. And as Steve reached the end of the room, turned, and then made the lure skip across the floor behind him again, Bucket brought his foot down. He leaned forward, he peered at this strange creature hopping across his living room. He turned his head upside down for a better look; then he spread his wings and flew down to settle silently just behind the lure. The thing bounced on. Curious Bucket, with his "diaper-full" walk, paced right behind it.

But just as he seemed ready to pounce on it, he hesitated. He bowed over it, his beak close to the feathers, and whether it was because they still smelled faintly of their former owner and that made him nervous, or because they smelled of some unpleasant millinery chemical, Bucket abruptly stepped back, and lost all interest. With one mightly flap, he returned to his door top.

Steve picked up the lure and wriggled it up the door. He nipped it quickly to Bucket's yellow toes and away again, but Bucket wouldn't even look at the lure.

After several days of Bucket's continued refusal to chase the pheasant lure, we were about to give up. We sat down early one afternoon and tried to think of some solution to the problem. Bucket, meanwhile, was struggling with a heavy ashtray that weighted down one of his beloved newspapers. The ashtray wouldn't budge. Bucket jumped inside the ashtray, and peered over the fluted edge at his heart's desire.

"Let's try to find someone who has already trained a big hawk to a homemade lure," Steve said, getting up to shoo Bucket out of the ashtray. "Maybe there is some kind of scent we can use to make the lure more attractive." Suddenly he stopped talking and stared hard at Bucket, who was now fiercely yanking at the corner of the newspaper, more determined than ever to gain possession of it.

Steve's eyes lit up: "A roll of newspaper tied to the line! It might be the one thing that Bucket will chase and 'kill' with no hesitation!"

We had our solution.

Steve worked Bucket in the house for two weeks with the plain roll of newspaper as a lure, and the bird loved it. Then Steve tried affixing a piece of cloth to it. That seemed to work, too. But when he added one of the pheasant feathers, Bucket was less inclined to chase the lure.

This went on for several days, with only half-hearted interest in the lure when the feather was attached; both of us were puzzled. Steve would let Bucket chase the paper lure with the cloth attached a few times, then he would add the feather and Bucket, more often than not, would refuse to play.

One evening, Steve was working Bucket and I was in the kitchen fixing ten-month-old Eddie's soy milk formula; he was allergic to regular milk. He could easily hold the bottle himself by this time, so I gave it to him while I cleaned Bucket's chicken gizzards. When I finished, I turned to see my darling son dripping with formula. It was drizzling out of the broken rubber nipple, and Eddie was splattering it with his hands all over the high chair, the floor, the walls, and himself. I got the child and the high chair cleaned up and knelt to wipe the floor when in hopped Bucket with the newspaper lure, feather attached, in his claw, and Steve in hot pursuit.

Bucket sloshed through the spilled formula, thoroughly soaking the lure. When Steve attempted to replace the soggy newspaper with a fresh roll, the bird snatched away the wet lure, and Bucket wouldn't give it up. He seemed to approve of the decidedly strong odor of the soy milk formula. It was a familiar smell to him, of course, because of Eddie, and now perhaps it masked whatever smell the pheasant feathers had that Bucket had objected to.

We made another lure, this time from a rag, into a pouch stuffed with cloth which we had soaked in the soy formula and allowed to dry. Then I sewed on as many feathers as possible, making it look as much like a pheasant as I could. Steve affixed the lead line, and we tried it out.

Bucket took to it gleefully, so well, in fact, that when his exercise time with it was over and we put it in the cupboard, he sat and banged on the cabinet door, trying to get at his new toy.

Gradually, we began to substitute pieces of chicken gizzards for some of the cloth stuffing. Soon we stopped using any formula-dipped cloth as stuffing, and filled the pouch with clean cloth and a whole fresh chicken gizzard. Bucket chased it at every opportunity.

Finally it was Steve's day off, a typical Bay area November day; the gray morning fog had burned off by noon, leaving the sky a watery winter blue. Steve felt it was time for some field training.

Man and bird walked to the flat meadow near the airport and with jackrabbits in the audience as usual, long ears visible here and there in the grass.

Steve let Bucket fly for a while to work off his first exuberance, then he called him down. The chair had long since been dispensed with, and the bird flew directly to Steve. When he was quietly resting on Steve's shoulder, Steve laid a paper bag containing the lure on the ground and jiggled the line attached to the lure. The rusty feathers wiggled out of the bag and onto the grass, looking very much like the real thing.

Bucket took one look and sprang for the treasure, but before he could reach it, Steve gave the line a yank and made the lure jump across the grass. He made it jump again and again until with a mighty tug, he pulled it to him with Bucket unable to catch it afoot, taking to wing.

Quickly Steve squatted down and began to swing the lure around and around in every-widening circles.

Bucket swung after it on its first turn and overshot it. Around and around went the lure. Bucket's eyes never left it, and he took to the air again, going in what seemed the wrong direction. Steve almost stopped swinging for fear the untethered hawk had taken off.

Anxiously Steve stood up. Bucket was now at the other end of the field. Steve's abrupt movement frightened away a young bunny with enormous ears, whose long back legs propelled it away in a hurry. Bucket swung around from high in the air and went into the magnificent stoop for which hawks are famous. The brown wings almost closed, the tail too. The bird's whole body seemed to flatten and elongate as he dove, feet pressed tightly back, and every feather sleek, down close to the skin. He screamed. The attitude of the dive was long and direct. Bucket would not be denied his treasure this time.

Steve had never seen the maneuver before. In his delight, he forgot to swing the lure. It fell almost on top of the fleeing rabbit, and whether the hawk mistook the rabbit for the lure in his excitement of the chase, or he suddenly decided that bunnies might be fun, Bucket swerved and took off after the rabbit.

Five feet above the rabbit's back beat the mighty wings. The black talons were extended now, spread ready for the catch. The rabbit had laid his ears flat and was running at full speed. Halfway across the field he swerved and sped past a clump of bushes that could have been a sanctuary. On he ran, zigzagging this way and that, with the hawk exactly above him. The rabbit made it through a broken wooden fence. The bird rose slightly to clear it, then dropped again.

In the center of a small depression in the field about twenty feet from the fence, the rabbit stopped in his tracks, and sat with his mouth open, trying to catch his breath. Bucket overshot him, not braking fast enough, but then one square-tipped wing drooped, the other rose, the brown body pivoted, and the bird swooped back for the kill.

He landed right in front of the creature, nose to nose. He went into his mantle, he screamed, he flapped his wings, but when the rabbit did not react, the hawk just sat there, his frustrated cries telling of his disappointment that this new friend wouldn't "play" anymore. Bucket didn't know that bunnies were to eat.

Finally, Bucket turned his back on the rabbit and jumped to Steve's shoulder to begin a mournful chirping in his ear. When Steve once more attempted to entice Bucket to the lure, the bird paid no attention to it.

Steve's hunt training of Bucket went on, sans lure, and the bird loved it. Nothing seemed more fun to him than a rabbit breaking from the grass and Steve launching him after it. He would take up the chase with purpose, but when the rabbit either made it to the safety of a bush or just tired and refused to run anymore, Bucket would land, disgruntled, and then Steve would have to pick him up.

But after a few months, Bucket began returning to his master's shoulder after the chase, for which Steve was grateful. However, never once did Bucket ever actually finish a hunt with the kill that would have meant his success as a hunter.

Steve and I came to the conclusion that the bird didn't kill, although he was capable of doing so, because he didn't want to. He was a civilized member of society, after all. He was well-fed on succulent chicken gizzards. He didn't need to eat a living wild animal still in its fur wrapper. How could we expect him to!

The Falconeering Society of California informed us of a solution that was employed by every hawk handler since the beginning of time. When a bird was expected to work, it was not fed the day prior to the hunt. It flew hungry, and when it made its kill, then it got to eat.

Bucket have no supper? We had cut him back to one meal a day, so that his evening feeding was of more than passing interest. It was important! And if it was delayed, he would hang on the screen, demanding to be let in, or if already in the house he would come stalking into the kitchen, jump up on the counter and look for the bowl in which his dinner was supposed to be warming. If he couldn't find it, he would then fly to the top of the refrigerator and firmly sink his heel claws into the door's gasket, shrieking displeasure. If that didn't work, he would seek little Ah-Soh's aid by springing over to the cage and shaking it furiously until the cockatiel was forced to join his cry. No. No way in the world could we deprive Bucket of a meal! It was no solution for us, so the "chase the rabbit" game continued.

8

AH-SOH AND BUCKET by this time were getting along as well as could be expected. Each rather tolerated the other instead of being real friends, or so we humans thought.

One day I was listening to a radio show on which listeners could call to ask questions to be answered by other listeners. A caller that day was the daughter of a bedridden, elderly woman. Her mother had had a canary for years. It had kept her company in her lonely room. It had sung to her, and it had chirped to her when she spoke to it. She had loved it very much. The canary had that week succumbed to old age, and the poor old woman was now distraught. In addition, neither she nor the daughter could afford to spend the money for another bird. She quietly asked that if anyone listening had any kind of small bird they could possibly give to her mother it would be a great kindness.

I remembered how empty the house had seemed after our parakeets Shmo and Jezebelle died, and how much the arrival of Ah-Soh had meant to us. Ah-Soh, being his feisty little self, had pushed our sorrow away.

That evening, as I told Steve the story, Ah-Soh was swooping around the house. Steve looked over at me and said, "She should have a bird like Ah-Soh, better than another canary. In a quiet room with nothing else to do, I'd bet he would even learn to talk." The cockatiel's father was a great talker so we had expected the young bird to have no trouble learning. But Ah-Soh wouldn't talk.

He would reply to a direct address with all sorts of whistles, he could whistle whole melodies culled from several of our records, and little Ah-Soh could also communicate his exact wants without any trouble at all. The only thing he didn't do was speak English. We often wondered if he expected us to learn his language instead.

"We do have Bucket . . ." he continued, "do you think she'd take good care of him?"

"Maybe we should at least make the offer and then if he's not right, we'll at least have done what we could?"

And so we agreed. I called the woman I had heard on the radio and discovered a very nice lady indeed. We were the only ones who had responded and she started to cry. Following a long conversation it was decided that Ah-Soh, cage and all, would go to stay at the old woman's home for one week. And if the mother decided he was too much for her, the daughter would return him.

She came the next afternoon to pick up little Ah-Soh. A pleasant middle-aged woman with quiet eyes and her hair in a bun, she traveled the ten miles by bus. On introducing her to Ah-Soh, I discovered she was a bit afraid of birds. Picturing the combination of nervous lady, feisty cockatiel, and two-foot-square cage on a busy city bus, I offered to drive her home, but she declined the offer. She had arranged for a neighbor to pick her up on his way home from work. I gave her a cup of tea, chatted about "that big thing outside"—Bucket—and soon her ride arrived, taking Ah-Soh to a quieter world where he could be king all by himself.

(The elderly woman took immediate pleasure in him, and he accepted her. When I called a few times to see how they were adjusting, I was assured the bird was happy, and I could hear him whistling and carrying on in full and cheerful tones. The last I heard, they were still trying to get him to talk.)

Bucket, upon discovering that the cage he'd tormented so much was gone, searched all over the house for it. He would stop in the center of each room, peer all around exactly as if he were looking for something, and then not finding it, would go on to the next, to repeat his head-turning. After he'd made the rounds half a dozen times, he would bounce atop anything high, the dresser tops, the bedroom curtain rods where Ah-Soh sometimes had perched, the tall bookcase where Ah-Soh had liked to sit. But when the six-pound creature landed on the flimsy, slatted room divider, just as the small bird used to do, it flew into fifty-some pieces, flinging hapless Bucket into the living room. Bucket *never sat* on the divider. We knew something important was wrong. And when he picked himself up and flew to land on the counter below the telephone where Ah-Soh's cage had stood we knew what the trouble was.

Poor Bucket. Ah-Soh *had* been a friend. The big bird sat in the empty spot next to the wall for a very long time and seemed to brood. His soft eyes which should have been dilated in the evening light were narrow as if he were focusing on something just before them, his feathers were slightly fluffed as if to protect himself from the cold. The whole time it took me to reassemble the divider, I talked to him, but he didn't even seem to listen. He just kept on sitting there as if he expected the little bird to materialize and dart at him to drive him back to his rightful place. He refused to move even when Steve brought out the lure. Steve picked him up and took him into the living room. I put the night's chicken gizzards into the warm water.

Bucket was eating five of them a day now. Every two days I laced them liberally with Avitron. He liked the vitamin even though it smelled just like cod-liver oil, and he would lick it off first before applying his beak to the meat. We didn't have to hand feed him any more, and he'd been eating on his own for several weeks. One day when his dinner had been delayed he just hopped up to the warming bowl and helped himself, carrying off the giblet to the closest green wing chair. He'd been so proud of himself, not even hiding the evidence beneath the humped over wings that I had not the heart to scold him. I threw a bath towel over the chair and he settled back on the cushion with a second purloined gizzard and cheerfully began to tear it into smaller pieces.

This night as I spread a plastic sheet on the chair under the towel tablecloth, I wondered if Bucket would eat. He was sitting beside Steve on the other green chair but he wasn't watching the pink rubber mouse Steve was using to distract him. He didn't even eye the evening paper which lay on Steve's lap. Bucket was truly upset. I added an extra drop of the vitamin, hoping for the best.

But I needn't have worried. Bucket never neglected his tummy.

He dug in, claws as usual holding the gizzard down while his beak tore delicate morsels off and his pink tongue lapped them neatly into his mouth. I hoped the meal would change his mood.

And it seemed to. When he had eaten his fill, we noticed that his eyes were calm and his feathers smooth. He wiped his beak, cleaned his dirty claws of all signs of his dinner. He settled on the wing of the chair Steve sat in and began his nightly preening, occasionally drawing his beak through a strand or two of Steve's hair when the notion crossed his mind. This was one of the continually endearing things about Bucket. It could be that in the wild, members of a hawk family help groom one another. We had occasionally seen the parakeets, Shmo and Jezebelle, do this for each other. But more than a few times as that evening passed Bucket suddenly swiveled his head, obviously still looking for his "little brother."

The next day I had to take Eddie to the doctor's office for his checkup, and as there was little fog that morning, I thought Bucket would do just fine in his cage while we were gone.

Steve got the call from Mr. Mac at work: "Your hawk is out of his cage and is terrorizing Mrs. Raymond's chicken yard. She just phoned me. She wants you to come and get him." Mrs. Raymond's house was three blocks from ours.

But when Steve arrived home he found Bucket sitting peacefully inside his cage, and soaking, dripping wet. The bird quacked happily at him and lumbered out to jump to Steve's shoulder and then to shake himself, dog fashion, all over. Steve wiped his face and talked to the hawk for a while. Putting him back into the cage, he shut the door and worriedly wondered what to do next. About this time, Eddie and I returned.

"Bucket got out of his cage. You've got to be more careful to lock it. Who knows what kind of trouble he's caused this time!" Steve was quite upset.

I blinked and finally managed, "But I did snap both catches. I checked twice to make sure. I don't understand how he got out, unless someone was up here . . ." Just then Bucket casually threw himself at the cage door and pop, it opened.

"Bucket got out of his cage, honey," I said and laughed at the disbelieving stare on Steve's face, adding, "You've got to be more careful."

When Steve explained what had happened, we both went to Mrs. Raymond's, taking Eddie with us. Mrs. Raymond's house was small, neat and pink, just like herself. She was about sixty with gray braids coiled around her head, and today she greeted us in her bathrobe.

"I'm afraid I got wet," she excused the robe. "The hose nozzle backsprayed when I turned it on your, ah, pet. I'm sorry I had to do that but I couldn't wait any longer for someone to come, and I couldn't see any other way to chase him out of my hen yard. I hope he's not hurt. . . ."

"No," I assured her. "A little water just probably taught him he wasn't welcome here. But how are the chickens?"

To our relief she said, "They're fine. It was the strangest thing though. He just flew into the backyard and tried to sit down beside my hens in the chicken coop. Just walked right into the coop like he belonged there. And jumped up onto the first shelf. The poor chickens went crazy, squawking, running around out in the yard, but your hawk just sat there like he couldn't understand what they were doing. Strangest sight I ever saw! And me standing there with the egg basket not ten feet away from him. I flapped my apron at him, told him to 'shoo,' but he screeched at me; so I ran and called your landlord. When I came back outside after talking to him, your hawk was standing in the middle of the chicken yard just watching my chickens huddle up together in a corner of the yard. He didn't like my rooster, but he didn't seem to want to bite any of them. He was quacking just like a duck. Almost as if he wanted to be friends. Like he was lonesome or something."

"Bucket did lose his little companion yesterday," I explained to the woman. To him one bird might look much like another, even a chicken.

As Mrs. Raymond began to understand that the hawk was a pet, and that he was lonely for his little friend she became very warm toward us . . . and to Bucket.

"Oh well, now you're not to worry about my chickens—my old hens don't lay much anyway. And you watch that bird of yours now," she added, as we turned to leave. "I wouldn't want him in my backyard again, but it's not every neighborhood that can boast a hawk in it."

And so Bucket had made not an enemy but another friend, and shortly thereafter also gained a padlock for his cage.

On Thanksgiving that year we were invited up to Rough and Ready, a small community in the Sierra foothills. We got up early for the two-hour drive, and bundling Eddie and Bucket into the car, off we went. It was a mild morning, somewhat cloudy, but the predicted rain never came, and the sun came out. Eddie sat in my lap playing and looking out the window, while Bucket sat on the back of the front seat as usual and viewed the scenery too.

As usual our car was attracting a lot of attention from other holiday travelers. Everyone was staring and pointing to the car with the child and bird who were side by side looking back at them. Occasionally, the fenders of their cars would drift towards ours. Again and again Steve had to honk and swing the steering wheel in evasive action. Swearing under his breath because he then had to watch the other side—and often there'd be someone swerving towards us on that side too. Finally he pulled over to the slow lane so that he only had to watch one side, drove slower and let everyone else hustle by. At last we escaped the freeway with relief, vowing to drive it again only in the dark.

When we were approaching the zigzag curves that would take us to the next lap of highway, we saw ahead of us a slow-moving heavily laden truck. Traffic was light and the speed limit on this road was fifty, so Steve speeded up a bit to pass the truck. As he stepped on the gas and swung out, the way appeared to continue on straight; however the road we were traveling on curved abruptly to our right, the truck blocking the fact. Steve was forced to continue on straight ahead, through a stop sign and onto what turned out to be a side road. There wasn't any danger of a crash for there was no traffic coming either way, but there was a Highway Patrol car parked just before the stop sign.

Steve sighed; he looked at me. I shrugged, and he pulled over. The blinking red light caught up to us, and the policeman got out of the car.

When he reached the driver's window—Steve had cranked it down a bare two inches—he knocked peremptorily on it and told us to please roll down the window all the way.Through the crack Steve said, "I'm sorry, I can't."

"Why not," demanded the officer.

Steve pointed to Bucket. The officer stooped down and peered into the car. "Hawk," Steve apologized uncertainly.

Bucket then screamed. His wings humped in full mantle, the brown feathers on his neck swelled, the small ones on his head flared up, and he raised one drawn back set of talons, menacingly, in the officer's direction. The patrolman took a hasty step back. "Ah . . . well . . . could you step out of the car?" he asked tentatively, as if afraid that not only Steve would, but the menacing hawk as well. With a protective hand around Eddie, I held on to Bucket's jess as Steve opened the door. Bucket lunged, but he could only jump to the driver's seat, where he sat and screamed the whole time Steve talked with the officer.

We got off with a warning to be more careful.

The trip continued on to Rough and Ready without further incident. As we pulled into the driveway, Pat came out to greet us, followed by Dale, her husband, and Sean, the older boy, Tim, and Sioban, the youngest. The little girl waved.

We took Bucket into the big, pleasantly scented by mince pie kitchen and settled him atop the door to the laundry room, spreading newspapers all around so Bucket wouldn't mess up Pat's new floor.

The kids, of course, were fascinated with Bucket, and he was being the perfect gentlemen although we were watchful for any small hands that might get too close. When Timmy climbed on a chair to touch him, Bucket only called our attention to his predicament as he drew away, making himself as unattainable as possible.

While Pat and I cooked and talked, Dale and Steve took Bucket outside to fly him to keep him from becoming restless. When the big wings had stretched, Steve allowed him to perch on the rooftop for a while.

Pat and Dale had banties, chickens hardy enough for the wild-country surroundings of Rough and Ready. They were sheltered in an old shed, but they weren't cooped. They continuously escaped, taking to the trees, and only came down at feeding time. Dale and

Steve were sitting on the porch stairs talking, and Bucket was sitting quietly on the roof minding his own business, when the little rooster took flight from his tree, and with an amazing amount of noise from so small a throat, dive-bombed the peaceful hawk, passing a bare foot above him.

Bucket squawked and flapped into the air. The rooster turned and dove again, smacking Bucket on top of the head. Bucket landed on the other side of the roof, tangling his lead line around the chimney top in the process. Unfortunately, he also surprised one of the banty hens roosting on an eave. The hen flopped around like he'd attacked her, crying in a dreadful voice. The rooster sprang to her defense, thoroughly enraged, and flew into Bucket with spurs to the fore. Bucket scrambled to defend himself, black talons snatching at where the rooster had been, but it was obvious that hung up as he was, the feisty little banty was certain to be the winner.

Dale ran for a ladder while Pat and I pitched pebbles at the rooster, making him swerve and miss his target.

Finally, with Dale steadying the ladder, Steve reached the roof. Shooing off the rooster, he untangled Bucket's line. Up onto his shoulder jumped a frantic Bucket, ducking and screaming at the banty. Man and bird gingerly descended the ladder together, Steve still fending off the rooster.

Once off the roof, we thought the battle was over, but the banty thought otherwise. He kept swooping at Steve's head trying to get at Bucket who hopped from one of Steve's shoulders to the other, sharp claws skittering, keeping Steve's head between him and the banty's flying spurs. Steve hastily hunted for a protected place to put Bucket until the rooster calmed down. Dale pointed to the rabbit cages—complete with occupants. Steve nodded and into mama rabbit's cage went the obviously terrified hawk. His mouth was open. He was panting. His head was scrunched into his neck, and his eyes darted in all directions at once.

The fat black and white angora buck in the next cage grunted at the visitor and in one long leap moved to the opposite end of the structure. The even fatter, brown angora doe twitched her nose at her sudden house guest and then seemed to think over the situa-

tion, while her seven babies hopped around here and there paying no attention at all to Bucket.

He flinched as the mighty little rooster twanged the cage and flew off again, but then he seemed to breathe a sigh of relief knowing that he was safe.

When the doe decided she wanted to sniff him, he let her approach, but when her pink nose got too close he warned her off with a small cry and a slight bridling of neck. She took the hint, backed off, and went on about the business of feeding her babies.

The doe was Pat's particular pet. She watched the rabbit cages with a more than slightly appalled stare, expecting Bucket to eat her mama bunny and perhaps a baby or two any minute.

"Bucket won't hurt her or the others," I assured her. "He and rabbits are old friends. If she was running, he might chase her, but . . ." I told her how he hunted rabbits outside the airfield. Mollified, she just shook her head, and we returned to the house for Thanksgiving dinner.

Bucket behaved so well away from home that we took him with us many places. Sometimes Steve would have to go into work on his day off, and he'd take Bucket with him to visit. The hawk created quite a stir among customers and help alike, but he never caused any trouble.

On one occasion, Steve was forced to slip into his role of department manager briefly and disappeared into the back room. Bucket, untended, decided to seek out a more desirable perch. Somehow he managed to slip the knot of his line and he flew to the top of the liquor department's tallest beverage cooler. Customers gaped at the hawk calmly preening himself, and work was carried on rather half-heartedly as employees tried to keep at least one eye on the boss's big bird.

Bob Hartman hurried to fetch Steve. When Steve peered out of the back room and saw that the chair on which he had perched Bucket was now empty, his face paled. Bob, grinning, pointed to the cooler. Bucket saw Steve and chirped, and then to the "ohs" and "ahs" and "what a gimmick!" and "when's the next show!" of the delighted crowd, the huge wings unfolded and with a flap Bucket sailed down to land happily on Steve's shoulder.

On another occasion Bucket was actually invited to a store, a small but exclusive men's clothing shop in our neighborhood called Stone's. As I wandered one day from counter to counter looking for a Christmas gift for Steve, one of the younger clerks offered to help me. When I looked up, his face lit in recognition.

"Aren't you the lady who owns that big bird down the street?" he asked.

When I nodded, he continued, "Wow! I've been looking at him morning and night, coming and going from work. Is he tame? Friendly? Does he fly? Is he a falcon?"

His questions came faster than my answers. Mr. Stone, the owner, passed by, and became embroiled in the conversation, because he, too, had often seen the bird. Another clerk joined the group and told us that just a few days before a local newspaper columnist had been in the store and had mentioned seeing what looked like an eagle perched on a roof top nearby, and wishing he could have a closer look.

"Hey," chimed in the young clerk. "Could you bring your

hawk in the next time Mr. Fiset comes? Then we could *all* get a look at him up close."

The shop was very crowded three days later when I came in with Bucket. I could see that it was not the best of times to bring him there, but I had promised. I stood near the cash register against the wall. Bucket drew his foot up under his chest and his eyes followed this one and that with interest.

When the young clerk finished with a customer, he came over and smiled broadly, reaching his hand out to Bucket.

The hawk peered suspiciously at the extended fingers, but when I reassured him he let his tummy feathers be petted.

"He's so soft," exclaimed the clerk, "and look at those feet!" Bucket had put down his foot, his long black talons curled around my wrist, almost completely encircling it.

And again the questions flowed, "Is he really so tame you don't need to use a glove?" "Can anybody handle him like that?" "What does he eat . . . do . . . hunt . . ." and so on.

Then, as though on cue, the columnist, Bill Fiset, was approaching the cash register. With a garment in hand, he stopped about five feet away and eyed Bucket. Although he had mentioned that he would like to see the "eagle" up close, it rather looked like he was not quite prepared to have someone fulfill that request so suddenly.

"This is the bird that lives down the street," the clerk said by way of introduction.

Mr. Fiset looked a little dubious as he handed the garment he carried to the cashier for packing and prepared to pay for it. Bucket decided that he had sat still long enough and raised his wings high to stretch his back muscles, then stood on one foot, stretching out one long leg, claws drawing closed into a perfect fist; the man warmed.

"Is he an eagle?" he asked.

"No, a hawk," I said, "a red-tailed hawk. His name is Baku but we call him Bucket."

We chatted for a minute or two; then as he paid for his purchase, he asked, "And you keep him outside all the time?" I shook my head, saying, "Just during the day."

It was an amiable enough encounter, but the columnist's casual pleasantry betrayed no special interest in Bucket. I thought no further about it.

However, several days later, about 5:00 P.M. the most curious thing began to happen on our street. There was a small traffic jam! First one car, then another, and another, stopped in the middle of the street in front of our apartment house. The drivers craned their heads towards our windows, it seemed, and Bucket on the roof screamed and screamed at the strange sight. I went out onto the porch to see an orderly procession of cars that would stop a moment, occupants staring up at us, and then drive on by. It went on until about seven o'clock, then ceased, only to be repeated the next night, and for several nights thereafter.

On the third evening, finally, I got bold enough to go downstairs and approach one of the cars. I had long sinced realized the target of the attention, but was at a loss as to what was causing all this sudden interest in Bucket. Bucket had lived with us for almost two years, and this had never happened before.

The car I approached was driven by a nice-looking middle-aged man who was so interested in watching Bucket that he barely noticed me step up to his window. When I told him I was the bird's owner, though, he readily answered my question.

"There was a line about it in the *Tribune,* in Bill Fiset's column."

All this had resulted from my innocent little trip down the block to Stone's store? We never did get to see exactly what Bill Fiset had written in his column. But no matter. That uneventful meeting had led people who cared to our hawk to share a moment of his special magic.

Late one morning I set about baking fruitcake with little Eddie. His job was to eat any boiled raisins that missed the bowl and fell on the counter. Bucket was out on the roof, enjoying the unusual warmth of the early December day.

When the cake was in the oven, and the child cleaned up, I had turned to wash the mixing bowls, but I heard an unusual sound that seemed to come from the direction of the stairs. I turned off the hot water and listened. It was repeated. It sounded like something was being bumped or knocked against the landing.

I rushed to the porch, but saw no one on the stairs or on the landing. I looked up at the roof to see where Bucket was. He was on the street side, and madder than heck about something. He was in full mantle and his eyes were pinpoints of fury, but oddly enough, he wasn't shrieking. He was trying to make himself inconspicuous as he did before an attack.

I started to the front rail of the porch but didn't take more than three steps before a rock whizzed up from the street, missed the roof and landed on the stairs.

I dashed to the landing, yelling, "Hey!" and saw three children perhaps twelve years old, standing on the parking strip. One was larger than the others, with close-cropped hair. One was chubby with a little boy face. And the last had hair so bushy it seemed to stand up from his scalp in all directions. And each had a supply of rocks in his hands. The biggest boy was just pitching one.

"And just what do you think you're doing?" I demanded. But too late, the missile flew to the roof. I heard it fall as if it had hit its mark, although Bucket didn't make a noise. Afraid for the bird, I yelped, "Hey, stop. You'll hurt him. He's a pet!"

"He throws them at us!" he returned in self-righteous tones. "See, he just did it again!"

Bucket was obviously knocking the fallen, offensive rocks off of "his" roof as he did with anything he didn't like there. They landed on the concrete just beside the building, twenty feet from the kids.

These had to be the same kids that had so upset Mrs. Greenwood before. But with my mind still full of the pleasant time of baking fruitcake, I was unprepared, taken aback in fact by their boldness. They continued to taunt both me and Bucket and I was very close to losing my temper. I reached up and grabbed Bucket's line, giving it the signal yank I used to call him down at dinner time. He cooperated beautifully. He spread his big wings and flew down to me, settling lightly on my head, as usual. I urged him over to my shoulder. He spread his wings around me, took his defensive stance—the black talons glittering sharp in the sunlight—and finally he screamed.

The one with the bushy hair who hadn't said a word tugged at the arm of his taller friend as if to say "Let's go," but his friend shook off the hand, held his ground and flung a stream of obscenities up at us.

I gazed down at the boy—the other two had deserted him and were already nearly thirty feet away. He stood there, red in the face, hurling insults, and I realized that it was partially my fault that he couldn't back down and leave also. I should have taken Bucket inside the house immediately. I gritted my teeth and pointed down the street.

He looked where I was pointing and yelled after his friends. Then he flung the rest of the rocks in his hand at me, turned and belligerently sauntered back to the sidewalk to follow the others just as Steve's car pulled into the driveway. Steve sprang out, a rifle in his hand.

The kid's face blanched, a wet spot bloomed on his pants, and he took to his heels.

Steve shook his head and called up to me, "Are you alright? The rocks didn't hit you?"

I pointed to Bucket, "Bucket caught the only rock that came close!" And the bird still held the golf ball sized missile in one big foot. He had snatched it out of the air like a baseball player might grab a fly ball. Steve came up on the porch and when he patted Bucket's tummy the bird raised his foot and dropped the rock into Steve's hand. Then he shook out his feathers as if pleased with himself and went into his quacking act.

"I had to go to the post office for the store," Steve said as we went inside, "so I thought I'd swing by Nel's and pick up that rifle he fixed for me and then come home for lunch. I didn't even realize I had it in my hand when I got out of the car. Sure scared that kid, didn't it!"

We never saw those three boys again. I suspect Steve left a permanent impression that made the boy hesitate to even come on our street, and perhaps he'd learned a lesson and would be more respectful of other creatures in the future, if only out of fear of how owners might react.

9

ONE RAINY FEBRUARY MORNING, I discovered we were getting new neighbors. Old Uncle Herman, who lived across the street, had passed away a month before and now a rental van was pulled up in the driveway of the red brick triplex next to Jim Ellis's sporting goods store. As the furniture was being unloaded, I saw a woman carry three wooden animal-carrying cages, one at a time, each large enough to hold a medium-sized dog, into the first floor apartment. I wondered how Bucket would react to three dogs living across the street from his territory. . . .

One afternoon during a break in the weather—it had poured for days—I was out on the porch sweeping water from the deck. Eddie sat just inside the door in his red walker watching me, and Bucket sat on the roof, happily sunning himself after the days of house confinement. I saw the new neighbor come out and sit down on the stairs leading to the upper apartments of her building. I hadn't met her yet so I thought it might be a good time to go over and introduce myself.

I was just laying down the broom when I heard Bucket's claws make a funny noise on the gravel of the roof, as if he'd clenched them while still standing on them. I stepped to the porch's side rail to look up. He was furiously mantled and he screamed the most terrified call I'd ever heard. He launched himself straight off the roof and went full tilt for the street.

The lead! He'd never stressed it like this before. Would the sixty-pound test line hold? I held my breath.

It stretched. It didn't snap. It pulled him back down to the rooftop. He bounced off it again and began to strike in terrible fury at the tarpaper and gravel of the rooftop. He jumped, he flapped, he flew, striking out with those flashing talons, and all the while that terrified, terrifying, eerie scream filled the neighborhood.

People began to come out of their houses: Mrs. Greenwood, Mr. Mac, George. Even the dour, retired Henry and his wife, Blanche, stepped out onto their porch next door to us to see what all the noise was about.

Henry turned to me and called out, "There! That's what's the matter!" He pointed to the woman across the street. "She's got a snake! Would you look at that . . . a big ugly SNAKE!"

And sure enough wrapped around the slender woman's waist was a snake, its big, narrow head resting on her shoulder. Its coils were dull green, the same color as her blouse. I didn't know much about snakes, but I thought it might be a boa. She was standing up now, staring at the flamingly angry hawk, as if she couldn't believe her eyes.

"Now, Henry," said Blanche, trying to hush him.

"Don't 'Now Henry' me!" he snapped. "I saw those three cages she moved in with. Want to bet that one snake didn't come in three cages? Want to bet *what* came in three cages? *Three* snakes, that's what I bet!" He stomped inside.

The woman across the street sat down again and began stroking the lapped coils of the six-foot long creature. I thought that anyone who would even dare handle a snake as big as that must surely be able to keep it under control.

I called to Bucket. He had stopped his frantic, futile efforts to attack the snake way across the street, but he was still screaming. He had never seen a snake before, but instinctively he had recognized a natural enemy and had reacted. I was thrilled by the promise of it.

At first he wouldn't respond to my call. He stretched himself against the line, leaning as far toward the enemy as he could manage, and his screams now changed pitch. Instead of being terrified, they were now just belligerent. His first fright was over, he had put his enemy on guard, and had given warning to his neighborhood friends, his flock, so to speak. He was beginning to relax. Coaxing him, cajoling him with soft words and repeated tugs on the line, I finally convinced him to fly down to me. And when he sat on my shoulder he began to tell me all about that fierce monster across the street. I praised him for his bravery and cleverness and then put him into his cage.

Speculating a moment as to whether or not the snake lady would want company while she sat with her pet, I shrugged—she *was* outside after all—I picked up Eddie and went over to meet her.

She turned out to be a friendly person. The snake, she said, was a python, not a boa, and basically timid, though short-tempered at times. She did indeed have two more companions, and they *were* boas. They were mottled tan and brown in color and even larger than the python but less excitable. If this one was the worst of the three, I thought, gazing at the lazy green coils, even Henry would have to admit there wasn't much to worry about. And they worked for a living too. The lady was an exotic dancer; the snakes were part of her act.

As the days passed the neighborhood got used to the snake lady sunning her pets—the snakes needed sunlight as much as birds and kids. However, Bucket, who had become very sensitive about strangers in his territory, never did get used to them. Every time they were brought outside, he would kick up a fuss, trumpeting his "intruder alarm" for all the neighbors to hear and heed.

And since he couldn't get at the snakes across the street, he began to take out his frustration on other "snakes" he had previously taken for granted: Eddie's stuffed-animal snake; the tail of the Dan'l Boone hat Eddie had been given for Christmas; and his favorite target, the vacuum cleaner hose.

Bucket had never much liked the roaring monster that ate up his carefully shredded newspaper bits anyway. When I used it, he preferred to be outside. When that was impossible, he would retreat to the door top where he would stay out of its path until it and its noise had gone.

But on a rainy Saturday after his first encounter with a real snake, a glint came to his eyes that I hadn't seen before. When I rolled out the tank-type machine, Bucket immediately jumped to the top of the front door which I had left slightly ajar to let in the rain-freshened air. He sat and narrowly eyed the machine; then his eyebrows wiggled and his eyes sharpened suspiciously.

I turned on the machine and began to peacefully vacuum when Bucket suddenly screamed. I then found myself in the midst of the silliest battle imaginable. The brave protector spread his wings and dropped onto the vacuum hose. Claws flashed, beak snatched against the enemy and he "killed" it, exactly as he had wanted to do with the snake across the street. Then, with the hose almost seeming alive in his claws, he bounced around the living room, the vacuum tank rolling after him, and screamed at the machine as if it were chasing him. He dropped "the snake" and pounced on the tank. He attacked it, black talons kicking out at the metal top making chalk-against-blackboard noises—jump, kick, land, again and again, until there were toe prints all over its shiny surface. I quickly pulled the plug out before he decided to attack the cord, and tried to undo the hose. As I did this he sprang to my shoulder and spread his wings around me, protecting me from the snake. In a huff, he swooped up and around the living room again before dropping to the hose and snatching it away.

The coiled wire inside the brown plastic hose made it act like a spring. Boing, boing, went Bucket and his snake as they bounced all over the room. And then, over went the tank, and its contents spilled out on my new salt-and-pepper tweed rug.

Setting the tank on its wheels again, and having had about enough of the bird's ridiculous shenanigans, I tried to reclaim the hose. But Bucket would have no part of that, and I got the impression he was not being so hawklike after all. His eyes were gleeful and crafty. He was not going to share his hose even with me, and he bent his wings over it and dared me to take it. There was no doubt about it, he knew now that he had not killed a snake but *my toy*. And he wasn't about to give it back to me, that was for sure. I glanced around the house, searching for something to distract him with, but all I saw was a newspaper. I wasn't going to give him that—it was because of newspaper scraps I was vacuuming. Then I saw Eddie's four-foot long, yellow, fuzzy snake lying on the kitchen floor. It was tightly stuffed, and very real looking as such toys go. I glanced over my shoulder to see where Bucket was; he was eyeing me from beside the door to Eddie's room.

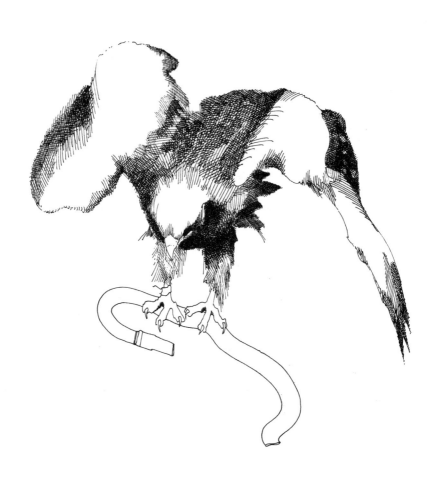

I went by him into Eddie's room and closed the door, then sneaked through the connecting rooms into the kitchen. Bucket was still gazing at the door through which I had gone. Perfect. Hiding myself from his view on my hands and knees, I picked up the toy snake, slid it tail first through the kitchen doorway into the living room, as if it had crawled there. Then I hissed.

Sure enough, Bucket attacked it. As soon as I felt his claws in it and heard him go into his "kill" screaming, I wriggled the snake a moment, then backed up until I reached the pantry. I jumped up and ran through the bedrooms and out the door into the living room to quickly gather up the vacuum hose before Bucket decided he wanted both "snakes." And he did, of course, as soon as he saw me. I made it back into the bedroom and shut the door!

Opening it a crack I saw that my bird was now standing on the vacuum itself, rocking the tank with all the force of his beating wings. It was going to spill again any minute, I just knew it! I dashed around to the kitchen and, crawling, gave the toy snake a tug. Before I could wriggle it twice, Bucket had it in his clutches again. He killed it, he trampled it, he went around and around in a circle with it. But I watched only a second before I crawled quickly into the pantry, then raced around again, this time to snatch up the tank.

Bucket then claimed the box of attachments and began picking out the bristles of the dusting brush. Back into the kitchen I went to wriggle the toy snake. Pounce, Bucket got it. Zip, back around into the living room for the attachment box. I'd won! Then I looked at the hose. It really had been killed. Its entire length was punctured by his busy talons. All my craftiness . . . for nothing.

If the aggressive creature had been able to inflict damage to such relatively sturdy material, how much worse off was the toy snake going to be? Sawdust!

Bucket was now sitting in his nest with the toy snake, busily picking all the fuzz off it with his sharp beak. Only a little sawdust was trickling out of it. I thrust the useless hose toward him, wagging it, saying "Come on, come get this snake . . ."

He took one look and bounded out of his nest. Big wings flexed, he came for the hose, still clutching the ragged toy snake in one foot!

I jerked the hose behind my back. He landed on the rug close to me, dragging the snake behind him, but its fat head had snagged on the table-top nest and with a mighty plop the nest fell to the floor behind him.

He glanced back briefly at the noise, but then immediately jumped and snatched at the hose behind my back, still holding the toy. Around and around the room we danced, he darting behind me, me turning and backing away. Finally, I knew I had to do something else, so I pitched the hose into the far corner by the couch; as Bucket hopped after it, I grabbed the toy snake by the tail and pulled; it came free and I gathered it up into my arms.

Bucket stopped, started to come back for it, but then realizing he'd lost that one, turned and leaped the remaining length of the room to the hose and sank his claws in it. He remained there on the rug, killing the hose all over again, occasionally glancing over his shoulder and warning me away in no uncertain terms. His face and his voice were no longer playful.

I took the toy snake into the bedroom to my sewing table, and sat down to hand-stitch its wounds shut. When it was back in Eddie's playpen—its tail a little shorter and a bit of stuffing gone here and there—I swept up the mess in the kitchen and gathered up Eddie and my purse to go out and buy a new vacuum hose.

The new hose was readily acquired but getting it into the house unmolested proved to be a difficult task. The hose had been too big to wrap so the salesman had just tied it into a coil with a piece of string. Not thinking, I walked in the door. Bucket spied the new hose immediately and from where he sat, amid pieces of the old hose now strewn all over the floor, he launched himself at the new hose in my hand, dragging along what was left of the old one as well.

I took one look and hastily shut the door again. Then stood outside in the rain, one arm full of precious new hose, the other full of child.

No, it wouldn't do. I dropped the hose on the porch and went into the house; it was *my* house after all.

I dried Eddie off and put him in his highchair with a cookie and his unspillable cup full of milk. Then I dried myself off too, and made a cup of coffee. I sat drinking it and looking at the ruined nest, now stuffed into a cardboard carton ready to take downstairs to the garbage cans. Over the months it had become a huge, wondrous thing; Bucket had brought many treasures to it. It had disrupted normal kitchen life considerably but we loved Bucket and he had seemed to love his nest, so we had made many adjustments, setting up food preparation and dining arrangements in other parts of the house.

When I next looked up, a rather forlorn Bucket still sat on the floor by the door clutching his snake. He had dropped his serious air, and was all ready to play again. He came into the kitchen, chirping and cackling, jump-hop he came. And he passed his ruined nest without a glance.

When he reached the table, the hose didn't—it caught on a chair and recoiled out of his grip. Bucket gazed at it a moment, seemed to shrug, then forgot it. He hopped up to my shoulder. Shaking his feathers, chirping in my ear, he leaned forward to see what I had in the cup. He cackled again, as though telling me he too wanted something to drink. I got up to get him his drink.

So we had, at last, reclaimed our table, and Bucket never tried to build another nest there. In the wild, if a hawk's nest is knocked down from a tree by high winds, or whatever, the bird will never rebuild in that tree, considering it no longer a suitable homesite. Bucket reacted just like his wild brothers would have done. But even though we got our table and our kitchen back, we kind of missed the nest. An era had passed.

Gradually the days became warm and the end of April approached. I went back to work part-time for Walter. With the ceasing of the rains, Bucket's temper began to change—it got shorter and shorter. The mockingbirds who nested in the apple tree didn't help matters much. Every time I'd let him out of the house in the morning, Bucket would fly up to his roof and the smaller birds would try to attack him. Beige wings with white badges would dive-bomb the brown head, sometimes even trying to get at the soft vulnerable place where his head joined his neck. Their beaks were long and sharp; I had no doubts that if they could make it to just the right spot, they could kill Bucket.

I took to pitching pebbles at them. I got a water gun and filled it with soapy water to squirt at them, drive them away, but still they came back.

Then one day in May, Bucket took charge of the situation.

I was inside doing house chores and Eddie was at the screen door looking out, when I heard some unusual sounds. I went to the door. A distressed mockingbird was flapping around on the porch with a broken wing. As I watched it, it stopped struggling and lay still.

I stepped outside to pick it up and heard more noises coming from the roof. I looked up, shielding my eyes from the sun with one hand. I saw two large mockingbirds and two smaller ones. They were attacking Bucket with a vengeance, an angry flurry of small wings around his head. I reached for the water gun I kept handy on the rail, but just then Bucket spread his brown wings, and flapped. One swift foot darted out, and he picked the smallest menace right out of the air—and killed it. Then he sat there patiently, head drawn into his neck, waiting for the next to come into his range.

My heart was in my throat. He'd taken the next step necessary if he was ever to survive in the wild.

Bucket sat watching the other mockingbirds, now wary, flying in wide circles around him. I couldn't see what he had done with his victim, but he hadn't pitched it off the roof as he generally did with things he felt didn't belong there. But would he eat it? Did he realize yet that such prey was to be eaten? My curiosity was killing me. But perhaps it was better to leave Bucket alone just now. The roof was his domain, and perhaps if he wasn't disturbed he might eventually take that next step toward independence. I let him be.

Steve came home a little early that evening. Bursting with my news I told him right away about Bucket's momentous deed. A huge grin spread over his face, and he ran for the ladder. Normally, when Steve came home, the bird would come off the roof to chirp and cackle a cheery hello and then would stick around, hoping to tease Steve into playing with him or to get him to take him to the flying field. But today Bucket greeted Steve and returned at once to the roof.

I held the ladder as Steve climbed to the roof, and then he hesitated. "Bones," he whispered, then he looked down laughing and added, "*Bones!* All over the place!" It hadn't been his first kill after all!

"There must be a dozen up here. And you should see Bucket," Steve said, laughing, "he thinks I've come up to steal his latest meal, he's hiding it just like he hides his toys."

I steadied the ladder and Steve came down. Bucket peered over the eave, one big foot clutching a prize. The bird quacked, an inquiring lilt to his voice, and then he poised the foot directly over Steve's descending head. The talons opened and a rather gory part of a carcass dropped on Steve's hair. Then the hawk went into his head-bobbing routine. He had been a host on his rooftop, he was happy, he had shared his meal with a guest.

Steve shook whatever it was off his head, and jumped the remaining two steps to the porch, a bit green in the face. I, too, felt a moment's queasiness.

Later Steve said, "Just think. Bucket can hunt on his own now. He'll soon be ready to leave us. When we're really certain he can recognize prey in the wild and feed himself, then we can put him back into the sky where he belongs." Before that moment, the bittersweet reality of Bucket's leaving us forever had never really hit home.

10

THAT JULY WE were able, together with Bucket, to attend the Exotics Unlimited meeting. Attendance together had been a little sporadic, depending on work schedules, baby-sitters, and Bucket's moods. The summer fog burned off early, bringing a nice day, and the meeting was at a convenient location, Leona Lodge, a recreation department facility in the Oakland hills, not two miles from us. There were only two other cars there when we arrived: Shirley Nelson's station wagon, and a van belonging to Marge and Earl Sparrows, the owners of the leopard, Schezada. The big spotted cat was sitting peacefully beside Earl, and I saw that Marge had a cast on her arm.

Marge was a lovely woman, with attractive gray streaks in her dark hair, and she had a hearty laugh. As we prepared for the arrival of the other members, I asked her about the cast. She patted it, saying, "Arthritis, that's what it is," and she went on using both hands to nimbly open a folding chair. I took the chair from her and said, "Here, it must hurt you to use that arm. I'll do this."

She giggled and leaned over, whispering, "Schezada had kittens two months ago, two of them, black as can be, and so ornery now that she's finally let them out of their box. I was feeding them yesterday, when one decided my arm might taste better. Earl rushed me to the hospital emergency room, with blood all over the place!"

I must have looked shocked, because she added, "Well, that's the chance we take, you know. If we minded getting bitten in the process of civilizing the babies, we'd raise house cats, not leopards. These two are coming along fine—one is already getting used to us, she purred in my arms this morning; the other is still just a little nervous.''

I thought of the times Bucket had accidentally or (occasionally) intentionally snapped at either Steve or me, and what those times had taught us about living together. Even people we knew well sometimes couldn't understand why we didn't get rid of him. I understood what Marge was saying.

More members were arriving with their animals, many of them cougars. Most of these animals had been born in zoos and deemed excess. They had been given to people who would give them good homes, and they reflected that love. The cats were as comfortable about being there as were their owners.

The speaker for this meeting had just finished surveying the wild cougars in California. There was a moratorium in the offing to prohibit the hunting of cougars, as it was a diminishing species. The state had assigned him to the task of finding out just how many of these big cats were left. He began to tell the club about his work. He was not exactly a timid person, but he was unnerved a bit by so many wild animals in the room. Slowly he seemed to forget about them, and warmed to his speech. He gave a brief description of what he'd been doing, live-trapping cougars and tagging them for the count. Then he launched into a colorful tale of one big cat he'd chased for a whole week, though it had often seemed to be chasing him and his co-workers instead.

He didn't pretend that he hadn't found some aspects of that experience scary, and went on to say how he had gradually come to respect the animal. He had just begun to tell us how large that cougar was, when the man who owned Samson, the biggest cat in the club, walked in with his pet.

Samson was huge, pushing two hundred pounds, and still growing. He walked like the butterball he was, and his tail was as big around as my upper arm, so heavy it almost dragged on the ground behind him!

The speaker's eyes bugged out, and he halted in mid-sentence to stare. He swallowed once, deliberately, and said slowly, "I take it back, that wild cat was big, but now I've seen the biggest one I've ever seen."

We had a good representation of the different types of cougars at this meeting. There were two from the south, called pumas there, dark gold and desert-colored, leaner than their northern brothers. There were the medium-sized, northern and California cats with their gray-gold color, who made up the majority of our cats.

One of these, a youngster by his lingering baby spots, was about twenty-five feet from where Bucket and I sat. Steve had perched the hawk on the back of my chair and gone to sit a little way from us and talk to a friend. As the bird seemed happy and was quiet, I hadn't been paying much attention to him. The young cat was a striking animal, perfectly formed with the deep chest and long legs that identified him as a high-country cat and indicated he would be good-sized when mature. I noticed him particularly because he seemed to be getting restless. From laying in one spot too long, I thought. He would sit up and then lay down again, sometimes shaking his head as if protesting the lack of activity. His master, a trim young man with sandy hair, leaned over to scratch the cat's neck. He calmed down, and rolled over on his back and began to play with the man's shoes.

I turned back to the speaker as he showed slides of the net-like traps with which he caught the animals. In the middle of his explanation of how they were strung over a tree, the young cougar I had been admiring began to meow. A strange noise, somewhere between a burp, a chirp, and a house cat's voice. "Meowup, meowup." Turning to look, I found he was much closer than I remembered; then I was distracted from him, as Bucket was also getting restless, his wings flicking. I petted his tummy, talked to him quietly, and after a final shake of his wings, he stepped onto my shoulder and settled down.

A few more minutes passed, and Bucket stepped back up to the chair. I murmured to him and absently brushed my hand over the yellow feet. Then I heard the cat meowup again—just once—but much louder than before. I looked up to find the cat reclining not eight feet from my chair, and Bucket was in full mantle, ready to fight.

143

The cat sat up, drawing his haunches up to his front feet instead of the other way around, then lay down again, having advanced another three feet closer to us. His master, concentrating on the slide show, just moved a little, automatically easing the pull of the leash on his arm.

I watched the young cat draw himself up again, then lay down, this time nearly on my toes. He lifted his gray-brown head, the tip of his pink nose almost level with mine and his yellow-brown eyes stared straight at Bucket with a look that said, "I've almost made it . . . a delicious looking bird . . . just another foot or two and. . . ."

I took a strong hold of Bucket's lead by the jess and cleared my throat, trying to attract the attention of the cat's master. Finally he looked, but by then the sly cat had sat up again and lifted one paw, as a kitten would to play with a dangling string. Innocent eyes gazed into mine and I could almost swear he was grinning. Bucket was drawing back his claws to strike.

"Well, well, what have we been doing," said the cat's master. Abruptly there was no happy, scheming cat facing me, only a very disgruntled one being pulled back across the room. When he lay down again beside his master's chair, he turned his head away and wouldn't even look at Bucket.

When the talk and slide show were finished, Steve rejoined us. "Poor Bucket, almost supper for a pussycat," he petted him. Shirley strolled over and said, "How come Bucket didn't screech? A caracara I once had would yell his head off at any animal approaching. And especially if he was ready to fight, as Bucket obviously was. . . ." I shook my head. "Our Bucket is the silent type, except when he's warning someone off he thinks might be of harm to me," I said.

Bucket was becoming more hawklike every day, but he was still very much the pet. He continued to play with his toys, the pink rubber mouse always the dearest, and of course, the newspapers. His behavior at the airport field didn't change much either: Rabbits were playmates, not prey. However, Bucket did now consider any small bird that picked on him his absolute enemy, no matter where it was.

One day shortly after the pet club meeting, Steve and I both took him to the hunting field. Bucket was busily harassing a scurrying rabbit, big wings tipping this way and that against the sky, when out from a clump of low bushes darted a small bird. It seemed furious and headed directly at Bucket as he passed the clump. It looked as if it would collide with Bucket's bright tail, but suddenly the little bird changed direction and smacked the hawk on the back with a gray-brown wing.

Bucket descended to the grass, and with the most puzzled expression craned his head in all directions, trying to figure out what had hit him. He wasn't left bewildered very long, however, for the small bird was soon diving on him, screeching and scolding, trying to hit him on the top of his head with its beak. Steve and I were momentarily afraid that Bucket had been injured or soon would be, but we needn't have worried. Bucket was the most adaptable bird. He waited coolly until the little bird's next pass. When it dove toward him he sprang into the air, deflecting the bird with the sheer surprise of his action. Then, airborne, he rushed after it. For the first time in his life, he was hunting from the air. And he had an amazingly good idea of how to do it. The small bird made it back into the bushes before Bucket could catch it, and Bucket landed, frustrated, atop the highest branch of the scrub oak.

The next small bird that objected to Bucket's presence wasn't so lucky. Soon Bucket wanted to do little else but chase little birds. He got very good at it. At the first sight of a small set of wings heading towards him, he would land. He would wait ever so carefully, silently and when the bird was almost above him he would lift with mighty flaps, and the deadly, incredibly swift talons would spring out; snap, Bucket would have the bird. Then he'd bring it over to us, showing it off, waiting for praise, before he devoured it.

This was unusual hawk behavior. Normally, they feed on small rodents, an occasional snake, or rabbit in the wild, seldom on small birds. And hawks only hunt and eat when they're hungry. Our Bucket was well-fed at home. He couldn't be hungry. Our very unhawklike hawk always had to show his differentness. He ate anything he caught. And he got fat.

I *thought* he was getting heavier—my arm seemed to tire faster when I carried him, but it was hard to tell for sure when his feathers moved with his emotions, and could make him fat or thin. So one day Steve and I decided to weigh him. We had weighed him twice before; when we'd first gotten him he had weighed just over five pounds and about a year later we found he had gained a pound, to six pounds and one ounce. Neither too fat nor too thin, we thought, the perfect size.

Steve brought the bathroom scale out on the porch. He weighed himself, then picked up Bucket and got back on the scale. After some mental subtraction, he blinked and looked back at the scale, saying, "Wow! That can't be right. Seven pounds three ounces? Naw, it can't be, I better do it again. . . ."

He tried it twice more, but the figures came out the same. There was no doubt about it, Bucket was not a hawk but a pig! A diet was hastily implemented. Bucket's supper was reduced to two chicken gizzards instead of the three we'd been giving him, and the weight began to come off. Soon he was at the ideal six pounds. He didn't seem to miss the third gizzard, or the ounces as they came off, but it seemed to us that he flew just a little faster and jumped at anything he cared to just a little quicker.

On another field trip, the newly trim Bucket was chasing rabbits in and out of their hiding places while Steve wandered down to a small creek. Finding a frog, he wondered if Bucket would be as interested in frog legs and he was in small birds. He whistled. Down came the yellow feet, wings and tail fanned out their widest, and pinion feathers swept back to brake his speed as he landed on Steve's shoulder.

Taking Bucket onto his hand, Steve then lowered him to the frog's hiding place under a clump of grass at the edge of the stream. The frog, needless to say, resented the intrusion of a beak into its shelter; it leaped. It landed two feet away in another grassy tuft and Steve was right behind it with the very curious Bucket.

But the frog leg question was not resolved, for Steve almost stepped on another creature who had taken refuge from both human and hawk, a pheasant.

Up into the air it fled—a bird even bigger than Bucket—in full cry. In the confusion of startled, multi-hued wings rising right under his nose, Steve flung up his arm and unthinkingly pitched Bucket into the air after it. Bucket was game; he'd never seen a real pheasant before, but a bird was a bird, after all, and thus the enemy.

The pheasant knew about hawks, however. He took one look behind him at the flashing hawk's wings, and he was gone before Bucket could get control of the situation, pheasants being power flyers where hawks are not. Red-tail hawks have more glide capability than power. Bucket looked around in the air for a minute or two, then came back to Steve, complaining loudly. Reflecting on the event later that evening, we came to the conclusion that it was a good thing Bucket hadn't caught up with that particular creature just then, and a very good thing that Bucket had lost weight. Had our hawk not been fit and gone after his natural adversary, the pheasant might very well have turned to fight instead of fleeing. A mature pheasant against an untried hawk could be deadly, because pheasants, like fighting roosters, have knifelike spurs on their ankles.

Late that year, we happily learned that another baby was on the way. Bucket, of course, was overjoyed. I'd quit my job and was home more and more. He didn't have to stay in his cage nearly as much; his temper immediately improved immensely. We were a bit slow to notice that, however.

One morning while I was in the kitchen, I heard Bucket start to cackle and then scream. Through his noise I heard, "Mrs. Wallig . . . Mrs. Wallig!" I recognized the voice of the milkman, who, never having learned to leave his bottles at the bottom of the steps, persisted in coming to the landing to be startled by the hawk. I dashed to the door wondering why Bucket, who had always played the silent hunter against this man, was now making such a fuss. The man was backed up as usual against the far railing of the top landing. Bucket, pulling against his line, stretched out a foot as far as he could, one talon just nicking at his victim's polished brown shoe.

"He's trying to eat my shoes!" cried the milkman pitifully. "My hat wasn't good enough today. Now he wants to eat my shoes!"

"He doesn't really eat shoes," I reassured him, trying to keep a straight face. The man was terribly upset. "He's just in a goofy mood and teasing you. He's even kind of friendly today." I picked up Bucket and he went into his chirping act, keeping one eye on the poor man's feet. I held the jess tightly to prevent any further puckish behavior, and said, "I think he wants you to pet him so he'll know you want to be friends. Would you like to?" When Bucket chirped, anyone could pet him. It was a peace offering, perhaps long overdue—but I didn't really expect the milkman to accept it.

The man hesitated and then, to my surprise, reached out and touched Bucket's soft, golden tummy. His expression melted into amazement, as if some wonderful wish had just come true.

"There. . . that's something," he said when he took away his hand, unbitten. "And that bird has been mean to me ever since I started to come here; now he wants to be friends? I think I've seen everything. . . ." He retreated down the stairs, talking to himself. Watching him drive away in his white truck, I realized that touching the bird had been important to him. I felt a little sad; two whole years he'd been delivering milk to us; I wished I'd given him the opportunity before.

Two days later, a young man delivered milk in his place. I asked about the older man. "Oh, he retired. He didn't say anything until he came in off his trip day before yesterday. Said it was his last trip, said he'd seen everything, and that it was time to enjoy the peace and quiet now. A lot of them do that," he added to my stupefied stare, "don't want people to know they're retiring, just suddenly retire. Say, the old man said you folks don't want your milk left on the porch. Said it was important. How come?"

I was astonished. The old milkman had told the new man to do what he himself had never remembered to do. Had that one fleeting touch of Bucket's breast feathers wiped away all memory of his nerve-wracking experiences of two years? I cleared my throat, blessing him silently, and pointed to Bucket, who this day sat in the house, looking out the front window at the street.

"I'll remember," the new man said, staring at Bucket. And he did.

Christmas came and went and the new year began very sadly for us; within six weeks, both Steve's and my father passed away unexpectedly.

Even Bucket seemed to know something was wrong. He wanted to be with us constantly during those grieving weeks. More often than not he would linger in the house, perched beside me or Steve, instead of sitting on the door top. It was as if he thought his presence would make us feel better, happier, and maybe even make us laugh again.

But then we finally could. We had a new little life among us. And while the child couldn't be expected to make us forget the two loved ones we had lost, a baby has a way of bringing joy even past sadness, all by itself.

Slowly, as we had done before, we introduced Bucket to Joseph George, and did all we could to help him accept the new family member.

Old Bucket looked down his black nose at the small person in my arms, and his eyebrows wrinkled as if he thought, "Gee, another one?" and then just went on about his business, preening himself.

One afternoon, when I'd been home from the hospital about three days, I was resting in the bedroom; the two children were napping and the car was at the shop so no one would think I was home, I hoped. I wouldn't be disturbed.

But I hadn't been lying down more than a half-hour when I

heard faint footsteps that made me sigh. From where I lay in the master bedroom, I could hear anyone coming up the wooden front steps. Someone was obviously coming. I was too tired for visitors just then; I decided not to answer the bell. It would be alright, the gate was locked and Bucket, on the roof, couldn't get past the top landing. I listened for the steps to stop at the safety point and for the bell to ring.

No bell rang; the steps continued past the gate.

With a few choice thoughts about people who pass through, or over, locked gates and don't heed signs plainly displayed before them—BEWARE OF RED-TAILED HAWK and DO NOT EN-TER—I got up and started toward the front door.

I assumed that whoever was coming had taken the sign as a joke, as some strangers had and in the past, and so were unwary. I wasn't moving as fast as normal yet, and the seconds it took me to go through the house seemed endless. Finally I made it to the living room, just in time to see the doorknob turn, and the door begin to open.

My mind was a jumble of conscious and semi-conscious fears. Fear that Bucket was now probably poised to spring from the roof with flashing claws on the unsuspecting stranger, and fear that the stranger was no doubt a burglar, taking advantage of a seemingly empty house.

Without really knowing that I'd even moved, I was at the door. I jerked it open, hoping to drag whoever was there into the house before the hawk attacked, as I knew he would, for he hadn't made a single sound. I could feel him waiting, coolly, for the intruder to get into the right position before swooping down off the roof for the kill. He would be perfectly capable of killing a human being: a claw locked in a temple, a talon slashing at a jugular vein. . . .

I was a little too late. Just as I saw that the burglar was two hefty teenagers, Bucket dove head first off the roof. When he struck, he screamed.

The first kid, hand still on the doorknob, blinked in surprise. He was luckier than he might have been. The black talons ripped the shirt off his back and left three, half-inch deep gouges that could have been in his neck if I hadn't pulled him aside by opening the door. Flinching, the kid flailed at the beating wings and tried to back away. Then Bucket turned him loose and went for the other boy.

The second kid turned and ran. He lost a pocket off his pants to a swiping claw as he disappeared down the stairs as if his feet hadn't even touched them. Bucket swerved after the first boy again, but he took a shortcut, beating his friend to safety. He ran right off the deck, over the rail, lit on the hood of Ruth's car in the parking area below, bounced onto the pavement, and kept right on running. Bucket trumpeted triumphantly.

Bucket now hopped to my shoulder and calmly began to tell me in his softly chirping, protective voice, that everything was all right. I sat down in the rattan chair to compose myself for a moment or two. When I was more in control of my emotions, I went inside and called Steve to tell him what had happened. Then I called a lawyer. I was certain I would soon hear from irate parents and/or the law.

But we never heard a word about it from anyone. Perhaps the boys had been afraid that too many questions might be raised for which they had no answers, so they'd told no one about the incident. We told no one either, especially not the police. It went somewhat against the grain, but we feared for Bucket's safety, and he could well be confiscated as a vicious animal if the authorities knew. We considered ourselves lucky to hear no more about it.

It was strange for two responsible people not to do what should have been done, all because of a bird. But even stranger was that during the remaining six years we lived there, though other homes around Walnut Street were broken into, burglars never again approached our little neighborhood, not even after our fierce friend was gone.

11

BUCKET WAS NOW FULL GROWN and healthy. The vitamin supplement he was still getting every other day had brought a sheen to his feathers that, when touched by sunlight, made them look like high polished, amber glass. He was well on his way to being able to care for himself in the wild too. But whenever I thought that he'd be better off wild now, for his sake and sometimes for the safety of others, I always backpedaled, reluctant to face setting him free. "Too soon. He doesn't know enough yet; other raptors will sense it and take advantage," and such. All the while, a lingering sadness colored my activities with the hawk.

The days went by rapidly—on the wings of a hawk, so to speak—with two baby boys to look after, as well as Bucket. Little Joey was a bright-eyed smiling two-month-old, and his big brother, Eddie, had become close friends with Bucket. The bird continued to ignore the newest addition, but he and Eddie had never had problems. Eddie never did things Bucket hated such as pulling tail or wing feathers, or trying to grab beak or feet. And Bucket, with the exception of the stuffed snake, played only with his own toys. However. . . .

I was feeding Joey his supper in the kitchen. Bucket was peacefully standing on his dinner, as usual, preparing to dig in. And Eddie was playing with his blocks on the living room floor.

Bucket chirped then squeaked interrogatively and I glanced up. A puzzled hawk watched his two-year old buddy stuff a raw chicken gizzard into his mouth. With a yelp I jumped up and ran to save my child.

Bucket, slick of feather and soft of eye, looked at me like I was the interloper and he chirruped, "If the kid wants one why shouldn't he have it? He's a good little kid, after all. . . ."

Nobody was ever invited to share Bucket's gizzards, but here was the bird calmly watching the child try to chew the rubbery thing. Well, good little kid or not, a piece of raw chicken that bird feet had been lately standing on was not my idea of good food for very small children.

"Come on, honey," I coaxed him, "spit bird's food out like a sweet kid. Not good for you, spit it out and I'll give you a cookie instead? Cookie. . .?

Just as I began to reach the point of total exasperation, Eddie reached into his mouth, and with the most peculiar gaze at me— "Mommy, you really didn't have to get upset; I was going to spit it out"—handed me the offending piece of meat. Then he smiled beatifically. All three of them gazed at me as if they were totally amazed by my agitated state.

With a word to the child, a pat to the still hungry baby, and a pet for Bucket, I shook my head over them then went to get cookie, bottle, and a new chicken gizzard.

The first two were easy: I got the cookie and the bottle, but there was no chicken left, just an empty bag of butcher paper.

Great, I thought, now what do I do? Seven o'clock at night, no stores nearby were open and who knew which distant ones would have a supply of gizzards. Bucket was hungry; if no food was forthcoming soon, he would quickly show me the advisability of scaring some up. I thought a minute, wondering if any of the neighbors would have a spare giblet or two, or even a chicken leg they might be willing to share. Then a jingle came into my head: "Don't cook tonight, call Chicken Delight!"

I picked up the telephone book, then the phone.

"Could you please deliver two chicken dinners, and put a *raw* leg in one of them? We have this hawk, you see," I added helpfully, "and he's hungry—I ran out of his chicken. . . ."

"Lady, is this some kind of joke?"

I'd been afraid it was going to be this way. The man was sputtering, but finally: "Okay, lady. Alright. Cooked or raw, it makes no difference to me. What's your address?"

Bucket had hopped from my shoulder and was sitting now on the front edge of the sink, peering into the bowl where his gizzards usually warmed.

"All empty, bird," I told him, "but you just be patient. We'll have your supper for you in no time."

He didn't believe me, of course. He thought I was just "dragging my feet." Supper was delayed; he'd just have to see if he couldn't hurry it up. Up onto the refrigerator he sprang to dig his talons into the gray rubber gasket.

I shooed him off. Back he went. Again and again, until finally in desperation I had to put him on the pantry door and tie the lead to the knob. He flew down the minute my back was turned and came into the kitchen again to stand on the floor beside the stove, raise his tail, and do what comes naturally to birds—all over the stove front—green and white ick. This wasn't the first time he'd been angry and got even, but never before had it been directed at me—on my stove!

Yet as I resorted to a rolled-up newspaper applied to the offending tail, I couldn't help but laugh. Bucket knew exactly what he'd done, and seemed to be taking great pleasure in the fact that I now had to spend some time on my knees, scrubbing. His eyes were bright and he smirked. He thought he was right, too . . . where, after all, was his supper?

"It's coming. It's coming!" I muttered at him, swabbing at the stove. I was still scrubbing when Steve finally arrived home. When I told him what had happened, he chuckled too, and then decided to put Bucket outside. But the vindictive little beast had only been outside a few minutes when the hand bell rang, immediately followed by our "watchhawk's" clarion call.

I started for the door, but Steve dashed ahead of me.

"The gate," he said, "I didn't know anyone was coming! It's not locked!"

A very bewildered looking young man stood backed up in the top landing's safety zone, holding out a steaming set of paper plates stapled together, as if he'd used them to fend off the bird.

"Are you okay?" Steve asked him. He told Steve he was unhurt; I breathed easier and as Steve paid him, I picked up Bucket, showing him the paper plates up closer. He couldn't know, of course, that they contained a raw piece just for him, but he smelled the chicken and must have known what it was, for he abruptly lost interest in the deliveryman. He leaped off my hand and to the rail on which I had placed the paper plates, and tried to pry them open with his beak.

"What is he—hungry?" the man asked, joking but a little taken aback.

"Oh, yes," I said, "and could you wait just a second while we check to see that our order is right? We wanted a raw piece for the bird."

The man watched curiously as we freed the plates from their staples.

"One piece, raw!" Steve chortled as he held up a small, plastic wrapped parcel. Then he nodded to the deliveryman. "Tell your boss thanks for us. We know this has all been a little out of the ordinary, and we really appreciate any trouble he took. And sorry to startle you," he added. "You're sure you're okay? No scratches?"

"Naw, he didn't touch me. I gotta go now . . . and thanks for the tip." He waved then left.

As Steve turned to pick up the plates he murmured, "Bet he'll have something to say to his boss for not warning him!"

Though hawks in the wild only eat raw meat, Bucket again showed that there were no hard and fast rules as far as *he* was concerned. From that day on he and Eddie often shared meals—if I didn't catch them at it.

A day or two after the Chicken Delight incident, Bucket was outside perched on the side rail watching Henry next door pull weeds from his garden, and Eddie was impatiently waiting for me to mustard his hot dog so he could eat it. Hot dogs were his favorite food by far.

I added some apple slices to the plate, and settled Eddie on a plastic tablecloth inside the front door in a pool of sunlight where he could play picnic as much as he liked. Tucking Joey into bed after he'd had his lunch, I went to the couch and my book.

A few minutes later I looked up and saw that Eddie had moved

and was now neatly stuffing a bit of hot dog, bun and all, and an apple slice under the screen door. Bucket, on the other side, bent his head to pick up the offerings in his beak.

I plopped down my book and jumped up to move Eddie's fingers to safety before they were mistaken for food and to watch what Bucket might do with his share of Eddie's lunch. Knowing his predilection for mischief, I was half-afraid the bird would decide to drop the bits of food down on the unsuspecting Henry below, just to see the old man jump.

But instead Bucket hopped to his cage top, and in one gulp, swallowed the hot dog, complete with mustard but without bun, then started on the apple.

I stared. He *couldn't* have eaten that hot dog, yet he had! What if it didn't go all the way down and he choked on it? What if it just lay in his crop and soured? A hawk with an impacted crop wasn't something I wanted to deal with; if it happened, he'd have to go to the vet for surgery. I wondered if I should call the vet right then or if I should just keep watching. He didn't seem to be having any difficulty swallowing, so the apple probably was going down alright which meant the hot dog wasn't stuck. But what about his digestive capabilities? As I went to take the rest of the apple away from him—at least he still hadn't eaten much of it— Bucket, all by himself, came to the conclusion that apple wasn't hawk food. He dropped it as I came up to the cage and then, with obvious distaste, wiped his beak on my blouse, leaving a streak the consistency of applesauce on my sleeve. Then he quacked as if to say, "Yuk! Hot dogs are okay, but that stuff is for parrots!"

I petted him and watched him carefully for a few minutes; he seemed to be just fine.

Bucket continued to share Eddie's lunches and he never did become ill. He would even eat a bit of tuna fish sandwich, mayonnaise and all, and thrived.

Something rather strange was beginning to happen, though, in the weeks that followed the first sharing of meals between Eddie and Bucket. Chicken Delight had been a nice change, so we began to call them every once in awhile. When we had home-delivered food, Bucket did too, for the shop's owner had remembered my voice and address and always asked if I wanted a raw leg with my order.

One evening a new delivery boy knocked not at the gate but on our front door. And he had a very interested hawk standing silently on the deck just behind him, also patiently waiting for someone to open the door.

Quickly we invited the boy in and gathered Bucket up. But the bird, it seemed, had no intention of driving away any intruders on his porch: Those big soft eyes were only for the paper-plated dinners in the young man's hands.

The next delivery was made by another man, and he also came directly to the front door. Bucket didn't bother him either, and again waited in line behind the man for the door to open. It happened two more times, with the deliverymen free to come as they pleased. I was truly bewildered. Bucket welcomed Chicken Delight as he had never welcomed even our best friends. And the most puzzling thing was that he was still just as nasty as he'd ever been to anyone else who tried to come on our porch.

We had decided, finally, that Bucket would allow anyone carrying the hot, aromatic chicken on his porch, but then one day that seemed to prove false. The chicken was the same, and the fries and rolls, too. Nothing could have smelled different to a hawk's nose. . . .

We were almost finished with our chicken dinner, when Steve asked for the tenth time, "Why did Bucket scream at this guy?" We had caught him below at the gate, after Bucket's screams of warning. I put the used napkins and bones into the bag the dinner had come in.

Steve's eyes were suddenly on my hands. "There *was* something different today . . . the bag!" The delivery had come to us not boxed as usual between stapled paper plates, but in two bags.

"Plates," Steve cried, "the paper plates mean something important!" Then he grinned. "Order chicken dinner for tomorrow night, be sure to ask that it be packed on plates, and take it off the plates before I get home."

The next evening the plates were ready when Steve brought Bob Hartman home with him. After a while, we put the idea to our victim. It took a bit of convincing, but Bob was a curious person and he finally said, "I don't know, folks; that bird is mean—*mean to me who was his friend!* I'll do it, but I do this only for you. . . ."

Bob left with the paper plates; a few minutes later his car pulled around the corner and stopped in our driveway. Steve had short-tied Bucket to his cage, giving him only enough line to reach the deck but not the door, so Bob wouldn't be in any real danger if the experiment didn't work.

Bob's steps on the last of the stairs were hesitant, his square chin raised as he came in view of the deck, and he held the plates as far in front of his chest as possible. Bucket started to scream and Bob winced, but then Bucket hesitated. Eyes squinted, focused wide, narrow, wide again, the head stretched out inquisitively with the beak making a solid line to the top of his brows, and then he changed his scream to a chirp, "What are *you* doing carrying those plates?"

Bob advanced carefully onto the porch, and Bucket let him come. The big eyes were soft, interest all on the "chicken dinners" in Bob's hands. When Bob made the door, the bird glided down to the deck and tried to stand in line behind the man! And from that day on, anybody with paper plates in hand that looked like chicken dinners could come and go on the porch with only a chirping welcome.

The problem of strangers who didn't have plates in hand still remained. Just as we couldn't supply every visitor with chicken-scented plates, we couldn't keep out everyone who ignored the warning sign on the gate below. One particular intruder's persistence posed a difficult dilemma.

The upper floor of the snake lady's apartment building was home to two families during this period. One was a woman and her little girl. We were soon to become well-acquainted with the child.

She was about four years old, with the typical independence of that age. She liked to escape her mother's eye, and also had a great dislike for staying clothed. Time and again we would see the mother racing down the street, blanket in hand, to retrieve the bare child. The woman's scolding seemed to do no good; as soon as Mama turned her back, off the little girl would go again.

Unfortunately, on one of these escapades of hers, the blonde, blue-eyed young lady decided to hide from her mother. She sneaked up on our porch. And discovered Bucket.

"Pretty bird," she said, "want to pet it."

Fortunately, I was there on the porch to hear her, and so could scoop up her little naked body before she could come to harm. I took her home and carefully explained to her mother about Bucket's emphatic territorial defense. I didn't know if it extended to a child, because Bucket was used to our kids, but I would hate to find out the hard way.

The woman wholeheartedly agreed, hugging the child to her. She explained to her daughter that she couldn't pet the pretty bird. It was a good try, but two days later I heard Bucket start to fuss. It was an odd kind of screaming, not one I'd heard before. Something like his territorial warning but crossed with his call for rescue. Apparently he was in a situation he thought he couldn't handle.

One glance out the window told me what it was. The little girl, fully clothed this time, was making for the cage, step by cautious step. Bucket was atop it, looking down at her. He was distressed—by her size, I suspected, as his eyes seemed to keep measuring the distance from her head to the ground—but his neck feathers were rising into the half-mantle that said, "Get off my porch!"

I hurried outside. I caught up Bucket and put him into the security of his cage, then took the child by the hand, back to her mother once more. I didn't hold with the idea of spanking children, but it was probably the only thing that would convince her not to visit us again.

Sadly, *nothing* convinced that little girl. Time and again I would catch her slipping over or under the gate. No threats or punishment seemed to scare her away; the fascination of Bucket was too great.

As the days passed, the bird had become more and more uneasy about the child's persistence. She was sometimes so quiet that Bucket wouldn't hear her coming, and if his back was turned, couldn't see her until she was almost all the way across the porch to him. One morning Steve and I were having a last cup of coffee before Steve took Bucket for his flying time at the airport. Bucket began to scream.

This was one of those days, because there again was the naked child not three feet from the cage. Steve's chair tipped over; with his longer legs he got outside before I did. He snatched up the child and turned his back, just a split second before Bucket completed his jump. Bucket crashed into Steve and landed on the deck. I picked him up. Steve took the naked child home and handed her over to her mother, who was already rushing down her stairs in pursuit.

When Steve returned, he put his arms around my shoulders.

"Afraid it's time to think about putting Bucket where he belongs. A child's safety is too important. . . ." I shook my head. He wasn't ready, I knew it! And I didn't want to lose my Bucket. "Sooner or later that kid is going to get hurt," Steve continued. "We can't let that happen! Besides, if it does, we'd lose Bucket anyway; he'd be confiscated for sure. At best we'd have to keep him caged in the house forever. I don't want that for him."

I sighed; I didn't want it either. And I knew that no matter what kind of personal feelings I had, no matter how ready or not Bucket was, we did have an insurmountable problem here. The child had twice tried to reach through the cage bars for the bird. I couldn't stop my tears, but I nodded.

"We can take him down to the airport field," Steve went on, "he's familiar with it, and there is plenty there for him to eat. There are even the wild hawks who hunt there to keep him company. Maybe he can find friends among them who will show him where they sleep at night, and," he paused and looked out at Bucket on the back rail, "maybe he'll even find a mate to help him hunt and teach him everything else he has to know to be wild."

Once at the field, in clear sunshine and soft breeze blowing in from the Bay not far away, Steve carried Bucket on his arm into the middle of the expansive meadow. We removed the jess—the piece of leather that had for so long bound Bucket to the world of man.

Then, bare-legged for the first time since babyhood, Bucket was launched into the sky that was his by birthright. He flexed his wings in their lifting rhythm, and rose higher and higher, until he caught a thermal current and began to turn in lazy circles, gliding, soaring, a silhouette of dark against the light blue sky, wing tips spread, and dusky red tail opening and closing whenever necessary to catch the next curling breeze.

Steve and I watched him for a long moment, and then as Bucket swung out over the end of the field, his head pointing away from us, we returned to the car, to go back to our now hawkless home.

But . . . some things are not meant to be. As we drove along the road beside the field, people driving towards us suddenly began to behave strangely. Heads were craning out car windows, traffic was pulling over to the side of the road, the cars were stopping. Everyone was looking at our car.

And then we heard the eerie scream, so familiar. We looked to Steve's left just in time to see Bucket drop down to the level of the car window, and fly beside the moving car, right into oncoming traffic, with no thought, obviously, as to what room there was for his wide, gold-glinting wings.

I don't think I have ever seen anything more beautiful than those wings at that moment, carrying the bird at thirty-five miles an hour right along with us.

And there was no doubt about what he meant to do: *Nobody* was going to leave *him* at any *vacant* field. He was just going to fly alongside until his family stopped the car and let him back inside where he belonged. What was this anyway, some new game? His screeching again and again demanded we stop and open the door. We stopped and let him into the car.

What could we do? We knew his stamina. And his determination to have his own way once he'd set his mind on something. He was perfectly capable of flying beside us all the way home.

Once inside Bucket chirped and cackled to both of us, smirking at his own cleverness. Back home, needless to say, we knew we still had the same problem, but how could we free a creature who wouldn't just go free? And I'm afraid we were exceedingly happy about the choice Bucket had made—for the moment anyway, until the reality of neighborhood life reasserted itself and the little girl again escaped the watchful eye of her mother.

We decided to keep Bucket indoors unless one of us could be on the porch to watch him; this worked well, although I found I was spending a lot of time outdoors. But just a week later it seemed that fortune of some sort was again smiling on us. It became apparent that the mother and the little girl were moving.

The story of the aborted release had gotten around the neighborhood, of course, but we didn't know if the woman was moving out of concern over Bucket's presence, or just decided to live elsewhere. At any rate I blessed her. It meant that Bucket could live unconfined again, and would have a little more time to learn *everything* he needed to know.

August slipped into the bustling holiday times of Thanksgiving and then Christmas. Visitors came and went with paper plates in hand, unmolested, and we all settled in for the rainy season. Things went smoothly.

By this time Eddie had accepted having a little brother and made the best of it, especially as Joey was now beginning to take more and more interest in the world around him. Even Bucket had gotten used to having the little one around. Everyone could sit in the living room now without any eyes hazarding mischievous glances from anyone else. The toys were an occasional problem, of course, so I couldn't trust the three of them alone with each other.

163

Bucket had decided anything he could carry away was his, in particular a squeaky, fat pig that Joey loved dearly. The bird would swipe it at every chance, then fly to a curtain rod or bookcase and sit there cackling down at the children, teasing them by squeaking the pig violently.

On sunny days the three of them would spend a few hours in Bucket's domain, the porch, and he didn't seem to mind a bit. In fact, it was almost as if he enjoyed sharing his territory with the little boys—his baby brothers. He would quack and chirp, and fiercely guard his toys atop the cage anytime Eddie's eyes rested on them. When the child would go back to his own business, Bucket would toss his spool or his ball, though never the treasured mouse, off the cage as if he wanted to play. I was right there all the time, however, and kept them apart.

Joey was soon crawling, but at six months was too young to realize that our porch wasn't the ground but a deck, one story in the air. The child kept trying to crawl off the deck edge.

One morning in February dawned sunny and warm. It had been raining the day before and the deck was still wet. I put Bucket outside and went to get the broom, to sweep the rain away so Eddie could be outside too. I hadn't been sweeping long when the new milkman came. He brought the bill as well as the milk so I went back inside to get my checkbook.

As I returned to the porch, Eddie tried to follow me. He was becoming impatient at the delay. I caught him and told him that the deck still wasn't dry enough and he would have to wait just a little longer. I shut the screen door, leaving both children inside looking out, and went down to the landing.

The scene with the children must have prompted the milkman to share his good news, for he told me then that his wife had just had a baby, their first. I congratulated the proud papa and we began to talk; the minutes began to slip by.

Bucket had been at the rail above me as I gave the check to the man, and he had been screaming every so often at this bottle-rattling fellow who never gave him a chance to steal the white hat from off his head. But when the screaming stopped, and the bird returned to his cage top to brood, I didn't give him any more thought.

The milkman had just turned to go, however, when Bucket screamed again, very close to me; I glanced up over the porch edge. Eddie had opened the screen door. Joey had crawled out. And Bucket, screaming nonstop now, had one set of his big black talons firmly clutched in the back of a tiny shirt—with child inside! Joey had crawled across the deck and was dangling three-quarters of the way over the edge of the porch. The only thing holding him in safety was Bucket who, bracing himself with his free leg, was rowing frantically in the air backwards with his big wings.

I flew up the seven stairs from the landing to the deck, around the rail, and across the porch to Bucket. I was suddenly there. Out of the corner of my eye I saw Eddie, scrambling into the house, trip over the door sill to land in a squalling heap just inside the door.

I fell to my knees beside the valiant Bucket, grabbed a handful of the knit shirt myself, then an arm, and finally the whole child was safe and sound, and a chirping bird sat on my shoulder telling me it was okay.

Eddie was still lying where he'd fallen. Maybe he was scared of me because he had opened the door when I had told him not to, or maybe the sight of Bucket grabbing Joey to pull him to safety had frightened him. But his little legs were twisted around one another and his hands were under his face; when I touched him he flinched. When I determined where it hurt, and got his Christmas present cowboy boot off, I saw a bruise darkening about halfway up his calf. I scooped him up and into the tub he went—a nice warm bath, which he loved, would make it better—with little Joey tagging along behind us as best he could.

But a half-hour later, the bath over and Eddie quiet and well-soaked, I discovered he still didn't want to stand up on his own. It was more than just a bruise.

I called the doctor who said he would meet us at the emergency room of the hospital.

I left Joey with neighbors and raced to the hospital with Eddie. There the doctor soon learned that Eddie had indeed broken his leg, a hairline fracture of the fibula.

As I sat in the waiting room, waiting for Eddie to come out of the casting room, I felt suddenly dizzy and I found it hard to breathe. I told myself that this was not the time or place to be silly and faint, so I tried to distract myself.

And I thought of Bucket. I hadn't even praised my feathered friend for his really glorious deed! Again I saw his rowing wings, so bright red and gold in the sunlight. Poor bird, he'd had to go against all the rules I had laid down about not touching my babies. And he'd even acted in direct opposition to normal hawk instincts—in the wild a nestling about to fall out was more likely to be helped along, pushed out, by siblings knowing that one less would mean more food for them. It was thanks to Bucket, only Bucket, that Joey hadn't fallen a whole story down to the concrete below. And I had just stuffed the hero into his cage without a word.

I vowed to make a special fuss over Bucket just as soon as I got home. I got up and went into the casting room and found the doctor almost finished. Eddie had recovered his smile and was laughing at the nurse making faces at him.

Joey, too, was safe. Bucket had been there, looking after all of us.

12

A S WINTER PASSED and the spring rain ceased, Bucket was allowed out on the porch again every day. He was glad of it. The porch with its available roof and good hunting was where he best liked to be. And the mockingbirds didn't let him down; they were nesting again and so very determined to drive him away. But I didn't worry about them anymore—he was fully able to defend himself.

One mid-morning, however, these small birds proved particularly annoying. I was running the vacuum but heard over its noise Bucket's hunting challenge. All month he'd been screaming at two really pesky birds. They seemed older then the ones who had fallen prey to him before—if their cleverness in evading the silent hawk feet could tell—and they had become a challenge. Whenever they stopped harassing him, and went to sit on the telephone pole again, he would scream, goading them on to try again. Yet the last scream had been ever so loud. I shut off the vacuum to listen. But the roaring noise didn't stop. Instead of the shrill tweety birds' voices, there was a dull, heavy, rapidly strengthening drone of some flying craft. The volume increased rapidly and the windows began shaking in their frames. My first thought was that there was a plane in trouble overhead. I dashed outside to see.

Not a plane. It was the Goodyear blimp. Very low, it hovered directly over our roof, and Bucket was now in the air, straining against his lead line, screaming at the top of his lungs, and going around and around in a circle with his unrestrained leg raised as if to kill this thundering intruder of his air space.

The blimp was often a silent, familiar object in the Oakland sky. Today it was so low I could see the people in the gondola, and see them pointing at our furiously flapping hawk.

Momentarily I was at a loss. What could I do to fend it off? The pilots had obviously found a new attraction, and couldn't guess that a hawk on a city rooftop was a pet, determined to defend his territory. They couldn't know that he might hurt himself. Then I wondered if they even knew how loud their motors were and how the vibrations might affect the building they hovered so close to. My windows *were* shaking! Both my kids, too, were crying in fright. . . .

I tried to calm the boys, then raised my hand trying to wave the craft away. The people in it evidently thought I was waving to them; they waved back. I tried both hands, pushing at the air with a snap of my wrists, as if by sheer willpower I could move the thing farther south. The people in the gondola just nodded pleasantly, murmuring to one another in silent pantomime of people having a good time. Finally, frustrated, I shook my fists at the darn thing. At last it slowly moved away.

When it was a good distance away, I tapped on the tight lead line and tried to call Bucket down. At first he wouldn't respond, just continued to try to fly after the blimp. But gradually his screaming died down, and on my third whistle he turned and closed his wings.

Once on my shoulder, he stood on both legs with equal weight. But as I couldn't be sure the jessed leg hadn't been uncomfortably overstretched, I moved the leather strap to this other leg. The rest of the day I watched him, on and off, for any sign of lameness, for any sign of hesitancy in using the leg to play with his toys, or jump for the tweety birds, that would mean he'd suffered a strained joint or tendon.

But even when he awoke the next morning, he was still fine. However, next afternoon the blimp again sounded in the sky. I raced outside, meaning to catch Bucket before he could sail up and try to attack.

It was much higher this time, and I breathed a sigh of relief. Surely Bucket couldn't object to something that far away. But, as I was considering the blimp, he screamed once, and was up in the air, way up, before I could react. He wouldn't come down. The previous day's performance was being repeated, but with a vengeance. I watched, I called, but I didn't reel him in, kite-wise, as I could have done, afraid to additionally strain, and perhaps injure, the jessed leg. All I could do was stand helplessly by, and watch, pray, and hope the blimp would soon go away. When it finally did, I convinced Bucket to come down again. He landed on his cage with only one foot, the unjessed one.

I petted him, talked to him, and finally he let me touch the leg he still wouldn't put down. It felt okay around the joint when compared to the other, but it did seem to hurt him. I rubbed it gently, giving those powerful muscle bulges and sinews careful attention, trying to find out if he'd torn something loose. Nothing seemed wrong, then I moved the jess and saw the problem. One of the lapped, yellow scales just above his ankle had been skinned. It was a minor thing, not bleeding, but enough to make him uncomfortable for a day or two. I changed the jess back to the other leg and then in a fury myself I stalked into the house and snatched up the telephone book. I would call the people who owned that blimp!

There was no listing for a Goodyear hangar among the Oakland airport's numbers. At last I settled for the terminal's executive offices. Finally reaching "someone who had information about the blimp" my anger cooled a bit. A man's voice came on, young and aggressive. I felt encouraged as I carefully explained my problem.

"Mrs. Wallig," he said in a bewildered tone, "I sympathize with you, but I don't see what you expect me to do . . . we have almost nothing to do with a private operation like the blimp. . . ."

"But what if the blimp comes back tomorrow?" I cried. "I'm sorry, I guess I sound rude, it's just that I'm really concerned over this thing. I realize that it's not your problem, but do you ever see any of the blimp's people? Even in a coffee room, maybe? If you do, could you mention the problem and ask them not to fly over my house? They could simply reroute it just six blocks away toward the hills—awash with wildflowers now—or the bay. It would solve the whole crisis."

"Okay, lady, you convinced me," he chuckled, "but I'm sorry that I can't promise anything. If I get a chance, I will pass along what you've said. Okay? I really can't do any more. . . ."

But the call proved to have been effective after all. The next afternoon, as I craned my neck for the first sight of the enemy, I saw it coming. It was a long way off yet but there was no doubt that it was on a different flight path. It could have been being towed by a car, so scrupulous was its path above MacArthur Boulevard, six blocks away. As I watched it turn, swinging ever closer to the hills banked with wildflowers, I wished that man responsible for the route shift could be on this flight. The glorious swath of yellow and purple above which the aircraft hovered was at its peak of bloom now. The wild beauty of millions of tiny flowers, vibrant against the new green of spring grass on the side of a sunny hill may not have been better than the sight of a golden-winged hawk, but it was surely the next best thing.

The blimp never did fly over us again, but one day a few weeks later something else did that reminded us that Bucket was ready to be on his own.

Eddie and Joey and I were downstairs, enjoying the spring sweetness of ground and growing things. I was pulling up weeds that threatened to hide the purple iris growing around the stairs, and the kids were playing with their little trucks and cars in the grass.

Bucket had stayed upstairs this time because he'd been unusually nervous for several days. He had taken to challenging every car that went past, and any person, cat, dog, paper or leaf that might happen to blow across his line of sight. Being off the porch seemed to distress him further. He now sat on the street side of the roof, brooding. Steve and I had tried to figure out what was bothering him, but the best we could come up with was that as it was spring, and Bucket was possibly coming into rut again.

I had just finished half of the flower bed and had stood up to rest my knees, when I happened to glance up at the roof. Bucket's stance had changed; no longer did he look like a feathered thundercloud, but was once again a cheerful fellow. His eyes were rapt on the sky beyond the roof and his beak was tipped up like a little kid's nose who can't quite see over the edge of the candy counter. Just then a big gray and white seagull appeared in Bucket's air space. The intruder was rather lower in the air than most gulls I'd seen around, I could see each feather of its pointed wings so white underneath, each toe on its gray feet.

It gave a mournful cry as it passed over Bucket's head. Instead of rising to protect his air space as I expected him to, Bucket sat there and began to talk. Not a screaming, but the squeaking cackle with which he welcomed both Steve and me home. His head punctuated each greeting with a nod, his wings at the shoulders opened slightly, revealing their inner whiteness, and his tail fanned out to its full width.

He was actually inviting the gull to his roof. And the gull knew what was happening; it turned and flew back over him, calling again, as if inviting Bucket into *its* domain. The gull's feathers seemed to shimmer in the sunlight as if it was displaying them to best advantage before what was undoubtedly an interested and interesting gentleman. Though there is nothing about a seagull that to me indicates its sex, this one had to be female . . . and husband hunting.

But for a hawk?

Bucket was himself assuming his handsome rooster pose, fluffing out his own feathers, and stretching up into a noble stance. He couldn't seem to figure out, though, why she wouldn't come down to talk to him. One eye kept peering up at her with brow drawn into bewildered wrinkle. She, I supposed, couldn't understand why he wouldn't come up to join her for a bit of aerial whoopee . . . red-tail hawks being known to copulate in the air. When she finally gave up her coaxing and moved on, Bucket sat for a long time looking after her. And then sank into an even deeper state of brooding than before.

The next day, the seagull again appeared and repeated her enticing maneuvers. But this time Bucket tried to respond. He made several half-leaps up off the roof as if he wished he could join her but still couldn't quite see why she wouldn't come to him. When she left, he puffed out his feathers as if cold, drew his head into his neck, and stared into the empty sky for a good hour.

The third day as soon as the lady appeared, he was in the air,

171

almost at the end of his tether, and beating his way in a circle. It was hard to tell what the seagull thought of this odd flight pattern of Bucket's. If she didn't come down to meet him, neither did she immediately fly away. She just kept calling to him from a distance.

As the days passed and the strange courtship continued, the feeling in the house grew uneasy. Bucket had begun to frown at Steve. Whenever he stood close to me the piercing hawk eyes stared at him.

About a week after the first sign of the gull, with Bucket becoming grumpier toward Steve by the hour now, even at last refusing to go down to the car with him for the usual flying time at the field, we sat down on the porch to try to decide what to do next. We had no more settled on the rattan chairs, close to each other, when Bucket came off the roof. He landed on my shoulder, wings shrouding me, and without a sound one foot snapped out. He took a swipe at Steve's wrist where it lay on the back of my chair. And then Bucket screamed, chillingly, demanding that Steve withdraw. Suddenly, we were defending poor Steve from the hawk as blood welled out of a skid gash on his lower forearm.

After his first attack, I at once swept Bucket off my shoulder. He lit on the deck, turned and flew into Steve's ankles, snapping and slashing with those black talons, screaming in defiance. Luckily, Steve was wearing high-topped riding boots, double-lined with leather. The angrily slashing hawk couldn't penetrate the leather, but Steve's trouser cuffs were taking one heck of a beating. And the creature was so aggressive that for a few minutes there seemed no way to stop him.

Finally, I got a foot on the tether and pulled it under my shoe until we had Bucket's jessed leg secure. Still he tried to strike at anything he could reach with the other. When he nicked my ankle and I yelped and jumped away, I lost the line again. It was the last straw for Steve. He dove for Bucket, hands snatching as fast as the claws. And up Steve came with bird legs firmly clutched in hand. He shook Bucket, trying to make him stop, while Bucket tried to get at the hands on his legs with his beak.

"Okay!" Steve gasped as the beak connected, "You want to fight? Stinker!" And he dumped Bucket upside down into the plants' half-full water bucket. The bird struggled at the first shock. Steve lifted him out. Bucket came up crazier than ever, and in even greater fury attacked Steve's hand with his beak.

Steve dunked him again, stirred the water with him like one stirs soup, then pulled him out, all the while admonishing him to quit. And finally, after the third time down, the bird seemed to get the idea that he wouldn't win this one. He started to attack the hand that held him, then hesitated, looked at Steve who was cursing under his breath now, and seemed to decide that he'd had enough of this treatment. He screamed a proclamation: I'm not beaten; I've lost a battle but not the war.

Steve held him on the cage top for a moment, half-afraid, I could see, to let the bird go for fear that he would decide to continue the war any minute now. Bucket's eyes were needlepoints in the tapestry of his drowned but still testy mantle. But at last Steve dared to let the unjessed leg go and he talked to the bird soothingly as he slowly tried to pet the dripping chest. Bucket held his ground but his head flinched, eyes widening and narrowing as he focused on the friendly but now somehow objectionable fingers that persisted in touching him.

It took Steve a whole hour to bring the bird around to tolerating the loving attention. I had brought them a soft towel, and Steve had dried off the evidence of battle from Bucket, but even after he was dry, he still took exception to Steve's hands. It was as if Bucket was just waiting to be alone in order to plot his next line of attack.

Watching the two through the window from the kitchen, I didn't know which one I was more sorry for or worried about. It was like seeing two old friends at odds, or a fight between father and son.

Later, Steve and I sat, avoiding each other's eyes, but finally Steve looked up from the small squares of gauze and tape on his hand.

"I wonder," he said, "what if he followed the seagull? Would he forget how to get back? If he did, then he would have to stay free."

"I doubt if he would," I said, "I don't believe that if he left the roof he would forget where it was. Remember the time with the chickens? He went to that lady's yard and came back, all by himself.''

"But in rut he might not pay attention to where he's going or how far he's gone."

"I think hawks must have a built in road map—the hawks who hunt at the airport don't live there, yet seem to manage to get wherever home is just fine."

"Then what are we going to do with him?" Steve sighed, "We tried to free him. He won't go!"

"Maybe we should take him to some place strange to him and let him go . . . maybe the time's right now."

And so it was decided that I would take Bucket, the very next morning, up to the Oakland hills where he'd been born, and release him in the hopes that the unfamiliar surroundings would prick his interest and draw him into exploring them. At least until I could drive far enough away to escape him.

It was a good plan; however, Bucket was Bucket . . . nobody made plans for him.

At eleven-thirty the next morning I parked my car at the top of a path that led down to a section of the hills heavily wooded with ruby-barked madrone, shiny green poison oak, and the duller live oak. A path curved to my right, bright in the sunlight, and then dropped downhill into the shade. The green of late spring stretched for miles but I could see that on some far-off hills the warm sun had already begun to turn the tall grass golden.

It would be an early summer, I thought as I brought Bucket out of the car. The hills looked dry even now, but just out of sight was the large lake formed by Chabot Dam. There was always plenty of water in it—it was the reservoir supplying most of the populated area between the ocean and the hills. A hawk would quickly find it.

I walked down the path; Bucket on my arm peered here, there, and everywhere at once. This place had scents and sounds he could probably only dimly remember if at all. And the hush around us was as different from the quiet of the airport field as the field itself was from our own apartment.

As I neared the curve of the path, already wishing myself in the cool of the shade, I heard tires crunch on the dirt and gravel; an engine idled up behind me. Rangers, I saw at a glance. The pale green pickup went slowly past us and pulled up just beyond the curve in the shade. The two men in it began to eat their lunch, but they nodded in a friendly way as I came abreast of them. Their eyes lingered on Bucket with interest.

I smiled back at them, feeling the sadness that had been with me all morning. No use prolonging it by stopping to talk. I marched on. I continued for a short distance over the crest of a small hill and down the other side. In a spot clear of overhanging trees I paused.

Once his jess was off, and I'd launched him, Bucket took to the air in excitement. I'd given him a hug goodbye, breathing in one last time the sweet watermelony aroma of his feathers. It seemed so like the soft scents of the wilderness that I had fond hopes of success. As I watched him hurrying his wings up past the trees, up into the cloudless sky, to become a small flying speck above me, I knew that I would never eat watermelon again without remembering the smell and feel of this hill country today and of the freshly bathed feathers that were now part of it.

As I puffed up over the path's rise, heading to the curve and feeling very bad indeed, I once more came upon the rangers, a half-eaten sandwich in each man's hand. Looking at me, they abruptly burst into howls of laughter.

My emotions at that moment were very touchy—I could have sat down and cried. I glanced down at the jess and line in my hand, and wondered what was so funny. I even looked down at my shirt and pants thinking that perhaps I had sprung a seam somewhere, and that *that* had struck them funny. Nothing. I then could only assume that they were laughing at an apparently careless woman who had gone down with a hawk and now returned without one. I altered my course a bit to avoid their truck, when the driver pointed. I looked to the top of the grade behind me. And there was Bucket. He hadn't even bothered to fly this time. He just trudged along in my footsteps as if we were out for a nice stroll.

I tried to shoo him off, but he just flapped, took to the air with those big wings, then landed on my head—and locked his big, dusty feet on my hair, 300 pounds of pressure in that locked clutch. Short of actually hurting him, there was nothing I could do.

I turned a prune-like face back to the rangers. They were unsure how to react, in laughter or fear. "Are you okay, lady?" asked the driver leaning out the window.

I assured him that I was fine, but that the bird was just nuts. "He'll turn me loose eventually," I told them, "but right now I'm the game he isn't going to let get away."

Bucket wouldn't even get off my head when I tried to get into the car. And so I just sat down behind the wheel—with bird stuffing himself between my head and ceiling—shut the door and started the engine.

This must have finally convinced him I wasn't going anywhere that he wasn't for he hopped down to his favorite perch beside my neck and complained to me all the way home. About his long walk, no doubt, as between chitterings and screams at any car we passed, he tried to lick that dust from his feet. Couldn't imagine why he was bothering, I was sure it was all on my hair.

That morning Bucket had hated Steve, and now tonight they were old buddies again, all signs of the rut gone.

"You tried?" Steve asked quietly as he reached to scratch the tummy beside his ear.

"He wouldn't go," I replied. I told him what had happened as we sat down in the kitchen for coffee and Bucket appropriated Steve's knee.

Steve gazed down at the peaceful hawk, now busy with his preening, and he looked sad, even wistful.

"Well," he sighed, "I guess it's over then . . . we'll never be able to set him free, because he won't go. Damn dumb bird!" Bucket hopped to Steve's shoulder, shook his feathers, and began to preen himself again, cackling in Steve's ear from time to time. "He attacks me. He bites me. I half drown him and still the next day he loves me. It's damn near more than a person can take. He's a house pet and his allegiance is to us. We are his family, and we made him that way. It's just a shame that we couldn't have foreseen it."

And so Bucket continued on with us. Eddie was three years old now, Joey was more than a year, and Bucket was four.

Downstairs, the hawk liked to perch on the red picket fence in the shade of Henry's rose bush. There he was hidden from the street, but he could still see everything that went on. In his normal mood when off the porch, he was the perfect gentleman—even tolerating the myriad of shrill-voiced children with inquisitive hands who began to appear as if from nowhere.

Not only was Bucket an attraction, so was Eddie's new tricycle. The small, red vehicle soon was a magnet that drew to our yard children I had never seen before. Everyone wanted to ride it, and when they weren't riding they wanted to pet Bucket. Most of the children were well-behaved and listened to our warnings. But there was one who would not.

Deidra was a rosy-cheeked child with chocolate skin and small pigtails. She lived around the corner. She was just three years old, but she roamed the busy streets at will.

When she first appeared, one bright afternoon, she not only seemed to be attracted by Bucket and the tricycle, but also by Eddie himself, if the constant hugs she gave him were any indication. And every day thereafter would find her at our front door asking if Eddie could come out to play.

Since Deidra was more interested in Eddie than in Bucket, Bucket was more tolerant of her, though the hawk still didn't like anyone on his porch. But as the child was oblivious to his screams, we were at a loss to see our way out of the problem. No child that age should be allowed to run loose on the busy streets but we suspected the little girl had some trouble or other in her home, or she wouldn't have been on her own; we felt it behooved us to look after her. On the other hand, there was Bucket. . . .

We tried talking to the child, explaining to her why she should just wait at our gate until we could catch Bucket, but Deidra just shook her head and said, "Oh, Buckie doesn't mind me; I'm his friend."

It takes two to make a friendship and Bucket wasn't interested.

I began to be alert every minute, listening for sounds on the stairs, and when one came, I'd dash out to Bucket. More often than not, there would be the little girl straddling the post, halfway over the gate, or going hand over hand up the stair rail to outsmart the padlock.

Even a visit Eddie, Joey, and I paid Deidra's mother failed to provide a solution. The woman, overburdened with a night-shift job that required her to sleep during most of the day and a teenage son in addition to Deidra, was not accepting responsibility for keeping her daughter away from the bird. Yet, she very indignantly expected us to keep Bucket away from Deidra! All I could hope was that the meeting had impressed the little girl with the danger of being too close to a wild animal.

Whatever hopes I had that Deidra would stay away were dashed the following day. She not only climbed the gate, but this time made a beeline for Bucket. I reached him a half a second before she did.

"Mama says I'm not to have anything to do with your birdie, that he'll eat me up," she said primly, brown eyes flashing mischievously at me. "But she said that about our dog too, and Killer likes me. He likes me to pet him and bites Gerald, my brother, when he tries to hit me. I'm going to make friends with Buckie so he will bite Mama if she comes to whip me again like she said she would."

I stood there appalled, gaping at the child; then I rapidly put Bucket in his cage and shut the door before the little hands could touch him as they were reaching to do.

"Honey, you can't want that to happen to your mother," I said then, "She loves you, mothers do, you know. But, also, if Bucket bit her, then the police would come and take him away, and we'd lose our little friend."

The next morning the child again tried to make friends with "Buckie." And morning after morning the siege continued. Bucket began to take definite exception to Diedra as she tried in every possible way to evade my constant watch. The times when she would run full tilt at him, to beat me to the cage, were the worst. He took to the air then. But when his big wings would lift, he'd go either to the roof to peer down at her over the eaves as if expecting her to come up after him, or he'd just fly in tethered circles high above us. Perhaps he knew she meant him no harm, I don't know.

He never made any attempt to hurt her, but he screamed as if he would, and I couldn't be sure he wouldn't one day dive at her. And I couldn't take the chance. Neither Steve nor I knew what to do. She was so determined.

One morning after an especially harrowing scene, I had occasion to call Shirley Nelson on pet club business. After a while, I mentioned what was uppermost in my thoughts these days, the problems surrounding Bucket. I told her we had even considered caging Bucket for good, maybe building a big cage around the entire porch deck and extending it up over the roof so he could still sit in his favorite spots.

"Something has to be done, Shirley," I moaned, "it may even come down to us having to move, though that might prove difficult because not many landlords are as tolerant and cooperative as Mr. Mac. And we can't afford to buy a house yet."

"Sounds like an impossible situation," she said after a moment's reflection, "have you considered placing Bucket with someone else?"

I *hadn't,* of course, nor did I want to.

"I don't mean to sound like the big bad witch, Gaird," she continued, "but you did tell me that you are afraid that Bucket can never be returned to the wild, that he's overdomesticated. That's an almost insurmountable problem, you know; it's come up before for club members. So, I can only suggest adoption, even though it might be hard finding someone suitable and willing to take on a big hawk like Bucket."

She paused. I was speechless.

"Look," she said, kindly, "I'll ask around if you want me to. If I find someone, then at least you'll have an alternative to the zoo—a home for Bucket where he'll be loved and understood instead of a prison."

Finally, I found my voice. "No. Not a zoo! That would be worse than giving him away."

I knew she was right. I glanced out the window at my now peaceful hawk atop his cage. Little Diedra had had an argument with Eddie over a toy so she had gone home for a while, but I knew she would be back.

13

AFTER DINNER THAT NIGHT, when the children were asleep, I sat down beside Steve on the couch to tell him about the new option for Bucket's life. When I had finished he stared at me, a parent, shocked at the very thought of *adoption*.

"I know," I said, "it's hard to take. But let me tell you what else I've done today. . . ."

In silence he listened as I then told him about looking up apartment and house listings in the newspaper, about the places I'd called, the prices, and the responses I'd received in regard to my query as to pets. Some landlords wouldn't even consider children, let alone two kids *and* a hawk. I had taken the children and visited the few that seemed to be likely that afternoon. Except for two places, none would do at all.

"And those two places?" asked Steve, staring now at Bucket who was perched comfortably on the front door, one foot up.

"One was a triplex. The other two apartments in the building had seven children between them. The other was a duplex on Bancroft, with no front yard but a backyard about like we have here."

"Bancroft's as wide as a freeway," Steve muttered, "too busy a street. I don't want to have to worry about the kids every minute. Wasn't there anything else? Like a place with a cyclone fence?"

I shook my head. "The place on Bancroft had a low fence, but the one thing I thought was good about it was that some previous tenant had had chickens and there was a rather large chicken coop left behind. It would have made a good cage for Bucket when we weren't home.''

"No," Steve said, "coop or not, it's too much to expect kids as small as Eddie and Joey to stay in a backyard. You'd have to watch them every minute like you do now. If we move, it should be to a place that's better for all of us than this one is. And anyway, honey, no matter where we go, sooner or later we'd have the same old problems with Bucket.''

I nodded, having to agree, then sighed, "And it's probably only going to get worse.''

We both glanced up at the peaceful creature. He regarded us with big, calm eyes, dilated to liquid softness in the dusky evening light.

"Even if we keep him in the house forever," Steve said, "or build that cage around the porch and roof, will it be enough?''

"I also called a building supply place today about materials for the cage. Just using two-by-fours, and chicken wire to cover the whole thing . . . at least a thousand dollars, probably more.''

"It's too bad," Steve growled, "poor old Bucket is like one of our kids. If only Diedra would stay home!''

I got up and went over to pet the big foot on top of the door. As I reached and touched the yellow toes, Bucket lowered the other foot, coaxing my hand to pet it, too. Then he stretched his wings and legs slightly, and as I turned from him, he opened his wide wings to parachute down on Steve's shoulder. He settled lightly, comfortably, beside the head which was reluctantly coming to a decision about the bird's future.

Steve gazed at Bucket for a long moment, then gave me a wry smile. "He's just a bird, you know—really. We're always putting emotions and thoughts into his beak, so to speak, but he's really only a creature and not a person. I wouldn't be a bit surprised, should Shirley find someone, if Bucket took to them like he took to us.''

I wasn't so sure and I couldn't accept the idea that Bucket wasn't going to feel something when he left. I'd lived in much closer contact with the bird than Steve had; I'd had more of a chance to watch all phases of his life with us. But maybe it would be bettter if now that Steve had arrived at his conclusion I supported his thinking. It might be easier for him in the long run.

Bucket suddenly leaned over to Steve's cheek. The big beak seemed about to give him a hawk kiss but Steve didn't see it coming and tilted his head to mine. Bucket just leaned a little further, but then, as if he felt rejected, banged his beak on Steve's ear, "Hey, how about me? Where's a little love for me, too?" Our "unfeeling" bird had been left out, and was now jealously demanding that Steve pay attention to him, too. As Steve objected to the smack on his ear, I patted his hand, saying, "He just wants his turn, honey. All us chickens need love."

For the next several days, I told myself sternly not to get so wrought up over a bird, but every time the phone rang I was in such a nervous state that even the quiet tones of its bell chime startled me.

Then one evening Shirley called. The moment was here now; I had to get hold of my emotions because it wasn't fair to Shirley to force her to listen to my addlepated moanings. I tried for a light tone, saying, "Anybody would think I was giving away my own child." My small laugh came out just a little crooked. "So, have you found any victims?"

My choice of words drew a chuckle from her, "Maybe a couple. One man said he might be interested, though he'd never had a bird before other than chickens. He has the facilities—about a half acre of land, fenced because of his cat. But a better prospect I think is the son of one of our club members."

"A kid? I don't know, Shirley. . . ," I began.

"Well, wait a minute," she said. "He's sixteen, a responsible kid, his dad says. They live on a farm in Sonoma County. Plenty of room for Bucket, and the kid has had hawks before. His name is Tim. He wants to be a falconeer but the small hawks are just too small. He has saved up fifty dollars already, doing odd jobs, toward buying what he wants."

"Well, we don't want to sell Bucket," I told her. "Just find somebody to love him."

"Now, think about it a minute," she said in a cautioning voice. "When a person gets something for nothing, or so I've seen, they often tend not to value it as much as if they'd paid good money for it. Why do people value a pure-bred dog when a mongrel is often just as good a pet? They have to pay for the breeds, that's why. They're more likely to take better care of the pure-bred too, give it shots, keep it from straying, give it medical attention. It might be a good idea to sell Bucket, especially to a kid, to help him value the bird more than he otherwise might.''

"It's funny, you know," I told her, "Fifty dollars is exactly what we paid for Bucket when we got him."

"Tim seems pretty grown up. And, too, of course, his folks are good people. They've been in the club a few years now, and their cat is in super condition.''

"Yes, and that's what's important: Bucket's well-being.''

And so I called Tim. It was a long conversation, and as we spoke I began to feel that he would be ideal for Bucket. He was bright, well-brought up, responsible, old enough to ask intelligent questions when he didn't understand something I said, and he was definitely interested. When I asked him if he'd like to come meet Bucket before making a decision, he said, after checking with his father, he could come the next Saturday.

Those three days went by much too quickly. I spent as many hours on the porch as I could just to watch Bucket. He was always at the peak of his beauty, anyway, in the summertime, but he was never as glorious as he was that summer. The brown wing tops were full of the glints of gold and auburn I loved. His head and back were rich and dark as chocolate, topped with swirls of amber icing. His tail was deep and dusky red with a dark brown band close to the end. The undersides of his wings were brightly banded in white and brown on the lower three-quarters, and edged with two inches of gray-brown; the top quarter all fuzzy rich gold. His proud chest was a symphony of pale gold and dark amber, spotted with teardrops of brown, giving way to the mottled dark gold of his upper legs. He was magnificent. All of him, even his yellow lower legs and feet shone as if waxed, and his black beak and talons, too. And the look in his eyes were kingly, soft of color and mood. He was Ruler of the Wind, and able to take the world in stride—a creature of the earth and sky to whom no man was master, only friend.

Each evening Steve took Bucket to the airport field for his flying. Although I almost begrudged every moment away from the bird in these final days, I couldn't accompany them. After all, I had Bucket to myself most of the day. Steve needed time alone with Bucket himself: time to watch him fly and wheel in the sky, to follow every nuance of his flight, and to watch the rabbits and little birds scatter. Then, giving the whistle, to have Bucket respond and come to rest so gently on his shoulder . . . all soft feathers and watermelon essence.

Saturday came. I didn't pay particular attention to the older man, but the boy, Tim, was tall and strong shouldered, blond, with a clean-cut, open face and excited eyes.

Bucket, as usual, greeted these strangers with his full-throated challenge, but he quieted down when I stood beside him, stroking his tummy. Tim stared at us, more so when I put my face to Bucket's head and coaxed him to give me a kiss; and when I put my bare hand under his claws, lifted him up to put him in his cage so we could talk, Tim shook his head.

"I don't believe it," he said. "I thought hawk handlers always wore gloves, a gauntlet. . . ."

"Not with Bucket," I smiled. "He's very careful with his big feet. Might be a good idea, though, for you to use one for a few days, if you take him, that is. That way both of you can get used to the other without any nervousness. He's a love, really, just let me tell you." Taking them into the house, I told them about Bucket's behavior with us, his inclination to sit on shoulders and heads, the highest perch around. I showed them his toys, and the battered newspaper my bird had appropriated that morning. And I warned them, too, about his dislikes: cats, small birds, strangers in his territory, mirrors, and, of course, snakes. The tale of our vacuum hose as well as the Chicken Delight plates drew a chuckle from the boy's dad.

At last I showed Tim the new lightweight small-ring flight jess I'd made for Bucket as a going-away present. The boy turned to look at his dad and asked what he thought.

"It's your decision," came the answer. "The bird looks great, but do you think you can manage such a big hawk?"

I suddenly wished that my own sons were as grown as this boy before me. If they were, Bucket could live with us forever. And this boy wouldn't now have such a look of wistful dilemma. It said that he *knew* he could handle such a bird, but if his dad thought it wasn't right. . . .

"It's your decision, Tim," said his dad again, as if he, too, saw what I saw; yet with fatherly gentleness he added his approval, saying, "But let's hurry it up . . . it's a long way home, and we'll both have a lot to do, reassuring your mother."

Tim nodded happily, then reaching into his pocket he pulled out a check, already prepared. And he grinned and said, "I'll go get the stuff."

I folded the check in half and put it in my pocket, wondering what "stuff" he was talking about. It proved to be a leather gardening glove, a hank of twine, and a large corrugated box.

I stared at the box and quickly said, "But Bucket rides well in a car. You don't need to keep him in that! Just let him sit on the back of the front seat. . . ."

"It was my idea," Tim's dad broke in. "I don't much care to drive all that way with a strange, wild creature loose in my car. What if he gets excited while I'm driving?"

I glanced from one to the other. Tim, afraid that his prize would be snatched away, was willing to do anything. His dad was adamant: "My way or no way."

Well . . . if it wouldn't hurt Bucket, I rationalized, I had promised him he'd never have to ride in a box on a motorcycle again, but this one would go in a car. That was better. But remembering the bird's behavior when Greg had released him from the box, I told Tim what to expect when he got home and not to take it as typical or characteristic of the bird's real nature. I also told him to give the bird time to quiet down when he came out of the box, and about the technique of stepping on the line until the bird was held securely to the ground, and from there offering the hand to pick him up. He said he understood.

I followed his glance to where Bucket sat in the cage. The big eyes were soft; he'd gone into a chirping mood. Tim said, "Since he's my bird now, guess I better start by putting him in the box myself."

I tried to step gracefully out of the picture, saying, "He's your bird." But I held my breath, alert for the first signs of the battle I knew was inevitable.

In his good mood, Bucket let Tim lift him out of the cage— anything to get out—and the boy moved well, calm and sure, to the box. But Bucket was going in no box! His legs spread wide, claws took secure hold of the box edge, and he looked to me, "Happy fellow or not just now, I still remember about boxes!"

I tried not to grin—the boy had looked at me helplessly; I waved him on. When he had tried twice more, each time offering the glove to the screeching beast, only to have him step back on the box edge again, I decided I'd better help before the situation got out of control. A chirping Bucket might tolerate a boy's advances, but no untried kid was going to maneuver him into a hated box, and Tim was on the verge of discovering it wasn't wise to force Bucket to do what he didn't want to do. The big eyes were no longer soft; the stance on the feet was now changing. I put my hand on his shoulder and said, "Tim, take a good look at your bird. See his eyes? When they're narrowed down like that, check his legs and feet. See how he's balanced himself—all his weight on one leg? When a hawk does that, the other leg is ready to clobber something, with talons attached. . . Why don't you let me help you, just this one time? You've just met him, after all, and I've had four years of convincing him to mind. Besides, then he'll more likely be angry at me, instead of you, and you're going to live with him from now on. . . ."

I had mouthed the words, but I hated the idea of it. I knew how Bucket would feel if I were the one to put him in the box. The sword was falling. There was nothing I could do. . . .

I picked Bucket up, talking to him, telling him what a bad bird he was being. He cackled and complained, then hopped off my hand to the box rim to begin tearing at the cardboard as if he would fix it so *nobody* could ride in it.

"Bucket, Bucket . . . you gotta go into the box," I told him. "They'll let you out pretty quick. Never mind. Here, in you go," and I swept the big feet off their perch so that he was forced to land in the box. Up he tried to come, but I put both hands on his wings and held him down. He struggled, and then his face canted up toward mind, to say, "What are you doing to me, Mama? Why?"

And then in an instant a shadow flashed over his eyes. I could swear he'd guessed his days with us were over. He opened his beak and he screamed at me. A scream of anger, betrayal, and hatred even, that mantled him and drove me to shout, "Somebody shut the box, quick!"

Tim stepped in and closed the cover; his father swiftly secured the box with twine. But the screams echoed and echoed from the box. Muffled now, and hollow, but not muffled enough that I couldn't hear them for many years to come, and as hollow as the hole Bucket's look had put in my world. My Bucket. . . .

"Don't fly him too soon, okay?" I said. "Let him love you first, before you take him off the lead."

"Three months before he flies unleashed, just like you told me, and then only wearing the small-ring jess. Don't worry," Tim grinned again, in the greatest of spirits. "We're going to make a fine team."

And so Bucket was gone forever, in a box, still screaming his hatred at me, on the floor of a blue station wagon.

As they drove off I was crying. I thought I would never stop. Even Steve couldn't help; opening the door not to be greeted by a welcoming cheerful chirp, his eyes too filled with tears.

We went on about our lives, of course, but there was always something in me that was waiting. Having been aware of almost every moment of Bucket's life for four years, I had expected Tim to call immediately to tell me how Bucket had taken his trip home in the box; how he had come out of the box; where he slept at their house; I wanted to know how he reacted to the people and the environment around him. Looking back now, I think perhaps it was better that Tim didn't call. Had he, the umbilical cord might never have been severed completely. And I might have gone to visit Bucket, as I so often ached to do, and might have disrupted the events that were taking place. I turned to Shirley, and she did have a chance to check in about two weeks after that sad Saturday. When she reassured me that all seemed well, all I could do then was wait for Tim to call me.

I immersed myself in household matters more and more—Eddie and Joey, their little friends, with cuts and bruises to be kissed and washed, medicated and bandaged; cookies to be baked and handed out; floors and walls to be cleaned; meals to be cooked. Time went by, and my thoughts always seemed to slip to my Bucket. His golden wings would flash in my thoughts; I saw him wherever I was.

Steve once suggested we get another pet, a dog or a cat, maybe. But he didn't really want one, and I didn't either.

Finally, when four months had passed, and still no word from Tim, I decided that the boy had had Bucket long enough, that nobody could think I meant anything other than curious interest by a phone call. I tried that evening, but nobody was home. The next day I tried again. Bucket had escaped.

Tim stammered, "I thought I'd done everything right. I thought Bucket loved me; he'd sit on my hand and my shoulder; he'd play with his toys with me. He didn't even argue too much when I wouldn't let him chase my little cat . . . I thought it was all right to . . . fly him," he blurted. "I'd had him three whole weeks! And he flew just fine on the line. He came down every time I called that last week. I didn't even have to tug on the line once!"

"And so you let him off the line. . .?" I sighed.

"He wanted to fly higher, so much," Tim said, sorrowfully, "I thought it was alright. . . ."

My immediate reaction was one of loss, of disappointment, but wasn't this what we had wanted all along? "Well, Tim, never mind—what's done is done. But what happened then? I would surely like to know."

"It was in the afternoon, after school. I'd got him out of the barn where I kept him—I've kept all my hawks there. It's a nice, dry place, and has an open spot for their perches. He was happy in there; it's peaceful, quiet, nothing to upset him or make him wild and mean."

I *had* told Tim that Bucket was house-raised, a family pet— was a barn home for him right?

"Anyway, I took him out to the yard in front of the house— I'd flown him for a little while that morning so the flight jess was already on his leg—and I let him fly on the line a couple times. Then I called him down again and took the line off. He flew for a few minutes right over my head as if he still was tethered, but then slowly but surely he climbed, until he was way above the tree in the yard. It's an old eucalyptus, very tall. When he got up that far I thought I'd better call him back. He looked so good just soaring up there, but I was afraid he'd get too high to hear me." He hesitated and cleared his throat, then said, "But he wouldn't come. I whistled and whistled, but he was already too far away, I guess."

I thought about the heights from which we'd called Bucket back. Not even the mightiest eucalyptus could grow that high. Bucket hadn't cared to respond.

Perhaps Tim hadn't realized how important it was for Bucket to be part of a family unit; maybe the boy hadn't known that family life was the way even wild hawks like to live—first they are nestlings, then fly on their parents' wing, and then they mate, for life, and raise clutch after clutch of young to make up their own family. In any event, Tim hadn't included Bucket in a family, so the bird had had nothing to hold him loyal to the call of man's voice. He'd answered the call of the open sky instead.

"Have you seen Bucket anywhere around lately?" I asked. "Maybe we could come up there and try to call him down? I don't know if it would work—it's been a long time now—but he *did* love us once: he might respond still. . . ." The words said, I heard again the scream of hatred Bucket had given me, saw his eyes, so betrayed. But even then I held firm to the idea. Bucket was an intrinsically quixotic creature. It could be that he'd gotten over his anger by now. And any try was worthwhile, if he was still alive.

"Well, Bucket has sometimes come back to the eucalyptus, but . . . well, it's too late!"

Abruptly I felt cold. I didn't want to ask, but I had to. "Why is it too late, Tim," I said.

"Because I don't want two of them," he answered with an odd laugh. "Bucket's mated. I only see him flying now with another bird. It's huge, golden—bigger and brighter then he is, if you can believe it. It's got to be female. My dad says that if I recaptured Bucket now, she'd try to join him, and I sure as heck don't want two of them in the barn to worry about . . . too much for me."

I was dumbfounded. Bucket was not only free, not merely alive, but *mated* as well. The bird *had* successfully returned to the wild—against all odds! A great personal satisfaction came over me. All the hours Steve and I had spent worrying, all the frustrations, all the love and hopes we'd had for the bird had not been to damaging effect, but had been good enough. Our bird was making a family for himself in a world that was rightly his.

Hawks come into rut in the spring, but during the winter before they make the first contact with the opposite sex, to be able and ready to build their nest in early spring. Bucket had been set free on just the right time schedule, to take up a normal life as a hawk!

"You know, I really hated to lose that bird 'cause he was the best. . .," Tim's voice cut back into my thoughts, "the biggest, the smartest, the quickest bird that anyone I showed him to had ever seen. And I showed him around a lot to the guys at the hawking club. But, now I think maybe he was meant to be free. The red tails in this area are very small; maybe now they'll grow to be as great as he is, one of these days. Wouldn't that be something!"

"Yes, it would;" I told him, "that's what Steve and I have always felt." Then I added, "But tell me, what about his mate; what's she like?"

"Well, like I said, she's big—so golden from the underside! When they fly together her wings seem a little broader than his and the one time I saw them sitting together on a tree limb, her head seemed higher, though not by much. The tops of her wings seem brighter than his too, and boy! You should see how they look when they fly! Around and around in circles they go, and if one picks up a twig from the tree or ground, then it's almost as if they play tag—way up high. If she has it, Bucket will swoop up to her and snatch it right out of her foot, then fly away like blazes with her in hot pursuit. She can't seem to catch him either, unless he slows down, or starts to go in a circle again. But when he does, and she tried to take the stick back, he lets her get her claws on it then he rolls over and over in the sky, both of them holding onto it. It's incredible—beautiful!"

"That's Bucket!" I laughed, "Teasing—hasn't changed a bit! And wow, how I'd like to come up and watch them play!"

"Well, why don't you?" Tim said, "On the weekend maybe? Then I can show you where I think they're living too. They always come from the same direction, you see . . . and. . . ."

"No," I said, "as much as I would love to see it, I better not do that, Tim. Bucket was a crazy bird. What if he recognized me

and then wanted to come home with me, spoiling this new life of his for himself." I knew we would never be able to put him out of our minds and hearts, but I added, "If he could forget us altogether, it would be the best for him. And listen, Tim, if I could offer a small bit of advice. . . ? Whatever you do, don't go near that tree, especially if there's a nest. Birds are funny about that. If the two of them didn't teach you why you shouldn't visit their private property, they might just abandon it instead, and not have time to pick another before it's too late to successfully lay and hatch eggs. Will you promise me you won't even try to find the nest? Please?"

"I can't," he said. "That's what I was about to tell you! I've already found it."

Bless him, I thought—just like a boy!

"You didn't climb the tree?"

"Oh, no! I can't. It's so tall it doesn't even have a knot or a twig for thirty feet up. No way can anyone climb it. I just saw the nest, can't miss it. It's the craziest mess, must be a good four feet wide—a gigantic pile of twigs and leaves stirred up with an egg beater! I hid in a clump of bushes on the side of the hill when I saw the two of them going to it. I was well-hidden; the birds didn't even see me."

"Thank goodness!" I said, thinking what a smart bird Bucket had been. Highest perch as usual—*nobody* was going to get into *his* house. "Now, there's one last thing, I said hesitantly. "Knowing Bucket, I can't help worrying. You haven't heard of anyone complaining of a marauding hawk in the neighborhood, have you?"

"No," he said, "when the bird first got loose, I asked people down at the local store if they had seen him or heard anything. Everyone comes in there sooner or later, and the man who runs it still says he hasn't heard a word about a hawk stealing chickens or anything like that."

Bucket's manners hadn't changed even in the wild. With such happiness filling my heart, I sat down to marvel over Bucket's triumph.

It was months before we heard from Tim again. But then one afternoon the phone rang . . . Tim. His voice had grown deeper, but his laugh was the same. "I'm really sorry to be so long in keeping my promise," he said, "but I wanted to make sure that everything was going to be alright."

"Why," I said, "has something happened to Bucket?"

"Oh, yes, *something's* happened alright. There's two more now—young! Both of them survived, will continue to . . . they're flying!"

Flying! Already. And I'd missed it.

Two little Buckets, flying around just like their daddy.

"Do they look like they're going to be as big as their folks, Tim," I asked softly, "and can you tell yet what sex they are?"

"It's a little too soon to tell," he said, "maybe after their molt is over. Already the gold is coming strong on their chests, and their tails are now almost all red. They seem to be the same size though. Let's see . . . I first knew they'd hatched about six months ago. Hey, wow! That makes them bigger than they should be, I think. Of course, I might not have seen them right away. And did you know that baby hawks peep, just like small birds' babies? And they chirp. These two are starting to cackle now too, and I even heard one of them scream the other day."

I was laughing. The boy had become so excited the words just tumbled out of him.

When he paused for breath I asked, "How well are they flying? I wouldn't have thought that they would fly at all at six months."

"Hey, they go pretty good. But that's why I waited so long to call you—once a young hawk is flying, its chances of survival are super. I didn't want to have to call later with bad news. Anyway, about a month ago they started to make short hops from one of the trees to another. Then I'd see them, all four of them, straggling along one behind the other for short hops. Now they fly in formation. Still not going too far from the nesting tree, but in perfect coordination with each other. The parent birds fly side by side, especially when they catch a thermal and glide, and the babies follow. All four making those lazy circles high in the air at sundown. . . . Well, no painter could paint it."

His words hit me softly. My wishes that he might be repaid some day for what he had done, I thought, might now be coming true in what he saw and felt.

I had seen Bucket, and other hawks, against a multi-colored sky, the sun setting toward the Pacific Ocean; brown wings outspread, feathered tips fingering the wind, head and back all glinting as the brown and gold turned warm red with the sunset and beak with its hook became a dark etching on the twilight. But the idea of the four of them all together like this. . . . Bucket and his family flew that day, for sure, in my mind.

Even now when sunset comes, and I get a glimpse of the broad wings of a red-tailed hawk against it, I don't just see one; there's a big golden female, two little ones, and Bucket, his sleek head canted back to them, calling to them as he used to call to Steve and me. . . , "Come on, I'm waiting for you. It's supper time."